UNLEASHED

Also by
KRISTOPHER REISZ

Tripping to Somewhere

UNLEASHED

KRISTOPHER REISZ

Simon Pulse
New York London Toronto Sydney

SIMON PULSE
An imprint of Simon & Schuster Children's Publishing Division
1230 Avenue of the Americas, New York, NY 10020
Copyright © 2008 by Kristopher Reisz
All rights reserved, including the right of reproduction
in whole or in part in any form.
SIMON PULSE and colophon are registered trademarks
of Simon & Schuster, Inc.
Designed by Mike Rosamilia
The text of this book was set in Electra LH.
Manufactured in the United States of America
First Simon Pulse edition February 2008
2 4 6 8 10 9 7 5 3
Library of Congress Control Number 2007933716
ISBN-13: 978-1-4169-4001-2
ISBN-10: 1-4169-4001-4

To my parents, Jim and Denise Reisz,
whose love guided me even while I forged my own paths

ACKNOWLEDGMENTS

I'm in debt to Michael del Rosario and Kate Egan for being smart, easygoing, and all around wonderful to work with. Ray Thornton shared his memories of the civil rights movement, and Leigh Ann Rhea let me hide out at her house while I was finishing this book.

Thanks to Wayne and Tanja Miller, Darren Cox, Josh Olive, and Leslie Crow for all those late nights at Pepito's, making a solitary endeavor feel anything but lonely.

And finally, Scott Oden, Lynn Viehl, and Holly Black have shown me not only how to face down the sometimes daunting realities of writing for a living, but also how to emerge with generosity, class, and sense of humor unscathed.

The course of true love never did run smooth.
—Lysander in *A Midsummer Night's Dream*

CHAPTER 1

"**I'm about to slap you if you don't shut up.**"

"Quit yapping, Keith," Scotty said. "You can't even lift your arm with that hunk of fake platinum strapped to it."

"I bought a nicer watch at Burger King once," Bwana added, covering his mouth with his fist as he laughed. "At least it had SpongeBob SquarePants on it."

Napkins and empty plates littered the table. Getting in one more night of jaybird chatter before the end of winter break, Daniel sat with his friends and his cousin Keith, a small riot wedged into the diner's corner booth. While his friends jostled one another, Angie curled her fingers through Daniel's hair. "Tell them," she whispered.

Nudging Angie's hand away, Daniel asked, "Seriously, Keith, why'd you buy that thing? You hope if you've got a watch with four dials, people might think you can tell time?"

"I can tell— Shut up!"

At the Galleria, Keith had spent his Christmas money on

an aviator's watch with sixty-second, sixty-minute, and twenty-four-hour dials set into the face. Now, flustered, he stumbled over every joke they threw at him.

"We're just messing with you. Relax. Let me see it." Reaching across the table, Daniel grabbed Keith's wrist.

Angie mouthed, "Tell. Them."

"Man, the numbers go up to five hundred. What kind of Korean junk did you buy?"

Keith snatched his hand back. "That's the tachometer, idiot."

"It's tacky, all right."

Before another swell of laughter could drown her out, Angie blurted, "Daniel got accepted to Cornell! He got in."

The booth went silent. Everybody turned toward Daniel.

"He got in," Angie said again.

Bwana stood up on the seat. He climbed over Geneva and Spence, then dropped back down to give Daniel a bear hug. Squeezing Angie out of the booth, both Bwana and Daniel spilled to the grimy tiles.

"When did you find out?" Bwana punched him. "Why didn't you tell anybody?"

"I found out a couple days ago. I was going to tell— Will you get off me?"

Bwana got to his feet just in time to smile at the waitress and keep her from kicking them all out. After folding themselves back into the booth, Daniel said, "I was going to tell you. It just hasn't, I don't know, sunk in yet."

"How do you already know?" Geneva asked.

"I sent my application in October and got an early decision slot."

"Aren't you excited?"

Daniel shrugged. "Yeah."

The table shook again as Scotty grabbed Daniel's head. "You got into Cornell! The Ivy League! Be excited," he told him. "Be running around buck naked, smoking a blunt, and telling Birmingham it can kiss your ass on the way out."

Grinning, Daniel pried free of Scotty's hands. "I'm excited. I promise. I'm excited."

Claws scraped against asphalt. Vapor trailed from muzzles. All around the wolves, the city was an opal, cold-burning with a million flecks of light.

A white water of sound—tires and grumbling engines— rushed along the overpass above. Val carried a spray can in her jaws, but she couldn't paint in wolf shape. Shifting into her human skin, she began slashing at the first pillar with black strokes of paint. Eric, still a wolf, brushed against Val's legs as she worked.

Misty loped down Clairmont toward a diner's parking lot. Hidden among mounds of dirty slush, she watched cars float past and kept a lookout for cruisers. Chunks of ice froze to the coarse outer coat of Misty's pelt, but they didn't bother her.

Val finished the first pillar and dashed to the second.

Above, Misty's twin brother, Marc, patrolled the expressway, padding ghostlike through the orange glow of street lamps.

A homeless man trudged along the overpass's narrow footpath. Seeing Marc, he stopped and held out a palm for him to sniff, cautious but not afraid, mistaking Marc for an ordinary dog. The man didn't see that Marc's rangy shape concealed more speed and strength than any pet. He didn't realize a wolf could tear the skin and sinew of his arm, shatter the bones, as easily as he could bite through an apple.

The man tried to scratch Marc's head. Ducking, Marc leaned against the guardrail to let him pass.

Misty's ears flicked toward giggling whispers. A couple stepped out of the diner. Strains of laughter and food smells, onions, sizzling oil, and meat wafted out the door with them. They hurried across the parking lot, the woman pressing against her lover for warmth. Before sliding into the passenger seat, she kissed him. Her voice dropped to a gentle hush.

Misty listened from between the cars. She remembered the way Andre used to whisper to her, even though he was a jerk. Suddenly, the wind that had plucked harmlessly at Misty's pelt stung her face cold enough to sear. She grunted, realizing she was a human again, the slush soaking through the knees of her jeans.

They shifted into wolves from the inside out. Before their bodies changed, Misty's pack had to let their minds sink to a primal, instinctive depth. Thinking about Andre or how good the woman looked in her red overcoat—thinking too human—yanked Misty back into her shivering human shape.

Closing her eyes, Misty imagined her wolf-self. She dropped her hands against the ground, but her fingers stayed thin and tipped with pearl white polish. Frustrated, she slapped the ground over and over until a speck of glass scraped the pad of her thumb. The ragged pain made Misty cuss. She sucked the cut, rocking back onto her heels. From the overpass, Marc sent up an alarm of frantic barks.

Misty turned and saw the cruiser coming down Clairmont. Luckily, Marc had spotted it before the police spotted Val and Eric.

Eric answered Marc with more barking. Fangs bared, he twisted around, snapping at the air. Val dropped to all fours and turned back into a wolf. The pair ran east. Bounding down the embankment, Marc ran west. All of them were on the opposite side of the street from Misty.

She tried shifting one more time, but it was no use. Giving up, she watched her pack scatter in different directions. Marc vanished behind a twenty-four-hour pharmacy. Eric decided to cross Clairmont and double back. Horns blared and the flow of traffic closed immediately behind him, leaving Val stranded on the far side. They were werewolves. They just weren't competent werewolves.

The cruiser pulled into the diner parking lot just as the couple in love pulled out. Misty slipped behind the building.

A single bulb burned above the rear door. Misty inspected her hurt thumb and stomped her tanker boots against the cold.

Listening to the Friday-night clamor, Misty waited. After a minute, she heard Marc howl. He was a couple blocks west. Zipping her jacket up above her mouth and stuffing her hands in her pockets, she trudged off to find her brother.

Daniel's friends wanted to know everything about Cornell. He gave them one- and two-word answers until the conversation finally drifted to their own applications at different colleges. It was past midnight when they left, sidling past two policemen coming in.

Daniel drove Angie home. On the way, she asked, "Why didn't you want to tell them about Cornell?"

"I was going to tell them. I just . . . I don't know."

"Is it that SAT thing?"

"No."

Angie sighed. "Daniel, you got into Cornell. So what if you had to hustle a little? I promise, everybody up there had to hustle somehow to get there. Including the teachers, probably."

"Yeah. Maybe."

"Everybody's happy for you. Me, the guys, your parents. Just be happy too, okay?"

"Okay."

"Promise?"

"I promise." He pulled to the curb in front of her house. The porch light burned, but the windows were dark. Their good night kiss turned into open mouths and teasing tongues. "Let's go up to your room," Daniel whispered.

Angie snorted. "My parents are asleep, not dead."

"We'll be real quiet." He kissed her again. "Two little mousies."

They stole through the kitchen and down the hall one careful, creaking step at a time. Angie's shoulders trembled with held-in laughter as they passed her parent's closed door.

In her bedroom, she put on music to cover the squeak of mattress springs. While a woman crooned in a studio-polished voice, Daniel pulled Angie's sweater and T-shirt up over her head. They had hushed, fumbling, giggling sex. Hands covered mouths and mouths tasted warm skin. Sweat filmed Daniel's back in the cool January night. By the time the CD came to the last track, he was reaching for his jeans.

"Stay awhile," Angie mumbled.

"I need to get home."

"No. Just a few minutes." Lying in bed, she reached for him.

Daniel kissed her fingertips, then her lips. "Sorry. I love you."

Mad he wouldn't stay, she answered, "Love you too, jerk."

Daniel pulled on his shirt and didn't say anything else. Stripey, Angie's stuffed tiger, lay in the windowsill above her bed. She'd had him for years, the nap of his fur worn smooth. Daniel tucked him into bed beside Angie.

"Congratulations on Cornell," she said. The soft words dripped venom.

"Thanks. Good night." Daniel gently shut her door and crept back downstairs. On his way through the kitchen, he noticed the box of raspberry strudel sitting on the counter. Cutting himself a piece, he slipped into the moaning cold and jogged to his car.

Daniel had been accepted by Cornell. The Ivy League. Everybody was happy for him, even if they weren't surprised. Since he was seven, people had seen something special in Daniel. He was always the bright one, the determined one, the shooting star who could rise above Birmingham and go on to great things.

When Daniel was in eighth grade, though, his dad lost his job with Pfizer. Then Mack was born. With three kids and nearly broke, his parents realized it wasn't enough to let Daniel's destiny unfold on its own.

Once his dad was working again, they nickle-and-dimed together the fee for a professional college consultant. Through high school, Daniel took advanced placement courses, volunteered as a peer tutor and at church, played shooting guard on the basketball team, and was a student representative before he could drive himself to the functions. He busted his ass, and when it came time to pick a college, he could have walked into almost any school he wanted.

But the brochure from Cornell had a satiny finish. It didn't feel like paper, almost like fabric. Inside were photographs of neoclassical buildings in far-off Ithaca, New York, their bluestone faces twisted up to spires and pierced by arches. The towers of Cornell seemed both somber and completely weightless.

Daniel's dad had never finished college. As a drug rep, he worked his natural charm to keep the family's bellies full. The army had sent Daniel's mom through nursing school. They paid the bills on time and had money left over for a few comforts, but Cornell lay beyond their dreams. Only shooting stars could ever reach it.

Daniel's standardized test scores might have weighed him down, though. After two rounds, they were okay but would hardly make anybody's eyes bulge. Reading up on the tests, his parents learned that, if Daniel had attention deficit/hyperactivity disorder, he could take them untimed, practically guaranteeing better scores. After working in Birmingham's sprawling medical industry for years, they knew plenty of "candy men," shady doctors who'd write prescriptions for Vicodin or Oxy-Contin for anybody paying in cash. Getting a psychiatrist to say Daniel had ADHD was a phone call away.

"Well? You have trouble concentrating sometimes, don't you?" his mom had asked one night after Daniel's brothers were in bed. He and his parents sat in the living room, all three of them pretending to watch a *Law & Order* rerun.

"You're a nurse, and you just figured out I have ADHD?"

She sighed. "I haven't figured out anything. We just want to find out if you do."

"C'mon."

"It's not cheating, Daniel. You still have to answer the same questions, right? And even if it was, people go to doctors for a lot worse reasons than this."

"I don't give a crap what other people do."

"We can't make you do this if you don't want to." His dad glared at the TV. "But you're not a kid anymore. And honesty counts for a lot less in the adult world than you seem to think."

Daniel was about to snap back, but his dad stood up and walked out of the room. Daniel realized this was making his parents sick. They knew it was wrong, but they wanted him to escape the crumbling city he'd grown up in. They had worked even harder toward that dream than he had. He couldn't let them down.

A week later, Daniel went to see a therapist. While his mom sat in the waiting room, the doctor asked him questions. Was it ever hard staying on task? Did he get frustrated easily? He gave the answers he was expected to, even though it made him nauseous. Thirty minutes later, he walked out with a signed form declaring him a sufferer of ADHD.

When they got home, Daniel's car was missing. His dad pulled it into the driveway that evening, and Daniel had a new sound system. MP3 compatible; 180-watt amplifier; and dual-coil, custom-fit subwoofers in the trunk. His parents wanted him to have something nice when he went off to college.

He retook the SATs, untimed this round, and did just as

well as everybody knew he would. He mailed his application off to Cornell and got their answer a few days after Christmas. When he showed the acceptance letter to his parents, they went ecstatic. His mom found somebody to cover for her at work so they could go out and celebrate.

His dad had probably been right. Angie, too. Nobody got anywhere without a little hustle. Still, the rush of pride Daniel had spent years working for never came. While everyone around him beamed, Daniel just felt exhausted and kind of pissed off.

Now, after a night filled with friends and laughter, the early morning quiet made his tangled thoughts worse. Finishing the raspberry strudel, Daniel worked the green-glowing controls of his new stereo until every rhyme Freetown spit made the steering wheel shudder under his hands.

Passing the diner again, Daniel crossed beneath the overpass on his way home. Below it, three of the support pillars bore the same graffiti tag: a stylized wolf's head, tongue lolling, fangs displayed. Daniel gave the leering wolves a quick glance. Drawn in profile, they watched cars curving off the expressway onto Clairmont. Then Daniel started thinking about Cornell again and forgot all about them.

CHAPTER 2

It was the last semester of their last year. An anxious energy electrified the whole senior class. They milled around the threshold of their lives, waiting to scatter off to wherever they would go, to become whatever they would become.

Misty walked into the school lobby, Marc trailing behind her. She spotted Val standing alone beneath the frost-stippled windows. Looking up, Val gave her a sleepy smile.

"Hey." Misty leaned against the wall beside her. "Where's Eric?"

"Bed. Some dumb fuck college sent Andrew a brochure."

Two years ago, marine officers had shown up at Eric's house to tell his family Eric's older brother had died. Since then, every few weeks, a college brochure or flyer from a Ford dealership where Andrew had gone to check out new trucks would appear in the mail, whispering about the man he might have been.

Misty sighed and wrapped an arm around Val. Exhausted

from comforting her boyfriend all night, Val needed comfort herself now. Letting her head drop to Misty's shoulder, Val yawned and said, "There should be a fine for keeping somebody on your mailing list after they die. Jackasses don't know what they do to people. They don't care."

"Still, it's cool Eric gets to sleep in whenever he wants," Marc said.

Val's head jerked back up. "Because his brother's dead."

"I know. I don't mean that part's cool."

Both girls looked at him, then at each other. "If you listen real close, you can actually hear the hamster wheel in his head spinning," Misty said.

Marc punched her. Misty punched him back.

"Well? We're werewolves," Marc growled. "And we have to come to school every day? It's retarded."

"Marc, you're just mad because you're a werewolf and you still don't have any chest hair, so just shut up," Val said.

"Oh, hell." Marc lifted his T-shirt, displaying a downy streak of hair running down his stomach.

"Aw, it's like dandelion fluff," Val cooed. "If I blow it off, do I get a wish?"

"That's the treasure map, baby. Leads all the way down to the pirate's chest." He started belly dancing. "It's okay, Valentine. Give in to your desire."

Val tried to shout, "You're so stupid!" but was laughing too hard.

"Don't make me show my nipples, Valentine. You know my nipples shoot love beams straight into your heart."

Squealing, covering her face, Val retreated into the corner. Marc chased her with hip-swaying steps. "All right, I didn't want to do this, but, pow! There's one. Pow! There's the—"

"Hey! Put your shirt on. Now!"

Mr. Fine, the vice-principal, pushed through the crowd toward them. Marc let his shirt drop back into place.

"What's the matter with you? Do you see anybody else ripping their clothes off?"

Marc fixed a bored expression on his face, staring off to the side through half-closed eyes.

"Well?"

"No."

"Then cut it out, or you're going to ISS. Clear?"

Marc shrugged.

Mr. Fine gave Misty and Val a warning glare, then stalked off. Once he'd walked away, the three pulled tighter together.

"Let's maul him," Misty said. "Rip his throat out."

Grinning, Marc and Val watched Mr. Fine over their shoulders. Then Val turned back to Misty. "Oh. Remember Monday I was complaining about Geneva Jones being in my health class? Wondering why bother since she's already got every crotch critter in the textbook?"

"Yeah?"

"Well, I should have kept my mouth shut, because the

very next day Angie Walton transferred into that class too."

Misty snorted. "There's probably a couple crotch critters named after her."

"I know. God, I hate both of them."

Daniel stood with his friends and lieutenants near the trophy cases, waiting for first bell. The lobby's commotion swirling around them, Angie squeezed herself against Daniel, her head nestled on his shoulder.

"Mr. Morning!"

Daniel stiffened at the sound of his name. Mr. Fine appeared, his right hand extended. "I heard you got some good news over the holidays."

Daniel shook the vice-principal's hand. "Yeah. I guess I did," he said, glancing sideways at Keith.

"Congratulations, Daniel. I know how hard you've worked for this. I know you're going to make us all proud."

"Thanks. I'll try." Daniel squirmed inside, but he kept the grinning mask in place as Mr. Fine slapped his back and rambled.

"Daniel Morning at Cornell. That's just wonderful. We all knew you could do it."

"Ew. That's gross," Geneva said.

They all looked up to see what she was talking about. Across the lobby, Marc Sandlin had his shirt hoisted to his chin, dancing around like a short bus kid off his Ritalin.

"Good job, Daniel," Mr. Fine said, already weaving through the crowd. "Come by my office later today. Can't wait to hear all about it."

"I sure will."

"Hey! Put your shirt on. Now!"

Daniel slumped back against the wall, watching Mr. Fine read Marc the riot act. Bwana mumbled, "I really didn't need to see that."

"Val sits in front of us in health," Angie said, motioning to herself and Geneva. "I wouldn't have changed classes if I'd known I'd have to stare at her back-fat all day."

While everybody snickered, Daniel slapped his cousin in the back of the head. "What are you telling Mr. Fine my business for?"

"What?" Keith asked. "He asked if you'd heard anything yet. Didn't know it was a big secret."

"You're such a suck up." He noticed Keith had stopped wearing his new watch.

First bell rang a minute later. Angie and Daniel shared a quick kiss, then hurried to their homerooms. In trig, Daniel used the parallax method to calculate the distance from Earth to different stars. He scribbled down notes and thumbnail diagrams, copying step-by-step the examples Mrs. Schiff put on the whiteboard.

With winter break over, at least Daniel could keep his mind busy. Getting lost in double-angle identities and the

Battle of Verdun, he didn't have time to obsess over the bluestone towers of Cornell or the slimy therapist who'd gotten him there.

He wouldn't have been so moody lately if he was still playing ball. Heading to government class with Bwana, Daniel mulled over trying out for the Big Red once he got to Cornell. Bwana laughed out loud. "Cornell sucks."

"It's the Ivies," Daniel said. "They're supposed to suck."

"They suck for the Ivies. Their last league championship was when? Like in eighty-five?"

"Eighty-eight. A mere twenty years ago. And they're just waiting for a good shooting guard. They're just waiting for me."

"You need to try out for rowing or something like that. Do they have squash up there?"

"Yeah, but—"

"They do? I was totally making that up. They really have a squash team? What about cricket? No, you've got to join the polo team."

As they walked into government class, Daniel changed the subject. "Which one? Jessica or Emi?" he asked, nodding at the Orr twins gossiping.

Bwana puffed his cheeks with air and let it out slowly, considering the question. "Jessica's ass. Emi's tits."

"How are you going to—" Somebody bumped into Daniel from behind. He stepped aside to let Misty Sandlin pass. They muttered, "Sorry," at the same time.

"How are you going to do that?" Daniel finished his thought. "Saw them in half and stitch the best parts together?"

"It's a hypothetical. So hypothetically, I can mix-and-match. Now, which one would I do, that's not hypothetical, because I could get both of them down to their skivvies before you slapped on your cologne. That's just reality."

They kept up the bored banter until Mrs. MacKaye appeared. After the class took their seats, she handed out a list of different forms of government. Everybody had to choose one from the list and write a three-page paper detailing its pros and cons. The class gave up a collective groan.

"Don't make it three pages, please?" Jessica begged. "That's too long."

Mrs. MacKaye sighed. "What do you want? To make a shoebox diorama? Make a little Stalin out of pipe cleaners and glitter?"

"Yes!" Jessica said, folding her arms across her chest.

"Come on, guys. When you go to college, three pages is the bare minimum you'll be expected to write for every exam. If you think anybody's going to hold your hand, you've got—"

Tires squealed outside, and an animal screamed. Twenty-three heads whipped around. At the bottom of the campus hill, a car drove down Nineteenth Avenue, leaving behind the dog it had hit.

The brown mutt tried to get out of the street. The class

watched it struggle up, crumple, then struggle up again. Daniel could see one of its hind legs was crushed.

"Oh, Jesus," Mrs. MacKaye said. "Oh, why do idiots let their pets just run around like that?"

"Should we call the police or something?" Emi asked. "I've got my phone."

Mrs. MacKaye hesitated, then pulled her eyes away from the window. "The main office can handle it. We've got a lot to cover, okay? Come on, guys. The main office can handle it."

The dog kept whimpering, but with the windows closed, the sound was thin. They could ignore it.

"Let's go over the instructions, okay? Zach, I'm not explaining this twice. Now, all these forms of government have been tried at one point or another. So when you write your pros and cons, I want actual—pay attention, Misty."

Misty Sandlin sat in the row of desks nearest the windows. Ignoring Mrs. MacKaye, she toyed with her lip ring and watched the dog.

"Misty!"

Rolling her eyes, Misty stood up. She walked past the teacher without a glance. Mrs. MacKaye yelled at her to sit down. Misty opened the door and vanished. The whole class sat stunned, listening to her boots thud down the empty hall as she broke into a run.

Suddenly, the spell of Mrs. MacKaye's authority shattered. Chairs scraped the floor as every student crowded around the windows. Misty reappeared, crossing the frost-silvered campus.

The dog had made it to the strip of dead grass between the curb and the sidewalk. Blood stained the snow. When it saw Misty approaching, it dragged itself toward her with its front legs. Misty pulled off her sweater. Kneeling on the ground in her T-shirt, she bundled the dog up and scooped it into her arms. Through the window, Daniel watched Misty rush the dog to her car while he, McCammon High's shooting star, stood with the gutless, gawking rest.

It took a minute for Mrs. MacKaye to get the class back under control. She sent a discipline slip for Misty over to the main office. They talked about the assignment some more and then the three branches of the federal government.

After third period, the story began spreading to people who hadn't seen it. When Daniel and Bwana told their friends they'd been in the same classroom as Misty, they wanted all the details, what she'd said and how she'd acted.

"She didn't act any way," Daniel told them. "She just walked out."

Listening to the hurt dog whimper, Daniel had felt sorry for it. He'd wanted to do something and had seethed at Mrs. MacKaye because she wouldn't. But Daniel had never considered going to help himself. All Misty did was walk out, but watching her, it had seemed as astonishing as if she'd swooped out the window and flown to the dog's rescue.

Daniel mulled it over through lunch and the last half of

the school day. By the time the three o'clock bell rang, Daniel could finally put into words what had been gnawing at him all week.

He hadn't wanted to cheat. Daniel blamed his parents for pushing him into it, but he could have refused. He could have answered the therapist's questions honestly. Walking into the testing room, he could have just not handed the proctor the form saying he had ADHD. Instead, hating every minute of it, he'd done exactly what they wanted him to do.

He'd gotten into Cornell, his dream school. But in the end, it hadn't been because he was bright or determined. Daniel was going to Cornell because he was obedient. Because he had never, not once he could remember, stood up for himself the way Misty had stood up for a mongrel.

There was a student rep meeting after class. Daniel was headed there when he remembered Mr. Fine had asked him to stop by. He really didn't feel like chatting with the vice-principal today, but he turned around, anyway.

Keith worked in the main office as a student aide. When Daniel pushed through the glass doors, his cousin had an elbow propped on the chest-high counter, scratching his head over some geometry problems. He glanced up when Daniel walked in. "Hey. What's up?" Looking back down, he started erasing an answer.

"Mr. Fine wanted to see me."

"Oh, yeah. It'll be a minute, though." Keith leaned over the counter grinning. "Misty Sandlin's in there now."

Daniel glanced at the vice-principal's closed office door. "Really?"

"Batshit crazy," Keith whispered so the secretary wouldn't overhear.

Suddenly, the door jerked open and Misty stepped out. Scowling at the floor, she walked around the counter, almost bumping into Daniel for a second time that day.

Misty and her brother were both nasty little things with personalities like battery acid. The last person to cross Misty had been her boyfriend, Andre Swoopes, last October. She'd locked him out of his house naked, then burned his clothes. But even though Misty was a vicious thug princess, she'd done something Daniel hadn't had the courage to do. Maybe never could, if he wanted to be a shooting star.

"So, uh, is that dog okay?"

"What?" She shot him a look as beguiling as a brick thrown at his head. Misty was half-black, her skin a sallow, almost sickly, yellow. Thick eyeliner gave the impression of a permanent flu. He guessed her lip ring was fairly new; the hole seemed infected.

"That dog," Daniel said again. "Is it okay?"

She gave a tiny shrug. "Drove him to a vet. They said he'd probably live, but they'll have to amputate one of his legs."

"That's good. That—that he'll live. Too bad about his leg, though."

"Yeah. He had a collar on, so they called his owners. Told them where he was."

"Good. That's good."

"Yeah."

They stared at each other. When Daniel couldn't think of anything else to say, Misty shrugged again. "Well, see you." She walked out of the office.

"I'll tell Mr. Fine you're here," Keith said, heading toward the vice-principal's office.

"Hold up a second." Daniel followed Misty into the lobby. Her brother and her friend Val lingered outside the main office. Daniel had passed them a minute earlier without noticing them.

"ISS?" Val asked.

Misty nodded. "Five days."

"Mom's gonna whip your ass," Marc laughed. "Gonna take off her belt."

"Don't tell her. I'll tell her when I get back from work tonight." Misty sighed. "Jesus. All this, and I've still got to be at the deli at five."

"You were right, we should have—" Val saw Daniel walking up behind Misty. Her eyes narrowed.

"It was just really cool," Daniel said. "I mean, everybody saw what happened and felt sorry for that dog, but nobody did anything. Except you. Too afraid to stick their necks out or whatever." Watching him, Misty's hard expression softened into something closer to bafflement. Daniel heard himself rambling but couldn't shut up. "I mean, it was just really . . . dashing."

That made the corner of her mouth twist upward into a smirk. "Thanks."

"Wow." Val tilted her head to one side. "You're very sensitive for a dumb jock."

Daniel nodded. "I can be. It gives me migraines, but I can be."

Misty had a gentle laugh. "Well, see you around."

"Yeah."

Misty, Val, and Marc headed outside. Marc held the door open for the girls like a butler, giving an elaborate bow as they stepped through. Val whispered a few words to Misty, then Misty glanced over her shoulder. She met Daniel's gaze and held it for a just moment before the door swung closed.

With two hours to kill before Misty and Val had to be at the deli, the girls and Marc drove to Eric's house. Eric was barefoot and rumple-haired, having just gotten up an hour ago. After he made sure his mom was still asleep, the pack started planning for next weekend, unfolding a map of Birmingham across Eric's bed. Black Xs marked where they'd already painted their sign.

"We're getting farther and farther from the furnace," Eric said. "From now on, we need to pick a meet-up point beforehand in case we get separated."

"Wouldn't get separated if everybody watched the streets they're supposed to," Marc grumbled.

"That cruiser still would have come," Misty said. "And

stop talking like a badass; you ran five blocks before realizing the police weren't after you. I was the one who spent an hour looking for you."

"Did you? Really? Gosh, Misty, that's so . . . dashing."

"Shut up!"

Before the fight escalated, Val cut in, "Misty, we better get going."

Misty and Marc shared their grampa's old Ford Lincoln, so Marc would drive it home now. Misty would go to work with Val, then get a ride home from her later tonight. The driveway gravel crunching under their boots, Val and Eric talked in soft voices, savoring warm touches against cold skin. Misty sat in the passenger seat of Val's car trying to ignore them.

"C'mon, Val. Ilie's gonna bite our heads off if we're late again."

"So? He bites our heads off no matter what we do."

Which was true, but Val gave Eric one last kiss then got into the car. Once they were on the road, away from the boys, she smacked Misty's arm. "What is up with Daniel Morning hitting on you?"

Misty shook her head. "He wasn't hitting on me. I don't know what that was about."

"He was babbling, Misty. You made him babble."

She smiled but said, "He's dating Angie Walton."

"So?"

"So, I don't know what he wants, and I'm not going to waste

my time trying to figure it out. If he wants to be friends, that's cool. But I'm not looking for a relationship now. Especially not with some overachiever jock with one girlfriend already. My life's too confusing as it is."

"All right."

Misty slipped on her aviators. She watched the passing city, then said, "But do you think he has those super-sculpted jock shoulders? I really like those."

CHAPTER 3

Years ago, Misty and Marc's church youth group had taken a trip to the Civil Rights Institute. Grampa had gone with them, and when Misty bragged that he'd been in the movement, the tour guide's face brightened. She asked Grampa to tell them about his experiences.

Grampa tried but got choked up. He was a deacon at church and a proud man. Suddenly embarrassed, he excused himself and walked outside.

Misty followed him, scared he was mad at her. But Grampa shook his head and asked her to sit with him on the steps for a while. They shared a few quiet minutes. Grampa said it looked like it might rain. Misty squinted up at the sky, agreed, and they settled back into silence for a while longer. Then Grampa pointed to a statue on the institute's landscaped campus. "That's Shuttlesworth," he said. "He was a crazy SOB." Then he told Misty a story in his quiet, stern voice.

When the National Guard wouldn't enforce integration

laws in Birmingham, Fred Shuttlesworth—a bootlegger turned shouting, jumping preacher—decided to do it singlehandedly by enrolling his daughter at all-white Phillips High downtown. When they arrived, a mob of Klansmen and other upstanding citizens were waiting. While his daughter Ruby screamed at him to stay in the car, the reverend climbed out and walked toward the front door.

"And he was smiling, Misty. Just grinning like they were all his best friends," Grampa told her.

The mob swarmed. It pummeled him with chains. It smashed the car windows. It stabbed Ruby in the hip before she beat it back with her purse. A friend who'd come with Shuttlesworth managed to grab him and make an escape. At the E.R., the physician took a second X-ray of Shuttlesworth's skull before being satisfied that he didn't have any fractures.

Covered in blood, Shuttlesworth laughed. "Doctor, the Lord knew I lived in a hard town. He gave me a hard head."

Grampa almost never mentioned the movement, and Misty had listened to every word of his story intently. She'd never forgotten it. Getting by in Birmingham demanded hard-headedness, in one sense or another. Grampa and the rest of the movement soldiers had known it. A generation later, Misty's mom had known it, working two jobs to feed and diaper twin brats. And Misty knew it now, growing up a stray in this tooth-and-nail city.

Misty's parents had married and divorced twice. Sometimes seeing a person is bad for you is a lot easier than shaking loose of them. While her dad drifted in and out of the picture, her mom dispatched for a trucking company by day and tended bar at a place over the mountain at night. At first, Misty and Marc would stay with their dad when their mom worked nights. Then he asked Rebecca and her girls to live with him. There wasn't much room left for his own kids after that.

When their mom was home, she was usually trying to catch a few hours of sleep between jobs, leaving Misty and Marc to raise themselves. Even at fourteen, as their mom scrambled around grabbing her purse and bartender apron, they still begged her to stay for just a little longer, just a few more minutes. They stopped after realizing how much harder they were making the whole thing on her. If she could have given her kids a stable home, she would have. All their mom could do, though, was show them how to survive without one.

Never let anyone see you cry except family. Life's tough; if you're not tougher, you'd better fake it. Never kiss ass, and never trust anyone who's kissing yours. And to Misty: If a boy calls you a slut, hit him. If he keeps talking, keep hitting.

Both Misty and Marc grew to resemble their mom, weed thin and just as stubborn. To kids at school with better families, with parents who bought them nice clothes and taught them to drive, Misty and Marc seemed feral. Misty didn't help much by telling Geneva Jones that, if she kept her mouth shut, it'd take people longer to realize she was an idiot. The next day, after Geneva's boyfriend told Marc his sister was psycho, Marc didn't help much either by head-butting him.

But a hard head was different from a hard heart. Even after she'd stopped crying when her mom left for the bar, Misty would sometimes jerk awake in the middle of the night and be unable to go back to sleep. She'd want to call her mom. They could have talked about anything, TV shows or what was happening at school. Her mom was busy, though, and couldn't talk unless it was an emergency. Curling up in the lonely dark, Misty wished her mom could look after them or that her dad wanted to. But her mom had taught her there was no point feeling sorry for herself; the rest of the world didn't give a damn.

As soon as she got her license, Misty applied for a job at Florence Deli, partly for the money, partly just to have somewhere to go. On her first day, Misty kept burning her knuckles pushing sandwiches into the oven. A girl named Val, who Misty sort of knew from gym class, stopped and showed her how to slide them in like hockey pucks while keeping her fingers clear.

Val seemed mousy and quiet at school, and maybe a little nervous around Misty. Once they got to know each other outside McCammon High's rumor mill, though, they grew tight. Soon, they were hanging out at each other's homes before work and smoking weed in the deli's walk-in cooler during their breaks.

Marc decided he was too cool to wear a fast-food uniform.

Instead, he spent nights roaming the city with his friends, and sometimes just by himself, exploring all its secrets. On the way to school one morning, out of nowhere, he turned to Misty and said, "There's this weird place near the viaduct. Like a closed up steel furnace."

"So?"

"It's just weird. It's like nobody's been there for years. Everybody's just forgotten about it."

"You really don't have anything better to do than kick around an old furnace?"

Marc shrugged. "It's just weird is all."

"Whatever." Everything she knew had just started cracking like ice under her feet, but she never heard a sound.

She started dating Andre a few weeks later, Doberman-sleek with a bottomless well of jokes and chatter. Misty was in love. Once, she and Val went to an army surplus store. Val wanted a peacoat, but they spent hours trying on bandoliers and gas masks, talking about Andre and Eric, a sweet, sad boy Val liked.

Misty saw a pair of tanker boots. They had leather straps and buckles instead of laces. Their thick rubber soles made her feel a foot taller and dangerous. At least until Monday, when Andre saw them.

"Letting your ghetto show, aren't you?"

"What?"

"What? People are going to say, 'Damn. She needs army

boots to squish those military-grade cockroaches at her place.'"

"C'mon. They're cool."

"If you're headed out to pick cotton. Why can't you wear normal shoes?"

"Because I'm not a normal girl." But suddenly, clumping around in boots a size too big for her, Misty felt her ears burn. When she got home, she took them off. They wound up forgotten in the back of her closet.

Andre could get frustrated with Misty's hardheadedness, scolding, "You want people to stop thinking you're a little hoodrat? Quit acting like a little hoodrat!"

Misty would apologize and try to be more sociable. And even if Andre's barbs stabbed too deep occasionally, she clung to him. She finally had somebody to call in the middle of the night. They'd talk about nothing in particular for hours. After hanging up, Misty sometimes lay in bed crying and laughing at once, flush with love and the wonderful feeling of belonging to somebody.

Last October, Misty and Andre, Val, Eric, and Marc went to buy from Charlie Say What, a pot dealer who lived in Misty and Marc's apartment building. Charlie wasn't holding that day, though, so they just drove around. They passed through the city's ugly side—warehouses and factories, women's shelters and AIDS clinics, all clustered together in the shadow of the viaduct. Then suddenly, Marc said, "Want to see something weird? Pull in here."

Eric steered into the empty parking lot of a machine shop.

A fence, curtained with dead honeysuckle vines and topped with coils of razor wire, ran behind the shop and stretched the entire block. Rusting metal signs were hung every few yards, reading PROPERTY OF VICTOR DEVELOPMENT. NO TRESPASSING.

As Marc started tugging at the honeysuckle, Andre asked, "What is this? The old furnace?"

Marc glanced at him. "Have you ever been inside?"

"No, it's an old furnace."

The names of Birmingham's neighborhoods, Ensley, Powderly, Owenton, were vestiges of factory-town fiefdoms, smokestacks stabbing a fume-blackened sky, dynamite buried in the roads to keep out union organizers. Most of that brimstone empire was gone, the mills and forges replaced by office parks. Traces of it remained, though, like old scars.

"Come on, Marc, let's go get something to eat or something." Val blew warm air into her hands.

"Just check it out. It's really—here." Marc ripped away the honeysuckle and revealed an opening someone had cut into the fence. Without another word, he scurried through.

"Damnit, Marc." Misty chased after her brother. Fear calcified in her stomach, waiting for security guards to rush up and arrest them for trespassing. Then she looked around and knew there were no guards or anybody else. The furnace complex had been completely abandoned to rot, rust, and lush new growth.

Great machines overgrew their crumbling brick control

houses. Brambles and kudzu overgrew everything. Rising around railroad cars and trestles, the scrub formed geometric blocks. Blast stoves and boilers seemed to blossom from the ground, unspooling tendrils of pipe.

Wooden walkways, most of their planks missing, led around the complex. Misty and her friends dared one another to climb to the top of the blast furnaces or down metal stairways sinking into lightless tunnels. Misty stepped through a window and into a long hall lined with identical machines. They were so huge, workers had scuttled up and down ladders to operate the controls. Their vast stillness made Misty aware of the gentle beat of her heart.

Holding hands, she and Andre wandered away from the others into an industrial grotto, the cold winter sun breaking through a canopy of I-beams and electrical conduits.

"This is actually kind of pretty."

Andre snickered.

"What? I mean, it's peaceful. It's nice."

"Sure." He eyed some empty bottles and a trampled sleeping bag in the doorway of one of the buildings.

Sighing, Misty heard Val's laughter on the wind. She and Andre rejoined the others by the mud-banked reservoir.

"Why'd they just leave this place?" Misty asked, craning her neck to look at the pair of towering blast furnaces that dominated the grounds. "Doesn't anybody at least want the land?"

"It's a con big companies play," Eric said softly. "After a

factory or whatever closes, developers go to city hall and say, 'Sell it to us cheap. We'll fix it up, reopen it, and you can brag about bringing all those jobs back.' As soon as they get the deed, though, they start doing economic analyses, environmental surveys, more environmental surveys based on the findings from the first surveys. They can drag that stuff out forever."

"Why? They're still not making any money off it," Misty said, but Eric was already shaking his head.

"Not yet. But eventually, this place will be so run-down, the city will condemn it. Then Victor Development can level the whole thing and build condos or whatever, which was their real plan all along."

"Oh." Wishing she hadn't needed Eric to explain it to her, Misty tried to think of something smart to add. "That's a crappy way to play the people who thought they were getting their jobs back."

"Yeah, but city hall's happy. The companies are happy." Eric shrugged and fell quiet again.

"Misty, check it out. That's like the perfect fairy-tale toadstool." Val plucked a mushroom from the dead weeds and showed it to her.

"Aw. It's cute." Cherry red and speckled with white spots, the same mushroom had filled every enchanted forest in every storybook Misty remembered.

"Um, actually, that's a magic mushroom," Andre said.

"Really?" Marc asked, suddenly interested. "So if you eat that, you'll start tripping?"

"I think so."

"You mean we've got free drugs just growing out here, and we've been giving all our money to Charlie Say What?" Grabbing the mushroom from Val, Marc raised it to his mouth.

"Or you'll go insane and poke your own eyes out," Andre added. "One or the other. Try it and see."

"Look, there's more over there."

"And over here," Misty said, turning in a slow circle. "Dang, they're every—didn't we just come from there?"

"Yeah. So?" Andre asked.

Mushrooms sprouted along the path leading from the grotto, a dozen or more pushing between the boards. Misty couldn't figure out how they hadn't noticed them a minute ago. She plucked one. The scarlet cap felt feverish in her cold palm. "It's hot," she whispered.

"Probably from all the toxic shit they dumped into the—"

Glass shattered inside one of the buildings. A few muttered, angry words and then silence. Misty and her friends' eyes twitched around at one another. The furnace wasn't totally abandoned after all. They started creeping back toward the gap in the fence. Dropping the mushroom, Misty broke into a dead run, her friends right behind her.

They rolled under the fence and jumped into the car. Once they were safe, unhinged laughter rose from their bellies. Tears squeezed from their eyes.

"That place was weird, Marc," Eric said.

"Deeply weird," Val agreed.

Misty wiped the mushroom's sticky residue off her pant leg. As Eric drove off, she twisted around to get a last glimpse of the tops of the twin blast furnaces. A dragonfly of fancy hummed between her rational thoughts. She imagined they must have taproots reaching down to the center of the world.

The sun had almost set. They started talking about getting something to eat again. Andre decided he didn't want to, so he and Misty said their good-byes and went to his house. They watched a movie and made sour-cream cake with Andre's little sister. Misty, who'd been doing the grocery shopping since she'd been thirteen, had no clue how Andre could assume baking powder and baking soda were the same thing.

Misty couldn't stop thinking about the furnace the whole time they cooked and ate. Getting home, she logged onto the Internet. She didn't expect any real answers; she was just curious. First, she Googled "Victor Development" but didn't learn anything except it was based in Boston. She tried "Birmingham steel furnace." There had been several steel furnaces in Birmingham, though, and she couldn't figure out which websites were about theirs. Finally, she typed in "Red mushroom with white spots." The top site was called *Herbal Magick*. Misty read for a couple minutes, then called Val.

Val had been asleep. Answering her phone, she mumbled, "Couldn't you hire another best friend to work the late shift? I already pulled a double today. I'm exhausted."

"I'm e-mailing you a link. Check it out."

Val yawned. "Is it that chimpanzee drinking malt liquor?"

"Get out of bed and check it out. Andre was right."

Modern biologists called their storybook mushroom *Amanita muscaria*, but the *Rigveda*, Sanskrit hymns written a thousand years before the Old Testament, praised it as a god. Warriors once drank a liquor fermented from its juices that made them fearless. They hurled themselves into battle snarling, slobbering, and biting their enemies.

Viking berserkers gobbled the mushroom caps by the handful, transforming themselves into bears. Druids had boiled it down into a salve that made them werewolves.

The mushroom seemed to have grown in the nooks and crannies of countless societies, silently offering seekers a chance to tear loose of every civilized impulse. The article ended with a warning. While *Amanita muscaria* was part of many peoples' cultural heritage, it was dangerous. Nobody should experiment with it, even in small quantities. Obviously, the article's author wasn't stuck in a rusted-out city, bored out of his mind.

None of them really believed in werewolves and all that; it was just something to do. But the myths surrounding the mushrooms and the strangeness of the furnace made the game more exciting. The next day at lunch, they started working out plans to return that weekend. Andre didn't say much. Afterward, he pulled Misty aside.

"You're not really thinking about this, right?"

"Why not?"

"Why not get high in an abandoned furnace? I can't imagine. That's as safe as eating cookies in Grandma's kitchen. Come on, Misty. My folks are taking Jenna to that majorette thing Saturday. I figured you'd want to spend some time just with me."

"I do, but can't we do this, then spend some time alone? It's going to be great, like going to a haunted house or something."

"Crackheads don't jump out and stab you in a haunted house, Misty. Use some sense."

Misty squirmed. Andre could make her feel like a raggedy stray easier than anyone. "Fine."

"Seriously?"

"Seriously."

"Good. You and me, little food, little music. That's how you want to spend a Saturday."

"Yeah."

Saturday, as Misty crawled through the hole in the fence, she told her friends she couldn't stay long but didn't explain why.

On their earlier visit, somebody skulking through the building beside the reservoir had scared them off. This time, Misty brought her MP3 player and a pair of plug-in speakers. The furnace grounds sprawled for acres. As long as they announced their presence loudly enough, they and anybody living there could keep out of one another's way.

Fiddling with her player, Misty chose Pins & Needles, mopey love songs at maximum volume. Val's cousin had done 'shrooms before, and Val was pretty sure they had to be cooked, otherwise they'd be poisonous. Building a small fire, they laid the scarlet caps on flat chunks of slag iron pushed close to the flames.

When it was cool, the slag seemed dull black, but the heat revealed jewel-tone impurities swimming within. And the ordinary-seeming fungus hid so much power, people had actually worshipped it once, sang songs and written poems about it. Misty and her friends made nervous jokes and watched the flesh of an ancient god darken to the red-purple of blisters.

When the caps were burned crisp around their edges, Val poked at one and asked, "Are we sure we want to do this?"

Surrounded by the crumbling buildings and all-devouring wilderness, their brashness had started to waver. Misty looked around at every sound. She knew some of them were the croaking voices of unseen people. "Maybe we should take them back to your house and eat them there."

Val shook her head. "My parents think I'm at work. We could go to the park."

"There's always cops at the park."

"I know," Marc said. "Let's buy a pizza, then cut the mushrooms up and put them on the pizza. Then we could walk—"

"You're such a moron." Misty sighed.

"What? What's so moronic about—"

Eric snatched one of the mushrooms off the hot metal.

Biting into it, he swallowed and forced a grin. "Screwed with the threads stripped now," he said, wisps of smoke rising from his mouth.

"Always the quiet ones." Taking a mushroom, Misty followed Eric down whatever path they were on.

The mushrooms tasted like iron and ash, as if they'd soaked up the blood of Birmingham. Misty choked two of them down, and afterward, her mouth got really dry. Then, muscles in her arms and thighs began to twitch. That scared her way more than dilapidated buildings. She started wishing she'd just gone over to Andre's house.

"No, no, I can't take this whining crap anymore." Marc wobbled to his feet and grabbed the MP3 player. Switching from Pins & Needles to Kanye West, he sent lyrics swaggering across the court of rusting demon-machines.

They started bobbing their heads. Eric told Marc to turn the bass down, and Kanye's zigzag rhymes sank below the crashing rhythm. Suddenly, they were standing, swaying, pounding their feet against the ground. The muscle twitches hadn't been random spasms. They were a wild dance Misty's body knew even though her mind didn't.

The smoke stung her eyes. Misty wiped tears away, but the earth's colors stayed watery and limpid. Nothing was real except for her, her friends, and their dance. Misty laughed, imagining her parents and grandparents, teachers at school, and even Andre reduced to shadow puppets.

Remembering the stories about werewolves, Misty began chanting, "I want to be a werewolf! Want to be a werewolf! A wolf! A wolf!" It didn't mean anything at first. Misty was just lost in the childish joy of yelling and being loud. But the others joined in. "Want to be a wolf! A wolf! A wolf! Want to be a wolf!" Then Misty decided she would.

She started howling and threw herself down. Claws dug into the earth. A warm pelt gathered around her. It was the easiest thing in the world. Taking a few unsteady steps, Misty barked for the others to join her.

One after another, they sank the unplumbed depth to all fours. Marc raced into the brush, sending up a tattered black pennant of crows. Misty tried to speak, but the words weren't there anymore. Finally, she managed, "H . . . ow?" And the instant she thought about the magic, it vanished.

Suddenly, Misty was balanced on her palms and the balls of her feet, watching wolves tear all around her. A frightened wail escaped her human throat. The monsters turned toward her, then shifted back into her brother and friends.

None of them moved for a long time. None of them spoke. After a while, Val got up and turned off the MP3 player with a shaking hand. She sat back down near the fire. Slowly, the rest of them huddled around her. They still didn't say anything, just watched the fire burn to embers. The furnace's homeless were silent now.

Marc flexed his fingers open and closed. "What the fuck did we do?"

Misty pressed her body against his without answering.

"We were tripping," Val said. "All that stuff about were-wolves. And Misty starts yelling. . . ."

"No. That felt real," Eric said.

"How do you know what changing into a werewolf feels like?" Misty shook her head. "None of us have done 'shrooms before. It was just a messed-up hallucination."

"No," Eric said again.

Misty was about to answer when her phone rang, making her jump. It was Andre. He'd called her twice already and wanted to know why she hadn't answered. Struggling to think straight, Misty apologized but didn't have a good answer, just telling him she was coming over now. As they scrambled for their stuff, Misty told Marc to get a ride home with Eric, then rushed ahead of the others.

Driving to Andre's house, Misty watched traffic float around her and almost blew a red light. "Shit." She stomped the brake. Her body jerked forward against the seat belt, but the Lincoln shuddered to a stop before sideswiping anybody. "Shit." Misty should have pulled over, taken a few minutes to focus, but she needed to see Andre. She needed his arms around her, far away from the furnace's delirium.

Eric was wrong. Eric had to be wrong, because no matter how real it had felt, werewolves didn't exist. Misty was certain of that all the way to Andre's house.

Andre was mad in that chilly way he got mad, lots of sighs

and heavy-lidded stares. Misty said what she was supposed to say, that she was sorry for being late, for going at all. Yes, she had sense. The whole time she talked, she felt something in the deepest chambers of her mind snarl and try to thrash free.

"If you want to waste your life with those jokers, maybe you should just go on."

Hairs on the back of her neck bristled at his threat, at every time she'd let Andre make her feel embarrassed and dumb. But Misty said, "No, I want to be with you. I'm sorry. I'm sorry."

She hugged him, kissed his unsmiling mouth, and that Misty-Underneath grew more furious. It hated Andre. It hated her, begging this boy for a few scraps of comfort. Finally, Misty couldn't control it anymore. It teased Andre with her fingertips. It whispered with her voice, "Hey. Let's do it outside."

Fifteen minutes later, Misty was mostly dressed on Andre's front lawn, holding her lighter to the tail of his shirt and laughing. "You want your clothes? Well, come get them."

Andre cowered behind one of the porch posts. "This isn't funny! Damnit, Misty, give me my Jockeys!"

"Misty, give me my Jockeys. Misty, dress cute. Come when I call you. Heel. Roll over." She whipped his flaming underwear at him.

"You're a crazy bitch, you know that?"

"Yes! Yes, I'm a bitch! And I'm a little slow sometimes, and I'm a little ghetto. But I am nobody's pet!"

She got in her car, drove past gawking neighbors, and disappeared into the evening. After several quiet minutes, she called Val.

"Hey, how'd it go?"

"I'm a wolf," Misty told her.

She met back up with the others. They took a walk and tried to figure things out. Wandering for hours, they talked one another through fear and disbelief.

"Just tell me how anything magical is happening in Magic City," Val demanded.

They all snickered at the city council's optimistic nickname for their home.

"Well? Does this look like Middle Earth to you?" Val waved her arms around empty lots and some men rolling bones in the light of a convenience store.

"No, it looks like the whole city is rotting," Eric said.

"Exact—"

"But mushrooms eat rot, remember? They thrive in the dank places filled with decay. And the only difference between *Amanita muscaria* and other mushrooms is that *Amanita* is a god."

After the steel industry collapsed, a slow bleed of jobs and families had left Birmingham echoing with derelict space. Besides the furnace, the city was filled with abandoned houses and factories, more every year. Entire malls stood as dark and empty as caves. Within McCammon High's castle-like exterior, holes in the ceiling plaster exposed wiring and duct work. Water damage steadily obliterated decades-old murals. As

Misty and her friends wandered the husk of a once-teeming metropolis, the idea that a rot-eater god had come to Birmingham didn't sound as crazy as it should have.

Val shook her head. "But it can't be a god. It's just a mushroom. Scientists have studied it, dissected it, and never found anything but, whatever, mushroom stuff. Chemicals and proteins and stuff. Nothing they couldn't explain."

"Scientists weren't dancing around their microscopes when they studied it, though," Misty said.

"So what? The dance was what made us into werewolves? The Kanye West song we've listened to a hundred times before?"

"I don't know. Just that the dancing and chanting, the furnace, it all felt magical. Not just the mushrooms. The whole thing felt like Sunday services."

Val laughed, but Misty had nothing to compare their transformation to except church. She didn't go every week like she should, and when she did she was usually bored and hot. There'd been a few times, though, when Misty had lost herself in the songs and shouts of praise. A trembling ecstasy had welled up inside her until it seemed like her skin would split open, shedding all her fear and loneliness with it. But those moments were few and fleeting, and the transformation had never been as total as what their ritual at the furnace had led to. For a few seconds, Misty had been reborn in body as well as mind and spirit.

Val worried some more, but they returned to the furnace

the next week and the week after that. Misty and Val started outlining their eyes in black, mimicking the dark rings around a wolf's eyes that blocked the sun's glare. Misty dug her tanker boots out of her closet. Eventually, she let Val pierce her bottom lip with a carpet needle.

Misty felt deeper changes too. Even with Andre gone, the nights didn't feel lonely anymore. Even with another story about her buzzing through McCammon, it didn't hurt when boys whispered as she walked by or when girls gave her wary glances. After all, they'd been right for years.

They'd been right that Misty wasn't a pampered, hand-licking pet like them, performing little tricks whenever a teacher snapped his fingers. They'd been right that she was something vicious and wild. They'd been right to avoid her.

Their only mistake was thinking she was a stray, half-starved and on her own. Through the winter, Misty's loose knot of friends tightened into a pack. Together, they were more at home in this hard city than any of their classmates. As Birmingham crumbled, it became the dominion of the rot-eater god and a hunting ground for wolves.

CHAPTER 4

"**B**ut the decorations have to be the school colors," Angie said.

"They're always the school colors," Claire groaned. "Let's do something different this year. Like reds and purples."

"God, no. Gross."

Her lunch tray pushed to the side, Angie leaned over a notebook already half full with phone numbers, prices, and other information about the basketball awards banquet. Keith watched her nibble the tip of her pen while she and Claire talked. Angie had the perfect bow-shaped lips and rose-pink tongue. Keith had dated whole girls he didn't love as much as Angie's mouth.

"Well, something different. Just not green and navy again," Claire said.

Angie turned toward Daniel. "What do you think?"

"School colors are fine." Daniel dipped a chicken finger in mustard.

"That's two votes for school colors."

"He's your boyfriend! He has to say that. And he's not on the planning committee, anyway."

Keith saw Daniel roll his eyes, but nobody else noticed. Daniel had been in a dark mood the last few days, his usual swagger replaced by brooding and a minimum of words.

"Let's put that off until later, okay?" Angie bit her lip with angelically white teeth. "Okay, Mr. Nguyen is taking care of the caterers, so we don't have to worry about that. He said to go to Gilbert Florists, but I'm going to call some other places today, see if we can get better centerpieces for the same money."

Even with a month left to prepare, Angie, Claire, and the rest of the planning committee had a major project on their hands. Held in the Tutwiler Hotel ballroom, with boosters footing most of the bill, the annual awards banquet was more elaborate than McCammon's prom. And the afterparty was legend. Keith had been listening to stories about it since ninth grade.

The ceremony was only for the basketball team and the players' dates. A few people managed to sneak in every year, but Keith had never had the balls to try. He'd never had the balls to try a lot of things.

Angie and Claire were arguing about the color scheme again when the bell rang. Following his friends out of the cafeteria, Keith reminded himself it was senior year; this would be his last chance. He interrupted the girls' squabbling with, "So you're going to get me into the banquet, right?"

Angie gave a single shake of her head. "C'mon, Keith. It's for the basketball teams."

"And the student reps."

"We're hosting it, and that doesn't really matter since you're not a student rep."

"Yeah, but you're in charge of the whole—"

"C'mon, Keith. I can't just let in anybody who wants to come."

"Yeah, but—"

Daniel sighed. "Angie, just get him into the stupid banquet."

"Why have you been so pissy lately?" she snapped.

"I'm not being pissy. Just get him in, okay? He's my cousin." Daniel tickled her, making her scowl crack. He bent down and kissed her neck. "Please?"

Angie laughed, then glanced at Keith. "We'll need help getting things set up beforehand."

"No problem."

"And if I need anything else, like somebody to drive decorations over or whatever, you're my little bitch."

"No problem. Thanks." But Angie was curling her fingers through Daniel's hair, and Daniel pressed his lips against her perfect mouth.

He'd gotten into the banquet. He'd gotten into the after-party. Striding to biology, Keith felt eight feet tall. He was thinking about asking Jessica Orr to go with him when Daniel jogged up behind him.

"Hey, Cousin." Daniel wrapped an arm around Keith's shoulders. They walked along, their heads bent close together and their voices low. "I need you to do some black ops for me."

"Like what?"

"Like getting me Misty Sandlin's contact information."

Keith snickered. "What? Sniffing around for a little gutterfuck?"

"No. I just need to talk to her about some stuff. You can get it, right?"

"I guess." Keith usually spent his student aide period inputting absences and discipline flags while everybody ignored him. No one would think twice if he printed something out.

"Cool. And just keep it quiet, okay?"

They bumped fists, and Daniel bounded up the stairs. Watching his cousin disappear, Keith thought about Angie's beautiful smile. Maybe he wouldn't ask Jessica after all.

A gutterfuck was a girl you could screw without even pretending to love. She could be fat, stupid, or pimply; she just couldn't be clingy. Her natural habitat was darkened back bedrooms during parties. Daniel had slipped off with gutterfucks a couple of times before, but that's not what he wanted now. He wanted to understand why Misty had saved that dog while he and everybody else had sat frozen.

He couldn't talk to Misty at school. His friends would assume he was chasing tail, just like Keith had. And Daniel didn't even want to think about this getting back to Angie. He'd considered getting Misty's number out of the phone book, but in four years of high school, he probably hadn't spoken a dozen words to her. If he called her out of the blue and started asking deep ethical questions, she'd think the whole thing was weird.

But Wednesday, Misty had mentioned working at a deli. If Daniel just happened to stop by, maybe he could charm her a little, get to know her a little, and see if there was something Misty knew that nobody had ever told him.

After school, Daniel met Keith outside the main office. He pocketed a folded sheet of paper, said a few words of thanks, then hurried to the debate team meeting.

They had a congressional debate in March and the district tournament at the state capital in April. Two sophomores needed to score a lot of points at the congressional to qualify for the district. While Mr. E., the debate coach, strategized, Daniel opened the printout Keith had given him, reading it behind his National Forensic League manual.

A student couldn't be held after class if she had a job, but the school needed a supervisor's name and phone number to make sure she actually worked there. At the bottom of the form, Misty's place of employment was listed as *Florence Deli*.

When he got home, Daniel did homework, called Angie, and spent an hour listening to more plans for the awards banquet. He and Angie had first hooked up during the party after last year's banquet, and Angie was stressing over every detail of this year's.

"It has to be perfect. This is so special for us."

"It's going to be perfect because it's so special," Daniel said, copying down key phrases on the Treaty of Versailles from his history book. "It's going to be perfect no matter how many yards of bunting there are."

"I know it's going to be perfect, but it has to be perfect, perfect, too."

After telling her he had to go, Daniel went outside to shoot hoops with his brother Fischer. They stripped down to their T-shirts despite the cold and coming dark. When their mom came out and asked if Daniel wanted supper, Daniel shook his head, glanced at his watch, and said it was time to get ready.

Before every semester, Daniel and his parents had a meeting with Mrs. Estes, his college consultant. Last summer, when he'd talked about maybe getting moved to first string on the basketball team this year, a tight-lipped smile had spread across Mrs. Estes's face.

"You know, Daniel. I was thinking it might be best if you focused on academics senior year."

Daniel nodded. "Sure, but I can be first string and still do that."

"But you can't do both well, you see? Your résumé of sports and extracurriculars is already very impressive. Now we need to show Cornell that you're just as serious about academics."

"I am serious."

"Good. Let's show them that." She wanted to take him off the team and, instead, have Daniel enroll in night classes at Samford University. Not only would he start getting college credits, it would get him acclimated to the college environment.

Trying to think of what Mrs. Estes would listen to, Daniel listed all the things he got out of basketball: leadership skills, teamwork skills, how to set goals. Mrs. Estes nodded and pretended to consider this.

"We all know how much sports have taught you, Daniel. But the hard fact is, your basketball game isn't going to get you into any of the colleges you want. You need another edge."

Daniel glanced at his parents. They nodded. "It might be a good idea, pal," his dad said. With all three of them behind the idea, Daniel had buckled once again.

Tuesdays and Thursdays, Daniel drove up to Samford University to take philosophy and sociology. Even if he still bristled occasionally that he'd gotten yanked off the team, it was interesting peeking into what college was going to be like. It had startled Daniel to be suddenly treated like an adult. At Samford, no bells or vice-principals herded students from one class to another. And if Daniel just didn't show up one evening, nobody would call his parents or expect a note.

Daniel took a quick shower and got dressed. From the top shelf of his closet, he took down the Core 205s he'd gotten for Christmas, their soles crisp white and never worn a step outside. Lacing them up and grabbing his book bag, he headed out.

His mom was in the kitchen. "You're dressed very nice."

"Why, thank you," Daniel said without slowing his steps.

"You sure you don't want anything to eat?"

"Not hungry."

"Daniel." She grabbed his arm. "Here. Take some trail mix, at least." She handed him a package of trail mix from the top of the refrigerator. He took it and kissed her cheek. Then, safe behind his mildly harassed smile, Daniel headed out.

Jostling with traffic up Twentieth Avenue, Daniel grabbed the can of body spray he kept in his glove compartment, dashing it across his chest and armpits. He pulled into Florence Deli's parking lot, checked his hair, and tightened his laces. Daniel had his dad's hustle and his mom's green eyes. This would be easy.

Florence Deli was a fast-food chain done in the same downtown style Starbucks went for, with brick walls, lots of blond wood, and employees decorated in tattoos and dreadlocks. Except everything was a little too tastefully matched and easy to wipe down. Walking up to the counter, Daniel wondered if the warm bread smell filling the deli was real or if there were canisters of the stuff in the back.

"Can I help you, sir?" The man standing at the cash register had an East European accent. He wore a manager name tag and a flashy gold watch that clashed with the deli's bohemian attitude.

As Daniel ordered a jalapeño chicken wrap and a Coke, Misty walked around from the back. She wore a yellow Florence Deli vest over a Tragic City Rollergirls T-shirt. She didn't notice

Daniel at first. Grabbing two sandwiches from under a heat lamp, she turned to place them on a woman's tray, then snapped her head around, staring at Daniel like a startled deer.

"Oh." Acting surprised to see her, Daniel gave a limp wave and smiled. "Hey."

"Hey." Misty didn't smile back.

"That will be six twenty-three," the manager said.

Daniel paid and pocketed the change, the whole time pretending not to be watching Misty pretending not to be watching him. When her boss headed into the back, Misty spoke again. "So what's up?"

Daniel shrugged. "Nothing. Just getting something to eat. What's up with you?"

Misty shrugged too. "Work."

Daniel nodded but didn't say anything else, giving her a chance to vanish on some imaginary errand. For a few seconds, Misty seemed to be considering it. Then her gaze drifted to the monitor overhead showing what Daniel had ordered.

"Oh, yuck." Turning, she yelled through the space under the heat lamps. "Ilie! This guy wants to change his order!"

"Do that then!" The manager's flinty accent came from an unseen prep area.

"I do?" Daniel asked.

"Last delivery of chicken was green," Misty whispered, sticking her tongue out in a quick, silent gag. "Like tuna? It's the same price."

"Sure. Thanks."

"No problem." She put in the new order. "It's a tuna wrap, now, Ilie!"

"Fine!"

"So you're just a Good Samaritan to everybody," Daniel said.

A glimmer of a smile started to surface. Misty quickly turned it into a sneer. "Whatever."

"So you got ISS for that thing with the dog?"

She nodded. "Five days." Val Reed appeared pulling a shopping buggy loaded with salads and slices of pie to restock the glass cooler. Misty gave her a subtle look but kept talking to Daniel. "Mom's pissed but . . ." She gave another shrug and let the thought trail off.

"Well, hey, Mrs. MacKaye gave us some more stuff about that paper we have to do. Actually, I've got my notes in my car, if you want to copy them."

One corner of her mouth twitched upward. "That's really cool. But I already took my break."

"Well, I have some things to do, but I could swing back by whenever you're getting off."

Misty narrowed her eyes and studied him.

"Or you could get them when you get out of ISS," Daniel backtracked. "I just thought maybe you'd want to work on that paper over the weekend. Or whatever."

"Have you ever even eaten here before?" she asked suspiciously.

If he insisted this was all coincidence, Misty wouldn't believe him. If he told her the whole truth, he might come off as a stalker. "Well, somebody mentioned you worked here. And, like I said, I was running some errands and figured, you know, maybe I could be a Good Samaritan too." He grinned. It was one hell of a charming grin. It had gotten Daniel out of—and into—a lot worse trouble than this.

His tuna wrap appeared under the heat lamps. Misty bagged it and handed it to him. "I get off at eight. If you're still out by then and want to come back, that's cool. But if you don't, don't worry about it."

"I'll come back. Thanks, Misty."

When he said her name, Daniel finally got a genuine smile from her. "No problem," she said.

"I told you. To give me some notes for government."

"No. What's he really want?"

"I don't know."

Misty and Val talked in circles through the dinner rush. When the stream of customers subsided, Ilie sent them into the back to wash a three-foot-tall stack of trays. They were still scrubbing away when he yelled from the front, "Misty! Your softhead is back!"

"Oh, God." Drying her hands on her vest, Misty ran. Daniel stood at the counter, his book bag slung over one shoulder, dark curls spilling across his forehead. Sleepy eyes watched her barrel out of the back, almost slipping on the greasy tiles.

"Softhead?" he asked.

"It's just a joke. Don't worry—"

"They chatter like crows all day. Val says you babble like you're soft in the head." Ilie busied himself closing down one of the cash registers. He glanced up at Daniel. "That's you, yes?"

"Uh, well, I guess maybe. I don't . . . don't really—"

"Yes, that's you."

Misty felt the tips of her ears burn. Seeing her squirming in place, Daniel laughed at himself and changed the subject. "Ready to get the notes?"

"Yeah. Great." She looked at Ilie. "Can I go?"

"Washing finished?"

"Val's got it."

Ilie let out a grumbling sigh. "Remember to clock out."

"Thanks, Ilie." She looked at Daniel again. "I'll just be a second, okay?"

Nodding, Daniel sat down in one of the booths near the windows. Misty still didn't know what he wanted, but she was glad he was here.

A minute later, Misty and Val slid into the seat across from Daniel. "Sorry about Ilie," Misty mumbled. "He's an asshole to everybody."

Daniel wondered what they'd said about him besides

being soft in the head, but he didn't want to embarrass Misty any more. "Where's he from, anyway?"

"Russia." Misty rolled the R in an over-imitation of Ilie's accent.

"Wow. So Mrs. MacKaye really stressed using historical examples. Other than that, it's your standard comparative essay. Did you get the list of suggested books, or were you . . . ?"

"I think I'd left before then."

"You can borrow mine." Daniel handed her the photocopied list.

"Don't you need it?"

Daniel shook his head. "I already checked out the books I needed."

"Very proactive." Val nodded, snacking on stale cookies. "No wonder you got into Cornell."

Misty's mouth dropped open. "You got into Cornell? Seriously? Holy shit, that's the Ivy League."

"Uh . . ." Daniel stared at her. She stared at a shooting star, a wondrous thing. He wanted to see what Misty's world looked like; he couldn't do it from high above. "No." Daniel forced a laugh. "Where'd you hear that?"

Val shook her head. "Can't remember. Just thought I heard somebody say that. Like, they accepted you early because you're so smart."

"No." Another laugh. "My parents wanted me to apply

there, but I don't know if I even want to go to college right away. Waste another four years sitting in classrooms."

"Yeah. Me neither." Misty said.

Just like that, Daniel had peeled off the shooting star, as thin and brittle as an old snake skin. "So you don't have any plans?" he asked.

She copied his notes while she talked. "Not really. I've thought about, like, backpacking through Europe or something."

"Wow. Where would you go?"

"I don't know." Misty lifted her head and thought about it. "On one hand, I'd love to see the Eiffel Tower and all the stuff I've seen on TV. But then, it'd also be cool to just wander around and not even worry about where you're going to wind up, you know?"

"Yeah, that's what I'd do," Daniel said. "Just let myself get lost somewhere."

Val got a call from Eric, leaving Daniel and Misty to go over the assignment. After she'd copied his notes, they ate stale cookies and talked about Mrs. MacKaye's class.

"She's been teaching government for what? Twenty years?" Misty asked. "But she hasn't had one student become president. I mean, how good a government teacher can she be?"

Daniel laughed. "It's a scandal."

"Misty!" From the counter, Ilie clapped his hands to get her attention. "Time to go."

"We're just sitting here," she said. "C'mon. You're not closing for another hour."

"All day, I fight with teenagers. I should have a tranquilizer gun. You clock out, you're somebody else's problem. Take your softhead and go."

As they gathered their things, she whispered, "Told you he was an asshole."

After an hour in the warm deli, the cold sliced right through Daniel's letterman jacket. Val was still talking to Eric. Glancing at Misty, she asked, "So are we doing anything?"

"Nothing to do."

"We could go see Charlie Say What."

Misty shrugged, then looked at Daniel. "So you have to go home or whatever?"

"Not really." His classes got out at ten. He couldn't go home until after then.

Misty grinned. "Want to drive around and smoke weed?"

They took Misty's massive old Lincoln, Daniel sliding into the front seat beside her. On the way to Eric's house, the girls entertained Daniel with stories about Ilie.

"Tell him about the girlfriend stealing his TV."

"Oh!" Misty banged her fist against the steering wheel. "Okay, Ilie starts dating this woman, right?"

"Who was so skanky. The first time she came up to the deli, I swear, I thought she was a hooker."

"Did you? Seriously?" Misty asked.

"Didn't you? God, she was like a chicken-headed alien from Planet Skeeze."

Misty turned down a street lined with bungalow houses painted cake-frosting colors. Daniel saw Eric waiting on the porch of one.

Andrew Polidari, Eric's brother, had been a senior when Daniel had been a freshman. Daniel hadn't really known him, but he remembered a big, laughing guy holding court in the weight room. He'd been killed in Iraq. A memorial plaque hung in the school's lobby now with a photograph of Andrew solemn in his dress blues. He stood at attention beside pictures of students who'd died in Vietnam, Korea, and World War II.

Eric was a rough sketch of his brother, gawky and stoop-shouldered, but Daniel recognized Andrew's features. Watching him dash toward the car, Daniel noticed Eric didn't wear the same black tanker boots Misty and Val wore. His were made for desert combat, beige with nylon ventilation panels. Daniel realized they'd belonged to Andrew.

Opening the car door, Eric saw Daniel and his eyebrows knitted together. "H—hey."

"What's up?"

They stared at each other until Val said, "Come on, babe, it's cold out."

Climbing in, Eric kept his glare fixed on Daniel. He started whispering back and forth with Val. Daniel pretended he couldn't hear them.

From the corner of his eye, Daniel watched Misty's easy grin. He could smell her shampoo. Then Misty glanced at him from the corner of *her* eye. Their gazes locked for just a moment before they both looked away.

Next, they pulled into Center Gardens Apartments to pick up Marc, who had the same reaction to seeing Daniel as Eric had. Then Misty cruised around to the other arm of the U-shaped apartment complex. Stepping out of the car, Misty grabbed Daniel's sleeve. "Don't stare. He's really sensitive."

"Sensitive about what?"

The apartment door opened, revealing one of the biggest human beings Daniel had ever seen. Misty gave him a hug. "Charlie! What's up?"

"Hey, what's up?" Charlie lifted Misty off her feet. In the light from the apartment, Daniel saw what he wasn't supposed to stare at. Somebody had sliced off both of Charlie Say What's ears.

"Can we trade some green?" Misty whispered.

"Say what?"

"Green," she said again, raising her voice.

"My favorite color." Charlie waved them inside, then stopped Daniel cold with a look. "You queer?"

"Uh . . ."

"You can't seem to take your eyes off me. I know I'm a good-looking sonofabitch, but I'm not queer."

"He's cool, Charlie," Misty said. "Let's do some business."

The apartment's air stank of pot. It made Daniel cough.

There were cases of Natural Light stacked against the kitchen wall, and Daniel guessed Charlie sold that, too. Two women sat watching a movie, hardly taking any notice of the customers.

Pooling their money, they told Charlie what they wanted, then told him again. He kept grunting, "Say what?" The mixture of menace and absurdity made Daniel bite his lip, afraid Charlie would break his jaw if he laughed.

After Charlie went through a beaded curtain, Misty flipped backward over the back of the couch, landing upside down between the women, squealing, "Elsa!"

One of the women tapped Misty on the nose. "How's your momma?" she asked in a sleepy, stoned voice.

Shrugging, Misty took a bowl of popcorn from Elsa's lap and twisted her head around to see the TV. "What are we watching?"

Charlie reappeared. He slipped Misty a Baggie, then they and Elsa chatted like regular neighbors. Daniel stayed in the corner of the living room with the others. Eric and Marc watched him. They had even less of a clue what Daniel was doing here than Daniel did.

He nodded at Marc's Miami Heat jersey. "So what do you think of DeWine so far?" he asked.

"That little bitch? Did you see the Wizards game?"

"Yeah. Where he kept trying to get through Kerry?"

"But he won't pass. They ship two great forwards out to Bum Fuck Egypt so DeWine can play with the ball like it's his left nut." The suspicion shadowing his face faded as he told

Daniel about the Heat game his and Misty's dad had taken him to in Atlanta last season.

After trading a few jokes about the Atlanta Hawks, Daniel mouthed, "Where the hell did his ears go?"

"Some prison thing," Marc mouthed back. "Do not fucking ask."

A minute later, they were back in the car. Misty tossed Eric the weed and a pipe from her purse. Eric carefully filled the pipe bowl as Misty rolled down Fifteenth Avenue. Lighting up, he leaned over to kiss Val and shotgun smoke into her mouth.

Daniel should have been in Dr. Byrd's class right now. At first, mental images of getting pulled over and having to call his parents from jail kept Daniel sober. But the heater blew eddies of smoke around the car as they threaded through dark neighborhoods. They passed the pipe back and forth, talking about music and teachers they hated. The careless abandon of Misty's world was as intoxicating as the weed. Before long, Daniel realized he was giggling just as much as the others.

"My old babysitter went to Hollywood, right?" he told them. "And she wound up doing all these straight-to-video slasher movies."

"Your babysitter became a scream queen?" Val asked. "That's so cool."

"Yeah, but, she was sort of topless in one, so now her family, like, won't talk to her anymore."

"How the hell are you sort of topless?" Misty demanded.

"Well, all topless. But it was really important for the plot. It was about a serial killer who stalked strippers, right? So obviously they needed strippers or the movie wouldn't have made any sense."

"Oh, my God. You actually watched it?" Misty croaked. "You actually watched your babysitter shaking her boobies in some crappy movie."

"Hell, yeah. Julie was my first love."

"Hey, Daniel, you're dating Angie Walton, aren't you?" Val spoke up from the backseat.

"Uh, yeah." The question had really been directed at Misty. Misty knew it too. Daniel caught her scowling at Val's reflection in the rearview mirror.

"You want to call her? We could pick her up," Val offered sweetly.

"Uh, she's on the planning committee for the basketball awards banquet. They're meeting tonight. I called her earlier, and she almost bit my head off."

"Angie's in health class with me," Val said. "She's really nice."

Daniel remembered Angie's comment about staring at Val's back-fat. "Yeah," he nodded, inhaling the scratchy hot smoke.

"Cop!" Marc yelped. "Copcopcop!"

Daniel looked up to watch Misty ease to a red light beside a squad car. Suddenly remembering to be afraid, he dropped the smoldering pipe to the floorboards. His chest started burning for air, but he didn't dare exhale.

They all stared straight ahead. Eric mumbled curses between clenched teeth. Misty fought to hold in a laugh. Watching her shoulders quivering with the effort, Daniel felt laughter surging up his own throat along with the clawing smoke. He smacked her in the arm, but that only made her clamp her hands over her mouth and double over in her seat. Daniel's eyes watered. He started getting dizzy. Risking a glance at the police officers a few feet away, he saw them talking, their words muted by the squad car's window.

Finally, the light turned green. Daniel struggled to hold his breath for a few more seconds while the police cruised up ahead. The moment he saw their taillights, smoke burst from his mouth and nostrils. The car rocked with wild laughter from the others. From the back, Marc reached over the seat and slapped his shoulder.

"Are you okay?" Misty touched his face. "You looked ready to pop a blood vessel."

Daniel hated coming off as a wuss in front of her and her rowdy bunch, but gulping down some air, he said, "If we're going to smoke the rest of this, let's get off the road or something."

"We could go to the furnace," Eric said.

Marc and both girls stiffened. Val nudged her boyfriend hard.

"What furnace?" Daniel asked.

"It's just that old steel furnace off First Avenue," Misty said. "But let's not go there tonight. Come on, Eric."

Daniel didn't understand why they were acting strange. "What? Is it scary or something?"

"No, it's cool." Eric grinned. "And it's about as far out of sight as anyone can get."

Daniel shrugged. "I'm in if you guys are in."

The ride became quieter, just a few hollow jokes and perfunctory laughs, as Misty drove north into a landscape of warehouses and small factories. She pulled into a lot choked with wildflowers, and headlights flared against a gate. Rusting signs declared it the private property of Victor Development.

"So how do we get in?" Daniel asked.

"With a key."

Misty took her keys out of the ignition and passed them to Marc. Climbing out, he rushed to unlock a padlock and unwind the chain holding the gate shut.

"So let me guess," Daniel said. "You're secretly the heir of the Victor Development empire."

"Yeah, right," Misty said. "We just sawed through the real lock and replaced it with our own."

Daniel nodded. "Clever mind like that, gotta be worth two or three empires."

They entered the furnace complex along a potholed memory of a road. Saplings grew to its edges, branches scratching at the car windows. Kudzu and honeysuckle wrapped around the industrial ruins like cloaks. Daniel had never imagined any place in the center of the city could be so quiet.

A wooden house stood at the head of the furnace complex, maybe the front office once. Now, the windows stood broken and the veranda had collapsed. A pair of lolling-tongued wolf heads, painted in dripping black, watched from the house's slat wall. Daniel had seen the symbol somewhere before but couldn't remember where.

"So this place is just abandoned?" he asked, staring around.

"It's a con big companies play," Eric said. "After a factory closes, they go to city hall and say, 'Sell it to us cheap.'"

"Oh, yeah," Daniel nodded. "Promise to open it back up, but then just get it condemned and build an office park or something. The Owenton Community Council's suing the people that own the Goodyear plant over that, aren't they?"

Eric stared at Daniel for a moment, then, without answering, chuckled and turned to look out the window.

Since the first ritual in October, Misty's pack had taken over the furnace. Val had worked out the wolf sign in art class and painted around the perimeter. The homeless living there got the message and moved on, scattering elsewhere.

Driving to the furnace with Daniel, Misty had fought to keep a calm face over her rising panic. A guilty voice inside her whispered that Daniel would take one look around and, somehow, know what they were.

Instead, she parked in the casting shed beneath the

northern blast furnace. They sat in the car with the radio playing, smoked weed, and bitched about school.

Eric and Daniel spiked their talk with subtle displays of advantage and dominance. Neither one would let the other think he was smarter or quicker-witted. But even when Daniel slid in the last word, Eric just smiled. Before long, Misty realized why he'd wanted to take Daniel to the furnace.

Daniel Morning was the prince of McCammon High. Since he'd walked into the deli, Misty had been a little terrified of him. She didn't know what he wanted, she didn't know what she wanted him to want, but she was still worried about saying the wrong thing.

This was their lair, though. The furnace guarded their secrets. No human boy could hurt Misty here. She felt almost as fearless as she did in wolf skin.

The conversation babbled across ISS, work, good weed and dumb things they'd done on it. Then Val and Eric started making out. The car became suddenly claustrophobic, filled with wet smacking sounds from the lovers and nervous shuffles from everybody else.

"Think I'm going to walk around," Marc announced, sliding out of the backseat.

Misty looked at Daniel. "Want to go to the top of the blast furnace?"

"Sure."

• • •

The casting shed stretched the length of a football field. Storms had torn away most of its roof. Following the blue LED glow of Misty's penlight, she and Daniel walked along a brick-lined trough running up the middle of the shed, where liquid steel had once poured from the blast furnace.

Watching the ground so he wouldn't trip, Daniel noticed paw prints crisscrossing the shed's dirt floor in every direction. "Better be careful. Some dogs have been living here."

That made Misty laugh.

"I'm just—"

"Why should I be scared? I've got a big jock to protect me. C'mon." Wrapping her thin fingers around his, she led him up some metal stairs.

The twin blast furnaces were visible from I-20 a mile away, two rusting ghosts watching commuters zip back and forth. Daniel had glimpsed them so many times, he hardly noticed them anymore. But now he stood at the base of one, craning his neck to see it rise up and swallow the moon. The blast furnace filled him with the same awe he imagined feeling among the bluestone towers above Ithaca.

The stairs ended, and they started climbing a ladder up the furnace's chimney, passing one catwalk, then a second, then a third. Icy metal rungs cramped Daniel's hands into claws.

Misty stopped near the top, waiting for him to catch up. She hung by one hand and one foot, her free hand resting on her hip. It was a very imperious gesture to adopt while dangling forty feet above the ground. "What's the matter?" she called down. "You're not afraid of heights, are you?"

In the pitch black, with the wind growing strong enough to pluck Daniel off the ladder like a dead leaf, yes. "No. I was just doing dead weights yesterday and pinched a nerve in my shoulder."

"C'mon!" She started climbing again.

Reaching the highest of four catwalks, their view stretched far beyond the furnace grounds. Years ago, Birmingham's leaders had commissioned a statue of Vulcan, the Roman god of the forge, to overlook their steel town. Daniel could see him standing at the peak of Red Mountain. In the darkness, highways had become molten rivers flowing through the valley.

Unhampered by trees or buildings, the icy wind lashed at them. Daniel and Misty squeezed into the mouth of an exhaust vent just large enough for both of them. Misty pulled her pipe out and packed it with the last crumbs of weed. Daniel cupped his hands around the lighter's flame to keep it from blowing out. He'd gotten her to open up some, to let her scowling mask slip a little and share jokes and beautiful views of the city with him. He figured it was time to ask.

"So when we were in Mrs. MacKaye's class and that dog got hit, why'd you go help it?"

Misty shrugged and passed him the pipe. The wind unspooled the smoke from her mouth as she talked. "Felt sorry for him, I guess. It's a dumb class, anyway."

"Weren't you worried about getting into trouble, though?"

Misty looked at him. She looked down through the catwalk's metal grate to the ground below. "I'm so stoned right now, I don't know how I'm going to get down from here. I'm not even worried about that."

His lungs full of smoke, Daniel's laugh turned into a hard cough.

"ISS isn't any more boring than normal school is," Misty said. "Who cares what room they stick you in if you're just going to be writing a bunch of definitions or whatever either way?"

"Yeah." Daniel stared out across the city. He was the shooting star, and he had his future to think about. He always had his future to think about. But Daniel wished, just once, he could sneer at the rules, just as openly, with just as much reckless grace, as Misty had.

"I do worry about stuff. Just important stuff," Misty said.

"What's important?"

"Marc. He's the one who's always getting into real trouble. Fights and stuff."

Below, they could hear Marc smashing bottles against one of the buildings.

"Dumbass," Misty added. "Got any brothers or sisters?"

"Two brothers."

"Older or younger?"

"Fischer's thirteen and Mack's five."

"Five?" Misty perked up. "Oh, I bet he's cute. Got any pictures?"

They huddled together on top of the world. Daniel tried to probe deeper into why she'd saved the dog, but didn't get any better answer than the one Misty had already given him. It had been an impulsive act. She hadn't considered the consequences before, or apparently, since. She started getting annoyed with his questions, so Daniel let it drop.

Instead, their conversation drifted back to globetrotting. They made up imaginary itineraries and lists of things they'd never seen. They wondered which country had the best castles and where you could drink at eighteen. While they talked, cars and people floated through the streets below like fish in an aquarium.

Sometime after the weed was gone, they turned to the subject of Misty's ex-boyfriend.

"When I started going out with Andre, I thought he was really mature and cool. Toward the end, though, I was pretty much dating him ironically. You know, like how everybody was wearing trucker hats a couple years back?"

Daniel laughed, rocking backward and banging his head against the exhaust vent. Misty winced at the dull *clang* it made. "Ow! Relax. It wasn't that funny."

"It was. But mostly you're just a lot different than I thought."

"Really, what'd you think?"

"I'm not sure. Just . . . different."

Misty's grin faded. "You know, I'm not some monster."

"I know."

"It's just people talk a lot of shit at school, and maybe I've done some stupid stuff, but, I mean, yeah, I set Andre's clothes on fire, but it's not like he was wearing them when I did, you know?"

"So why did you set his clothes on fire?"

She glared at him. "Because he pissed me off."

Daniel nodded. He watched her for another second, then felt himself leaning forward, felt damp-breath vapor and the soft resistance of Misty's mouth.

Misty closed her eyes as Daniel kissed her. His soft curls brushed her forehead. Her hand reached out to touch the firm muscles beneath his shirt. She wanted to sink into him, and that scared her, because it meant he could hurt her, even here in their lair.

Daniel pulled away, and Misty relished the slight ache left behind. "Just don't piss me off," she whispered.

CHAPTER 5

Leaving the furnace, neither Misty nor Daniel spoke much. After he'd waved good-bye, Misty didn't mention the kiss to Val or the boys, pretending such a small detail had slipped her mind.

She was still in in-school suspension Friday. The ISS room had bare walls and papered-over windows. Misty sat at a carrel with wooden partitions keeping her from seeing the other students around her. Nobody was allowed to speak or leave except to go to the restroom. The isolation had a crushing weight like deep water.

Her back aching from sitting hunched over, Misty did busywork until three. After school, she went to the deli. Every time the electronic door chime sounded, Misty would glance up, then silently scold herself for hoping it'd be Daniel.

Her shift was supposed to end at eight, but Ilie needed her to prep a bunch of dough for tomorrow, and she ended up staying past nine. When the day was finally over, Misty gathered with her pack at the furnace.

Not much of the stuff from horror movies turned out to be true. They didn't transform into wolfmen, walking on two feet, hands tipped with vicious claws. They just became ordinary wolves. The boys were disappointed about that, but Misty loved charging through the night on four long legs.

When they were human, they didn't crave raw meat or have tufts of hair sprouting over their bodies. It had taken five minutes to explain to Marc why getting shot with a silver bullet would hurt whether he was a werewolf or not.

And the full moon didn't have any effect on them. Only the ritual allowed them to shift. The rot-eater god's putrid eucharist turned their minds animal-pure, devoid of emotion or memory. Then their stomping, sweating, screaming dance summoned their most primal selves to the surface.

At first, the wolves had only emerged for a few seconds at a time. They just raced around the furnace grounds. Slowly, Misty and her pack had learned to suppress their humanity for minutes, then hours, at a time, and had begun venturing into the city.

Now, Misty crouched near the fire, its light turning her breath a pale, poisonous yellow. Watching the *Amanita muscaria* smolder, she remembered how desperate she'd been to show Daniel she wasn't a monster. Before that night with him, she hadn't realized that she wasn't entirely certain herself.

Val started turning up the music. Misty stopped her. "Hey. What if we're doing something really wrong with all this? What if the rot-eater god is really, like, the Devil?"

Eric was scratching spirals into the dirt with a piece of rusted metal. "Think you're going to hell?"

"Well?"

"For what? Dumping your prick boyfriend? Helping that dog the other day? When that dog got hit, how many good, Buckle-of-the-Bible-Belt Christians saw it, and sat there, and didn't do shit?"

Misty didn't answer.

"But you did," Val said. "Eric's right. Wolves aren't evil. Just strong."

Even before Misty had learned what lay beneath her skin, if she'd heard that dog whimpering, she would've felt the same urge to help it. She didn't know if she could have stood up, though, cowed by the thought of Mr. Fine lecturing her in the main office and Andre telling her she'd acted like a fool.

But now, even when Misty wore her human shape, she walked through school like a wolf—strong; proud—knowing she was something Mr. Fine, Andre, or any of the other yapping hand-lickers could never intimidate into submission.

"You're right," Misty told Val. After another moment of thought, she reached for one of the smoking mushrooms.

Soon they were dancing, letting the energy chained down in classrooms and crappy jobs break free. Misty's worry and wondering burned away. Her memory of Daniel's face burned away. The wolf heard Misty's chanting calls and appeared in the firelight.

Their clothes disappeared with their humanity. The pack tore naked through the streets. They didn't notice the cold; their pelts trapped body heat so well, the snow didn't melt on their backs.

Through the wolf's night-stalker eyes, colors were washed out to a eternal dusk, but Misty could see infinite flickering movements all around her. Birmingham was in constant, rippling motion like the surface of a lake. The wind filled with delicate blushes of scent. She smelled trash and exhaust fumes, a fire-gutted house blocks away and spring welling up beneath the frozen ground.

Even though people didn't see anything but a pack of big dogs, that was enough to make them wary and keep their distance. Val slipped back into human skin twice, just long enough to spray paint their sign on an overpass and the wall of a gas station. But mostly, the wolves just ran as fast as they could, moving across the city like a thunderhead. Southside belonged to them. Maybe rats, sneak-thief racoons, and humans scuttled along its edges, but it belonged to the wolves.

It was nearly dawn when *Amanita muscaria*'s magic began to fade, making it harder and harder to keep civilized thoughts from seeping into their minds. One by one, they tumbled back into their human skins—and tanker boots and hoodies—and were unable to shift into wolves again. The night's prowl was over.

Legs threatening to crumple with every step, they returned to the furnace for their cars. Val came home with Misty and

Marc. Prowling always left them famished. After getting to the apartment, Marc grabbed some food and vanished. Misty and Val stood in the kitchen eating cold fried chicken and licorice. And water. Before she'd become a wolf, Misty had never realized how delicious crisp, cold water was. They were still gorging when Misty's mom came home.

"Misty! Use a glass, damnit."

Misty lifted her head from the faucet, water dripping down her chin and the front of her shirt. Even though they were human on the surface, it took a while for their brains' language centers to wake up. Forming words was difficult; the sounds didn't fit right in their mouths. "Sorry," Misty grumbled. "I'm sorry."

"Why are you two still up? What have you been doing?"

Misty shrugged. "Mostly . . . on the computer."

"It must be nice to actually enjoy staying up all night. Just please be careful what you do online, okay? Please?"

Misty nodded.

Her mom started making herself breakfast. Reaching past Val for a cereal bowl, she asked, "Honey, what happened to your hands?"

Val's hands were speckled with black spray paint. She shoved them into her pockets. "Art project."

Luckily, after years of bartending, Misty's mom couldn't smell the smoke on their clothes. Misty and Val retreated to Misty's bedroom with more food. They freed their aching feet from their boots and hit the lights, still eating in the dark.

The wolf was hidden but not gone. Even though Misty could walk upright and speak with concentration, the wolf's simple hungers and austere philosophies bled into her more complicated human vision of the world. Drifting to sleep, Misty remembered Daniel but not what she'd gotten so anxious about. He had kissed her. Because of his heat and savory boy smell, Misty kissed him back. She'd taken a few seconds of pleasure from him. There was nothing beyond that.

Misty began to dream without realizing it. Her eyes closed, she listened to the wolf, her other self, pad into the dark room and settle down at the foot of the bed.

They slept past noon, until Eric called Val to check on her. Yawning and stretching themselves awake, Misty felt talkative again and finally told Val about Daniel.

Val, still in Misty's old Dora the Explorer sleeping bag, sat up with a jerk. "You kissed him? When?"

"When we went to the furnace Thursday. And he kissed me first. I was just being polite."

Val slumped back to the floor and hid her face under her pillow.

Misty laughed. "It wasn't a big deal."

"I thought you weren't into him," Val said, her voice muffled.

"I wasn't." Reaching down, she grabbed the last of the licorice. "I always figured he was just a leg-humping jock. But he's really kinda sweet. He actually likes talking about things besides himself."

"He's still got Angie."

"I know, I know."

"So?" Lifting the edge of the pillow, Val gave Misty a nervous look. "No matter how sweet and gooey he is on the inside, I don't want you to be his little gutterfuck when she won't give him any. You're way too good for that."

Misty stared at the ceiling and finished off the candy. Val had watched her tear herself apart over Andre, and she'd earned the right to worry. This was different, though. Misty was different. Misty was a wolf. "Maybe I'll make him my little gutterfuck."

Angie had soccer player legs, firm and tan even in January. She had a sunny personality, a belly-button ring, and that smile that made the whole school want her. And Daniel had her.

His friends were the best bunch of guys Daniel could imagine. He was destined for the bluestone towers of Cornell, and he had made his mark here. Trophies etched with his name and records would stand in their glass cases long after he'd left Birmingham behind.

All that should have been enough, but Daniel's night with Misty and her friends had awakened something restless inside him.

Their combat boots, which only Marc didn't wear, kept

the group distinct from the student body mingling around them. They didn't even have much to do with McCammon's other dregs, the stoners and skater boys in their Vans.

Despite all that, Misty's friends acted a lot like Daniel's own, just a little more desperate and a little more dangerous. Eric had something to prove, but Daniel knew lots of guys like that, small guys who knew exactly how small they were and hated the world for it.

Misty was the one who fascinated him, though. Unlike him, she didn't have a shining future waiting up the road. But she had furious pride and the freedom to forge her own path to wherever she pleased.

Misty was out of ISS Wednesday. Daniel looked up as she walked into Mrs. MacKaye's class, and they held each other's gaze just a moment too long. Then Misty took her usual seat by the windows. A minute later, Mrs. MacKaye shut off the lights and started a PowerPoint lecture on the Supreme Court. Daniel kept stealing glances at Misty.

He thought about Angie's soccer player legs some more, her taut calves, how ticklish she was behind her knees, gently biting her thighs. It didn't work. After the bell rang, he lingered outside the classroom, pretending to read a flyer for a summer biology program on Dauphin Island. When Misty came out, he said, "What's up? So, I've been thinking about you thinking about traveling after graduation. I know where I'd want to go."

"Cool. Where?"

"The Greek Isles. Keith told me about them a while ago. There's beaches that you can only get to by boat, and at night, like, the whole island turns into one huge party."

"Yeah. I think I saw something on TV about them. They seem pretty cool."

They both had first lunch period. They started walking to the cafeteria but only got as far the stairwell landing. Hidden from the bustle of the school, whispered voices and laughter echoed up and down the brick-walled shaft. They talked about skinny dipping in the Aegean Sea and other adventures Daniel would never have. At least not until he'd gotten through his undergraduate courses and nailed the LSAT. But by then, he'd be grubbing for a prominent internship or maybe a position on the *Cornell Law Review*. After graduating, some people spent a year just studying for the bar exam. And after that he'd need to begin planning his career. It wasn't like he could spend that time wandering Southern Europe and expect to get anywhere.

Misty, on the other hand, had apparently thought as far as buying a plane ticket and grabbing her toothbrush, happy to make the rest up as she went along.

She liked him, and Daniel knew a lot of it was because he'd lied, pretended to be as reckless as she was. He decided there wouldn't be any harm in pretending for a little longer. As far as anything sexual, he could keep his options open.

The bell rang. They'd spent the whole lunch period talking.

"Wow, I better go," Daniel said, jumping to his feet. He still didn't want anyone seeing them talking.

"Yeah, me too. Oh, wait." Reaching out, she started feeling Daniel's shoulders through his shirt. "Hm . . . not super sculpted, are you?" she said in a teasing voice.

"You mean traps and deltoids? No. I used to have them when I played ball, but I haven't been working out regularly like I used to. It takes a lot of free-weight work to harden those up."

"Hm."

"I mean, a lot of work. Like three times a week."

"Hm."

Daniel wasn't used to being appraised so unforgivingly. Ignoring the people already trickling up the stairs, he defended his ego. "Do you know how many girls want this body?" He rubbed his chest. "Dream about it?"

Misty eyed him up and down. "I bet. Narrow shoulders. Slim thighs. Give you some decent boobs, and you'd be gorgeous."

"What? No, I mean, want me."

"Oh, that's what you meant." She smirked, then turned and headed up the stairs. "Well, see you."

Daniel stood there completely baffled, kind of scared, and a little turned on.

A few days later, they swapped numbers. They always made sure to have some reason to call, usually a question about government class, but then they'd talk for hours about places beyond Birmingham or just their families. Daniel told Misty about getting yanked off the basketball team but switched one detail, saying his parents had made him quit because of his grades.

Daniel kept finding ways to slip out of his real life and go slumming with Misty and her strange friends. They never did much, but it felt like an adventure, anyway. Daniel would hang out at the deli, run by Charlie Say What's, and for a few wonderful hours, forget he was within arm's reach of the valedictorian's purple honor cord.

When he was with her, Misty would be constantly plucking at his sleeve or nudging his shoulder. Once, Daniel's shirt tag was sticking out. Without halting her stream-of-consciousness chatter about work, Misty reached around to tuck it back in.

Those brief, static pop touches thrilled Daniel. And judging from the sly smiles that followed them, Misty knew it. They never led to another kiss, though, or any of the other things they made him think about.

Eve had probably taught her daughters the same game, but Daniel wondered if any girl since the fall of man had played it with as much cool and confidence as Misty. Within a week, Daniel had given up any hope of screwing her, then going back to Angie. Misty was happy to have him around, happy to keep his excitement and desire stirred up, but nothing else would happen until Daniel showed her he was serious.

Since he continued calling, Daniel had to admit she was winning.

Sneaking around behind Angie's back was exhausting enough, but it also guilted Daniel into acting like the perfect boyfriend when he was with her. On the Sunday before Martin Luther King Jr. Day, Daniel went to church with Angie, then downtown. She needed to talk to the events coordinator at the Tutwiler Hotel, then do some shopping. Browsing through stores, Daniel held Angie's hand and whispered gentle things in her ear. When she saw a funky beaded purse she liked, Daniel bought it, saying it was just because he loved her.

Angie obsessed over the awards ceremony the whole time. With a week to go, minor details had her near tears. Plus, Claire had said something to another girl that got back to Angie, and now the two of them weren't speaking.

Daniel found the details dull. And he was dreading the ceremony a little. He looked good in a suit, and the afterparty was always worth recounting the next Monday, but last year, he'd gotten the Oliver Robinson Award, given to the player with the best scholastic ranking.

Oliver Robinson had played ball at McCammon before getting drafted by the Spurs. A bad shoulder ended his pro career, and he was a state legislator now. Mr. Robinson shaking his hand and giving him the trophy had made Daniel grin like a moron, not to mention the five-hundred-dollar scholarship that went with it.

He would have been first string this year. Who knew what he could have done? But his parents had pulled him off the team, and the only reason Daniel got to go to the ceremony at all was as Angie's date.

Driving home, they crossed the train tracks and a long clay scar that had been a major street before the overpass had been built above. Now, Baseemah Taxi Service parked their broken-down cabs on what was left of the road. Three of the cabs bore spray-painted wolf heads across their sides.

"Jesus," Daniel muttered as they bounced across the tracks.

"What?" Angie turned but didn't see anything except a few vandalized cars.

Daniel shook his head. "Nothing."

The tracks divided downtown from Southside. The wolves watched north, gazing across office towers and regional head-quarters. The same wolves guarded the furnace. Since Misty and her friends had taken Daniel there, he'd started to suspect they were the ones throwing the signs up all over the city. In the weeks since, he'd spotted it on store fronts and overpass pillars. Slowly, he'd begun seeing a pattern. Misty's crew weren't vandalizing random walls and weren't driven purely out of boredom. The wolf head only appeared near arteries of traffic flowing into Southside. They were slowly, steadily marking their territory.

Daniel had tried to guess why but didn't have a clue. Whatever their reason, they'd obviously spent a lot of time, effort, and risk on the project. Somehow the secret, like a locked chest, fascinated Daniel more than the treasures Misty had already revealed.

All the way to her house, Angie talked about the awards

ceremony. Daniel tried paying attention, but his eyes kept flickering to the mouths of alleys. He wondered if Misty was out there somewhere in her scuffed tanker boots. Nodding, mumbling vague affirmations to Angie, Daniel strained to see past the streetlights and glowing signs, down into the dark cracks of the city.

"Daniel?"

"Yes, Misty?"

"I really like you."

"Great, let's do it. Or should I just massage your feet while speaking in an Italian accent?"

Misty slapped Val's arm. "Come on. Be serious."

They sat in the walk-in cooler, having a dinner of cookie dough and weed. Grabbing the pipe from Misty, Val laughed. "Okay. Give me a second. . . . Gee, Misty, I really like you too," she said, lowering her voice.

"Way more than that cheap skank Angie, right?"

"Of course."

"Good. I have to tell you something, though. And you have to promise to listen to the whole thing before you say anything, okay?"

"Whatever you heart desires, my love."

"Okay. I am a werewolf. I know that sounds crazy—"

"Damn straight it does. Never talk to me again, you whack-job. I'm going back to the cheap skank."

"No, Val! He promised to listen."

"I don't care what he promised. He's not going to stick around after you tell him you're a werewolf. Either he'll think you're nuts, or even worse, he'll believe you and think you're about to eat his entrails."

Misty took a toke and shook her head. "See, I hit him with the werewolf thing first. Bang! Like ripping off a Band-Aid. Then I explain everything calmly and rationally, so he doesn't get scared and can't think I'm crazy."

"You're so fucking high."

"God, I can't keep my hands off him. But I can't . . . you know, until I figure this out."

"What's to figure out? Three weeks ago you were just going to use him for sex, then kick him out of bed and make him do your laundry or whatever."

Sighing and stuffing her hands in her jacket, Misty slumped against the corner. "That's, like, what I want to want. But—"

Ilie jerked the cooler door open. Val shoved the tub of cookie dough back on the wire rack. Ilie didn't care if they smoked weed, but he hated it when they ate his cookie dough.

"I need some Reuben preps," he said.

Val glanced at the time. "We still have five minutes on our break."

"I don't need them in five minutes. I need them now."

"I got it." Misty grabbed the carton she'd been sitting on and a pack of cheese slices off a rack. Ilie held the cooler door open for her.

"You waste all your money on drugs. Should save it. Go to university someday."

"And quit working here?" Misty asked. "Ilie, you're like a father to us."

Val's stoned laugh spilled out of the cooler as the door swung shut.

Since October, Misty had been a wolf. She'd only wanted food, sex, and some time to prowl with her pack. All winter, her life had been that beautifully, brutally simple. Then Daniel had walked into the deli, and Misty's human side started complicating everything again.

She'd never daydreamed about backpacking through Europe. But Daniel had said he didn't know what he was doing after graduation, and Misty needed to say something back. Traveling the world was the first thing that popped into her head. It was a ridiculous lie. Misty felt like a stray in Birmingham. Being lost in a distant city, surrounded by strangers, would terrify her.

But Daniel kept asking questions, so Misty kept lying. Somehow, she fooled him into thinking she really was that free. He looked at her like she was someone enchanted, like he had no clue she was just a hoodrat.

Slowly, Misty started believing her own fairy tales. It wasn't like there was anything here worth sticking around for. She could save some money and go wherever she wanted.

Making the Reuben preps, Misty laid a piece of precooked, presliced roast beef on a waxed paper circle, a slice of Swiss cheese on top of that, another slice of roast beef, and then another waxed paper circle. Ilie grabbed the first two she made, dropping them on the grill for thirty seconds before scooping them into rye loafs with sauerkraut and Thousand Island dressing.

"Ten more for tonight," he said without glancing at her.

Misty stacked them one on top of another. Meat, cheese, meat, waxed paper, meat, cheese, meat, waxed paper. While her hands moved automatically, she studied the Florence Deli logo on the cheese wrapper, an old-world skyline dominated by an orange-and-white domed roof. Misty had spent more than a year surrounded by its image—on the sign outside, on her uniform vest, as a watermark on every paycheck—but until a few days ago, she'd never been curious enough to find out what it was a picture of.

The dome was the Basilica di Santa Maria del Fiore, the Basilica of Saint Mary of the Flower, in the real Florence. Now, making Reuben preps and staring at the logo, Misty let herself imagine standing in Florence, Italy, seeing the actual thing.

The wolf was hungry for Daniel. She loved his strong arms and good smell. She wanted to bite him. Not hard. Just a little. Misty loved his eyes, the deep green of slow-moving rivers. As the weeks of conversations went by, though, Misty was falling just as hard for the reflection of herself she saw inside them.

Another kind of desire had started winding itself around

the wolf's urges like a vine. Misty wanted to be the woman Daniel let her pretend to be. She wanted to be clever enough and fearless enough to leave everything familiar behind, to explore foreign cities and see strange sunsets.

"Just don't stare," Daniel said. "He's really sensitive."

"Sensitive about what?"

The door opened, and Bwana and Spence got their first look at Charlie Say What.

"Hey, Daniel." Charlie bumped Daniel's fist. "Where's Misty?"

"She's working."

"Say what?"

"Working! Let's go inside."

Charlie glared at Spence. "You queer?"

"They're cool, Charlie. Let's go inside."

While Angie worried about centerpieces, Daniel decided to do some planning of his own for the awards ceremony. Namely, getting beer for the afterparty. He joked around with Charlie and Elsa while Bwana and Spence stayed very quiet in the corner.

As Spence carried a case of Natural Light back to his car, he whispered, "What the hell happened to his ears?"

"Some prison thing. C'mon, let's go play ball."

They loaded the beer in the trunk and headed to the park. Bwana asked, "Who's Misty he asked about?"

Daniel had hoped they'd been too startled by Charlie's appearance to catch that. "She's Charlie's cousin. She introduced me to him. I know her from church."

"Bullshit," Spence laughed. "It's Misty Sandlin. Don't lie. Somebody said you were asking around for where she worked."

"Are you for real?" Bwana started laughing too. "Danny Boy. Don't tell me you're that hard up since you left the team. I used to go to your house, there'd be girls camped out on the lawn. I used to follow you around like a seagull hoping for your scraps."

If they hadn't been cousins, Daniel might have gone and banged Keith's skull against the ground until the memory of printing out Misty's information plopped out. Daniel looked at his friends. There was only one answer they'd believe. "Well? She's got a nice pair of tits if you actually look at her."

"Need to be careful. Crazy one like that will bite a chunk off."

Daniel shook his head. "Just flip them facedown. They're like catfish; be careful how you handle them, they're harmless."

Daniel's friends didn't love him because he was a bastard. They loved him because he was so good at it. They crowed and tried to top one another's jokes. Inside, Daniel stewed over Keith. He never would have trusted the loudmouthed idiot except he'd needed him. He didn't trust Bwana or Spence much more.

"Just keep quiet, all right? I sure as shit don't need Angie finding out."

"We aren't going to say anything," Bwana said.

"Not even to Geneva. I'm serious, okay?"

"Yeah, don't worry about it, man."

At the park, they played one-on-one, but Daniel was out of practice. He kept missing easy shots and lost to Spence, then Bwana, in forty-five minutes. At least it gave them something to laugh about besides Misty.

After two more embarrassing rounds, it was past dark. Daniel said good-bye and headed to Florence Deli. He hadn't been to his night classes in almost a month. It was still early in the semester, though. Daniel figured he could catch up later.

Misty was wiping off tables in the dining area when Daniel walked in. Seeing her, he gave her his perfect lopsided smile.

Eric showed up a few minutes later. After Misty and Val clocked out, they went to hang out on the sidewalk, breathing warm air into cupped hands. Soon, Val and Eric decided to go.

"We're hitting the town tomorrow, right?" Eric asked.

Misty nodded. "I'll tell Marc."

Leaning close, Val said, "Just use him, then make him do the laundry."

Misty elbowed her but grinned, anyway.

"Bye, wolf girl," Val whispered, making Misty feel a little more confident.

Watching them pull out of the parking lot, Daniel asked. "So what do you guys have going on tomorrow?"

"Whatever." Misty shrugged. "Just run around."

"Spray-paint a few more taxis?"

She stiffened. "How'd you know about that?"

"I notice things."

Misty realized Daniel thought about her when she wasn't around. Maybe as much as she thought about him. Watching him from the corner of her eye, Misty knew she couldn't stand being inches away from him, but still miles away, much longer. She had to risk telling him what she was. When she opened her mouth, though, she couldn't force the words out. "So I read about this basilica in Florence," she said instead.

"Yeah? Thinking about going there?"

"Why not."

They sat on the cold sidewalk. Daniel was in a glum mood. After some cajoling, he admitted, "I went to the park with Bwana and Spence today, and the awards ceremony is Saturday, and I don't know, I just wish I could have played ball this year."

"It sucks your parents wouldn't let you."

Daniel shrugged. "It wasn't like I'd ever get a scholarship or anything."

"But that's still what you were good at. That's what made everybody cheer for you."

"Yeah." He scraped at a patch of ice with the heel of his

sneaker. "That's not what I miss, though. I miss pushing myself like that. Just running as hard as I could, whipping through all these other guys running as hard as they could. It's like . . ." He searched for the right words. Misty found them for him.

"It's like you can't let yourself think," she said. "You have to just let instinct take over. If you think, you'll stumble."

"Yeah. You ever play sports?"

"No, but I know what you're talking about." In her mind's eye, Misty was prowling the city, muscles and tendons singing like violin strings. "Going crazy from sitting still all the time. Wanting to just run until you're exhausted."

"Exactly. That's what I miss, when you can't even hear anyone cheering because the blood's pounding in your ears so bad."

Misty had gone to a few games. She'd listened to people chanting Daniel's name and watched him stride through the school in his letterman jacket. She'd never thought about what he got out of basketball except what she heard and saw herself. Misty studied Daniel's profile in the artificial noon of streetlights and storefronts, imagining him as a wolf.

She kissed him this time. She tasted his mouth and neck, and let her hands explore his chest. Daniel held her warm against the icy wind.

Then Misty's phone rang. She cussed, already knowing it was her mom. She lied, saying she was just coming back from Val's house. After hanging up, Daniel asked, "You in trouble?"

"No. But I better go." Misty stood up, and Daniel did too. Out of habit learned with Angie and other real girlfriends, he leaned forward to kiss her good night, then halted, not sure what to do.

Misty didn't know what to do either. Her face felt flushed and hot. Her mom had slammed the brakes on their make-out session but couldn't slow its momentum. She'd only sent Misty fishtailing.

"Hey, you want to come out with us tomorrow?"

Daniel made a soft murmuring sound. "Can't. I got some things to do."

"With Angie?"

"Yeah." The word came out as an apology.

"What do you have to do with Angie?"

"The ceremony's Saturday, and we still need to pick up some of the decorations and put together the gift bags. Plus some of the paperwork—"

"That sounds really boring."

"It'll be excruciating."

"Get out of it, then. We'll go run around instead. Let instinct take over." She grinned, knowing he wanted to. "Get the blood pounding in our ears."

Daniel hesitated for a few seconds, then nodded. "I can probably talk my way out of it."

"Cool. See you tomorrow, then."

"See you."

Walking to her car, it sank in that she'd just invited Daniel into the pack. She hadn't even asked the others first.

CHAPTER 6

Meeting up at school the next morning, Misty told the rest of the pack. They just stared at her until she started to squirm, until she wished one of them would at least blink.

"No," Eric said once he realized she wasn't joking. "There's no way that over-the-mountain dick is tagging along with us."

"He's not from over the mountain. He lives below Vulcan Park."

Birmingham sprawled through a valley. On the other side of Red Mountain, curtained from the city's smog, teacup mansions dotted curlicue streets. It was a fifteen-minute drive over the mountain into Southside. From Southside, the emerald green suburbs marked the borders of the known world.

Eric glared across the teeming lobby at Daniel, watching him laugh at something one of his daylight friends said. "He wishes he was from over the mountain. That's even more pathetic."

"Daniel's not like that," Marc said. "Some of them are like that, but Daniel's cool."

Marc was defending Daniel because they liked the same basketball team. Misty needed all the support she could get, though, so she kept quiet.

"I don't care how cool he is," Eric hissed. "We can never trust him. No matter how friendly he acts or how much he jokes around with you guys, he's a hand-licker. When trouble starts, he'll betray you."

"Betray us? To who?" Misty demanded. "The Spanish Inquisition? Even if Daniel did tell anybody, they'd never believe him. And he's not going to tell. Just because he's a jock doesn't mean he's a hand-licker." Misty recounted what Daniel had said the night before about missing basketball. He had the same maddening restlessness that had driven them blindly toward the furnace, toward release through *Amanita muscaria*.

Eric wouldn't budge. He refused to go to the furnace if Misty brought Daniel with her. Marc, though, was more excited about tonight than before. Val didn't say much until after the bell rang. Leaving Eric and Marc, she walked with Misty to her homeroom.

"You should have asked us before you invited him. Before you invited anybody."

"I know. I'm sorry. I wasn't exactly thinking straight. But you were right; there's no way to just tell him without him thinking I'm crazy."

"So you'll just scare the hell out of him, instead?" Val asked.

"It scared us too, at first, but we ended up loving it. Daniel will too."

"And what if he doesn't?"

"I already told you, even if he did try to tell—"

"I'm not worried about Daniel. I'm worried about you. What happens if he decides you're evil and never wants anything to do with you again."

"When I first told you me and Daniel kissed, you said I was too good to be his gutterfuck, right? If Daniel really has a wolf inside him, then he's not going to keep wasting his time with Angie. If he doesn't, then it was never meant to be or whatever, but at least I can quit wasting my time with him."

Val sighed. "Bring him then. I'll talk to Eric."

Misty hugged her. "Thank you. I love you."

"You really need to quit listening to me. I'm just making it up as I go along half the time."

Government class seemed to languish for hours. While Mrs. MacKaye droned on, Misty kept glancing at Daniel across the room. She silently recited, *He wants to be a wolf. He just doesn't know it yet.*

Lost in thought, she didn't notice Mrs. MacKaye had stopped talking until the teacher snapped her fingers in front of Misty's face. Startled, she whipped around to meet Mrs. MacKaye's sickly sweet smile.

"How about you stop ogling Mr. Morning and concentrate on passing my class?"

Stifled laughter rose around Misty. Mrs. MacKaye kept

her hand, tobacco beneath the scent of lotion, hovering an inch below Misty's nose. Misty wanted to grab it and twist. But she straightened in her seat instead, pretending to be entirely human.

After the bell finally rang, Daniel talked to Bwana as they stuffed binders into their book bags. Misty waited for Bwana to leave before walking up to Daniel.

"Hey. So you still want —?"

"Yeah. Do you want me to call you later or —?"

"Actually, Marc needs the car today. Think you could give me a ride home after school?"

Daniel almost managed to mask his nervous expression. She wasn't supposed to make demands on his time. "Just this once," Misty added.

"Sure. No problem."

"Cool. I'll see you at three."

"Cool."

Entering the cafeteria, they separated without a parting glance. Daniel slipped up behind Angie and wrapped his arms around her. Misty found her pack in the lunch line. Val had smoothed things over with Eric, but he was still sullen about the whole thing. Ignoring him, Misty told Marc to take the car and go somewhere, anywhere, just as long as she had the apartment to herself for a few hours.

The sensation of his skin shifting around him would scare Daniel at first. But Misty could get him through it, she could give him a reason to stay, and soon he'd see how beautiful he could become in the dark. Then, maybe, Misty could become beautiful in the daylight.

Daniel had already told his parents he'd be chauffeuring Angie around all day, so they wouldn't expect him home until late. At lunch, he told Angie he needed to finish a paper for one of his college courses. She was pissed, but Daniel promised to get to the hotel early tomorrow and help set up for the awards ceremony.

After school, he slipped through a backdoor, avoiding Angie and his friends, crossing the parking lot with quick, short-breathed strides. A few people shouted his name. Daniel shouted back but didn't slow down.

Misty milled near his car and smiled when she saw him. Daniel didn't smile back. He relaxed once they were heading down Thirteenth Avenue, away from Angie, the awards ceremony, and the shooting star. He felt himself become that other Daniel, waiting for sunset to hit the city with Misty and her lovable crew of graffiti-bombers.

"So what are we doing tonight, anyway?" Daniel asked.

Misty shrugged. "We'll find something. I just need to change first."

He drove to Center Gardens Apartments. Misty pointed to an empty parking space beside her door. "You can park here. Mom's still at work."

"Okay."

Across the complex, Charlie Say What sat on his stoop, drinking beer with a couple friends. Misty and Daniel waved. Then, unlocking her door, Misty led him inside.

Daniel had never been in Misty's apartment before. Ceramic knickknacks filled the living room. Everything was so proudly clean, Daniel could have built microchips at the coffee table. A white cat brushed against his leg, and Daniel bent down to scratch it.

"That's Lily," Misty said.

"Hey, Lily."

Misty crouched to pet her too, their fingers brushing each other's in Lily's short fur. After a few seconds of quiet, Misty stood up, playing with her lip ring. "Okay, I need to change. C'mon."

Daniel hesitated, watching Misty turn down a hall. "C'mon," she said again.

Daniel followed her into a room wreathed in fruity scents from lotions and makeup. The beige walls were covered with pictures cut from magazines and a pastel drawing of Misty asleep at a desk.

"Val do that?" Daniel motioned to the drawing.

"Yeah. And it only got a B; that's kind of insulting," Misty laughed nervously. "You like Pins & Needles?"

"What?"

"The band. They're okay." Misty dropped a CD into her

stereo. Piano notes filled the room, followed by winding lyrics about a girl on a train.

Singing under her breath, Misty started unbuttoning her shirt. Daniel glimpsed her storm gray bra, then turned to examine a column of snapshots between the door frame and light switch, the last things Misty glimpsed before heading into the world.

Most were of Misty and her friends. They stood in Wal-Mart sometime near Halloween in one, posing with the masks and plastic pitchforks. Val stuck her tongue out in another. One was of a black man and white woman Daniel guessed were Misty's parents, her and Marc infants in their arms. And one picture made him chuckle.

"Oh, my God. When was this?" Kids in Renaissance costumes lined up along a stage, a forest of tempera-paint trees and plastic ivy behind them. Misty stood in the center, wearing a pair of blue fairy wings.

"No, don't look at that. My whole face broke out from that stage makeup."

Daniel heard the rustle of fabric falling to the floor. "Seriously, when was this?" he asked.

"Ninth grade." Behind him, Misty was rearranging pillows. "It was *A Midsummer Night's Dream*. I played Puck."

Daniel stared at the fourteen-year-old Misty smiling out from the photo. She didn't smirk or sneer; she beamed without any caution at all. Her eyes glittered. "You remember any of your lines?"

"Daniel." Misty sat on the edge of the bed wearing nothing except her jeans. When he turned, she started to cover herself, then stopped and held her hands in her lap.

For years, he'd barely noticed Misty. When he did, all he saw was a scrawny, pallid thing. Now, Daniel couldn't imagine being blind enough not to see how rare she was. Misty's skin was the color of autumn. Even naked, with peering eyes and lips pressed into a thin, nervous line, she tipped her chin up, the mildest hint of challenge.

They started kissing. One of Daniel's hands tangled into Misty's hair. The other touched her shoulder blade and the knobs of her spine. Her armor of scowls and tanker boots stripped away, Misty's body shook a little. She trusted him, though. Misty didn't trust many people, and Daniel knew what a gift this was.

When she started unbuttoning his fly, Daniel pulled back. "Wait. Wait a second."

"Don't worry, I've got—"

"No, not that. It's just . . ." Daniel traced her collarbone with his fingertips. Its shape reminded him of the curving lines of spray-painted wolf heads, of Puck's butterfly wings. He forced himself to remember he was leaving the city for Cornell's bluestone towers in a few months, then on to even greater heights.

Misty had enough problems without falling for him.

"Daniel?"

He pulled his hand back. "I used to have this pet hermit crab."

Misty's eyebrows pinched together. "Oh . . . kay . . ."

"From Panama City. We used to go on vacations there a lot, and they sell hermit crabs in the souvenir shops, and one summer I saved all my money and bought one. I named him Herman. I was eight; I thought that was really clever."

Sliding her arms across her breasts, Misty's expression grew more mystified. Daniel talked as fast as he could.

"Anyway, I bought him, and had him for a couple weeks. Then one day I was cleaning his aquarium, and dropped him on the bathroom floor. Accidently. And he curled up inside his shell, but I figured he had that hard shell, so he was fine, just startled, right? But inside, he was really delicate, and me dropping him killed him. Even though he had that shell."

Unsure what response she should give, Misty went with, "I'm sorry? About your crab?"

Daniel soldiered on. "It's just you act really tough and like nothing bothers you. But I'm scared you're really delicate inside. Like Herman."

Suddenly embarrassed or angry or both, she turned to grab her shirt off the floor. "Jesus. You *are* soft in the head."

"It's just—"

"I heard you. You're clumsy, and I've got crabs. How did you ever hook up with Angie always babbling like a retard?"

A sour laugh escaped Daniel's throat. "I just tell her whatever she wants to hear. That's easy. It's telling the truth that's hard."

Misty buttoned her shirt and turned back around. "I've been dropped before. I'm not as delicate as that."

"I know, just—"

"But it's nice to be treated that way sometimes."

Daniel half-smiled and ran his hands through his hair. "Still, maybe I should go."

"No. Stay."

"Thanks, but I really think—"

"You promised you'd hang out tonight. Please? I'll keep my hands to myself. I swear." Misty held up her hands, showing him she was harmless.

Daniel needed to tell her who he really was. He hoped they could stay friends, but he needed to get back to his college courses, to Angie, to his real life. He needed to let Misty find a boy who could take her to see the *Basilica di Santa Maria del Fiore*. But one more night playing a delinquent couldn't hurt.

They decided to call Val and get something to eat. This time, Daniel waited in the living room while Misty changed. She came out wearing a snug knit cap and a canvas jacket with a factory logo stitched across the breast. One of the sleeves was held together with rough black stitches. Daniel wondered what they were going to be doing tonight that required an outfit that went past street style and neared postapocalyptic.

At McDonald's, Daniel tried to buy Misty's dinner, but she wouldn't let him. Even though their mutual self-consciousness eased after Val and Eric showed up, they monitored the space between them constantly, careful not to touch and just as careful to not act like they were avoiding touching.

They ate their burgers and refilled their drinks. Misty called Marc, who said he'd meet them at the furnace. She and Val went to the restroom together. Daniel didn't doubt Misty was telling her best friend what had happened earlier.

They refilled their drinks again and dabbed cold fries in ketchup. Misty and her friends were restless, waiting for something to happen.

Then Eric pointed at Daniel's letterman jacket and asked, "You're not on the basketball team anymore, right? How come you still wear that?"

"Because it keeps me warm?"

"Yeah, but it's more than that, isn't it? It's a uniform. It makes you a jock. One of the cool kids."

Val nudged Eric in the ribs and told him to play nice. Daniel answered, anyway.

"The time I scored eighteen points on a fucked-up knee makes me a jock, not my jacket."

"Okay, you earned it or whatever. I'm just saying it declares your loyalty to a tribe you're not really part of anymore."

"It doesn't declare—"

Eric leaned forward. "You walk up on two guys beating

the hell out of each other, right? One of them is wearing a letterman jacket like you, and the other is dressed like me. Now, you don't have time to figure out what the fight is about; you've got to rush in and help one of them. Who do you stand with? The guy wearing the jacket or the guy wearing boots?" Eric kicked the plastic seat with his dead brother's boot, making it shudder under Daniel.

Daniel forced himself to grin. "It's just a jacket, man."

"All right." Eric turned to look out the window. "Whatever."

Daniel didn't know if Eric was just screwing around or if he genuinely wanted to get under his skin. Either way, his talk about uniforms and loyalty contained a sliver of truth. Daniel remembered getting his varsity letter, striding through the halls with Bwana and his other teammates. He'd felt lifted up from the crowd, one of the chosen. Wearing that same letter a year after his last game did seem a little pathetic.

Daniel couldn't dwell on it long, though. The short winter day slipped away, and it was suddenly time to go. He and Misty climbed into his car. Alone again, they stayed on the absolute surface of things, reading bumper stickers out loud and complaining about the long light at Morris Avenue.

Misty examined Daniel's stereo. "This is aftermarket, right?"

"Yeah. I had it put in about a year ago," he said, leaving out the part about it being a gift for cheating on the SATs.

Misty ticked down the bass, filling the car with gut-quivering thumps. She turned it back to a normal level and said, "Nice. Good speakers."

"Thanks."

"You like me, right?"

"What? Yes. Misty, that's not—"

"I'm not talking about . . . about today. I mean in general. You think I'm a pretty good person, right? That I wouldn't do anything really bad."

Daniel stared through the windshield while he spoke. "That first time I went looking for you at the deli. Giving you those notes was just an excuse."

"Yeah? An excuse for what?"

"When you ran out to help that dog. I watched you, and I don't know . . . everybody thinks I'm this shooting star." He found himself wrestling ideas into words again, struggling to say what he meant. He didn't talk about things like this with his other friends. He didn't even think about them much. "But if that's true, I couldn't figure out why you did the right thing, while I just sat there."

Misty smiled. "I'm going to show you why tonight, okay? But you have to promise to remember everything you just said, okay?"

He was getting nervous. Misty's abrupt question made him realize that, whatever he was getting into, it was bigger than spray-painting walls. But he'd told Misty he couldn't imagine her ever doing anything bad, and it was the truth.

Marc was already at the furnace, and when they arrived, the gate was waiting open. Entering, the city's clamor sunk away. Without any streetlights to push back the night, it pooled into the furnace grounds like oil.

Marc crouched in the middle of the casting shed, feeding a fire with smashed pieces of an office chair. He didn't look up when Eric and Daniel drove in, only after Misty opened the door and yelled, "Marc! Let's use Daniel's stereo."

"What for?" Daniel asked.

"To dance."

Marc ran over with a handful of hip-hop CDs. "Hey, Daniel."

They bumped knuckles while Misty flipped through the CDs. "They about cooked?" she asked.

Marc nodded.

"Cool." She slid one of the disks into Daniel's stereo. Far from Pins & Needles's wistful rock, she picked a track snarling with club bravado, turning the volume up, the bass down, and asking Daniel how to make one song repeat over and over. Daniel showed her, then popped the trunk, where his subwoofers were. Music stripped to a deep, percussive pulse boomed against the shed's corrugated tin walls.

Getting out of the car, they walked to where Val was gathering pieces of something like dried fruit from the fire and passing them around. Misty pressed two of them into Daniel's palm. They were shriveled mushroom caps.

"Uh . . ." Daniel drank at parties and smoked pot occasionally, but he'd never done 'shrooms. He glanced around. Val and Eric hugged belly-to-back. She fed him one of the caps, his chin resting on her shoulder. Marc washed his down with gulps of orange juice he'd brought with him. "Uh . . ."

Misty stood on her tiptoes, speaking in Daniel's ear so he could hear her beneath the throbbing beats. "Please? Take them, and I'll never ask you for anything again."

Daniel couldn't go slumming with her or her friends again or return to this waking-dream furnace. He wanted to devour this last night with Misty, suck the marrow from its bones.

The mushrooms tasted horrible. Daniel gagged them down, then grabbed the carton of orange juice Marc offered. Around him, heads bobbed and boots drummed in time with the bass line.

The music was hypnotic and terrifying at once. It was the relentless sweep and boom of ocean waves. It was the earth's steady, sleeping heartbeat. Val started stomping around the fire. The others joined her, kicking up dust clouds. Daniel tried to laugh, figuring they were goofing around. But they put total, panting effort into the frantic dance. Their skin glowed like hot metal in the firelight.

Misty took Daniel's hand. Being led to the circle felt like being pulled into rushing flood waters. Daniel danced along with the choppy rhythm, his body not entirely under his control. High above, moonbeams slanted through gaps in the roof, interweaving with steel support beams. Daniel couldn't tell which ones were solid and which ones were ethereal. It wasn't important either way.

Misty and her friends started yelling, "Want to be a wolf! Want to be a wolf!" Daniel joined in without wondering what it meant, just relishing the feeling of shouting as loud as he pleased, over and over until his throat burned.

Marc's words broke into a howl. Daniel watched him stumble, then fall forward and change into a wolf. The transformation was beautiful and not particularly strange. Somehow, Marc had always been a wolf. Daniel just hadn't noticed before.

Misty escaped her human shape too. Then Eric, then Val. Eric chased Marc into the shadows past the fire. Daniel wished he could become a wolf too, and as soon as he wished, saw that he clung to humanity, not the other way around. It was as easy as letting go. Daniel sank into dense fur. The shed's musty smell blossomed open, unfolding into countless distinct scents—the other wolves, smoke, rust, dew gathering on grass.

He ran his tongue across long fangs and took a few careful steps on lanky legs. Distant fires filled the furnace complex with light, but only the palest colors. Daniel looked up and realized the fires were the moon and stars burning overhead.

A wolf grappled his neck with her forepaw and nipped Daniel's ear. He connected her with cocoa butter conditioner, a girl with a beautiful scowl. Her name was gone, though. He groped for it, finally garbling, "Mis—Misty!" The starlight faded to sparks as his human eyes returned.

Kneeling in the darkness and cold, Daniel was suddenly afraid. "Misty!"

He was knocked onto his back. Misty, normal again, straddled his hips. "Misty doesn't mean anything. A sound. Misty just a sound." The words were strained with effort and kinked by wrong inflections. "Don't talk. Or think. Just . . ."

Daniel didn't understand until she kissed him. He smelled her and tasted her. Raw sensation flooded him, unfiltered by thoughts of what they meant, what to do next, or even names for them.

"Just . . ." Misty turned back into a wolf. She bounded off him, then turned, watching Daniel, her ears cocked toward him.

What was happening didn't matter; it just was. Daniel forgot Misty's name, then his own. He let his confusion fade away and felt his body shifting around him.

Eric howled. Instinct told Daniel it was a mustering call. He followed the pack out of the shed, across the furnace grounds. Cold mud squelched between his toes. Brambles slashed harmlessly at his pelt.

People hid behind locked doors or huddled together below the brightest lights, abandoning vast, dark swaths of the city to the wolves. Daniel could only keep his mind primal for a few seconds at a time, making it hard to stay in wolf shape. Sometimes on four legs, usually lagging behind on two, he prowled alleys and chased sway-bellied opossums through storm culverts.

He helped Eric smash open a restaurant's Dumpster with a chunk of cinder block. In human skin and his letterman jacket, but crouched like an animal, Daniel ripped open garbage bags for bread dough, burnt beef tips, and handfuls of cake, shoving anything that smelled like food into his mouth. He refused to consider what he was doing, only how pungent and delicious it all was.

They roamed for hours, until the mushrooms' potency started to fade. Returning to the furnace, they followed the sound of Daniel's still-playing stereo to the shed. Even after Marc shut the engine off, a ghostly rhythm beat inside Daniel's skull. His muscles burned. Grime caked his jeans and crisp white sneakers.

Eric and Val were having sex in Eric's car. Daniel had cut his hand crawling under a chain-link fence. Pulling gauze and antibiotic ointment out of Marc's backpack, Misty gently bandaged his hand. Apparently cuts and scrapes were fairly common. Neither of them spoke or felt any need to.

Afterward, they hunched together, Daniel's hand resting in Misty's lap. Marc stretched out on the other side of the fire. A full stomach and the wavering heat of the dying embers lulled Daniel to sleep.

While his body rested, the wolf continued to stalk through the city in his subconscious, id and ego transformed into glass and concrete. The mushroom's strange drugs filtered out of his system, magic breaking down into simple amino acids and nitrogen. The wolf grew weaker, becoming aware that the fire had died and Misty's cheek nuzzled against his shoulder. Finally, reality pounced.

"Fu—" Daniel's head snapped up, startling Misty awake too. He'd been a werewolf. "Fuck. Holy, holy fuck."

"It's okay," Misty said. "It's weird. I mean, it's really weird, but it's okay." She touched him, and Daniel threw himself to the dirt to get away from her. He scrambled backward like a crab, then jumped to his feet.

Marc had woken up. Eric and Val opened the car door and peered out.

Daniel flexed his fingers and touched his chest. The muscles and ribs felt solid, but he didn't trust them. He'd been a werewolf. "What are you? What the hell did you give me?"

"*Amanita muscaria*," Misty said. "It's a mushroom that . . . it's kind of a long story. Actually there's this website. I should have printed all that out before tonight, but I'll get it to you, okay? The main thing is . . ."

Daniel ignored her. Staring around, he noticed wolf tracks around the fire. He remembered seeing them the first time he'd come to the furnace.

Better be careful. Some dogs have been living here.

Why should I be scared? I've got a big jock to protect me.

"Daniel," Misty tried to get his attention again. "The main

thing is this is why I saved that dog. This is why a lot of things. Calm down, okay? Please?"

Daniel looked at her. "I think I better go."

"No, Daniel, just calm down."

"It's really late, or early, or . . . I better go."

Misty and her friends—Misty and her pack—started talking all at once. Shaking his head, insisting it was very late, Daniel climbed into his car and found his keys in the ignition. When he cranked the engine, a blast of noise made him scream. The stereo's volume was still turned to maximum. Jabbing the mute button with a shaking hand, he backed out of the shed, leaving the werewolves behind.

Pale morning broke overhead. Crossing the furnace complex, Daniel finally saw it for what it was, a crack in the world. The brambles hid clearings where the Cherokee had danced and summoned spirits. The dank coal tunnels led to caves where Stone Age hunters had painted beasts from their dreams.

Somehow, Daniel made it home. Coming up the flagstone walk, his dad jerked the door open. "Where have you been?"

"Uh, out. Out with Angie." Daniel tried to squeeze past him, but his dad grabbed his arm.

"We called Angie. She never saw you."

"Okay. Yeah." Panic had dulled to a numb stupor and jumbled half-thoughts. He just wanted to go to bed. But then his mom came out of the kitchen with her Bible in her hand and her eyes rimmed red from tears.

"Daniel, where were you? You're filthy. I called your cell phone a dozen times. I thought you'd been in a car wreck or—" She couldn't make herself finish the sentence.

"Okay." He remembered something else he should say. "Sorry."

"I've been reading Psalm Twenty-three for hours, asking God to look over you. I called the hospitals. Your dad called Bwana at two in the . . ." His mom kept talking. Daniel's gaze drifted to the family photos hanging on the living room wall. His mom's framed Nurse Corps insignia and Soldier's Medal. One Xbox controller snaked from the entertainment center and across the carpet.

This house, his parents, all of this felt like it had been ten years ago. Daniel had plunged past everything he thought was real, then landed back where he'd started. It was confusing.

"Daniel!" Grabbing his chin, his mom jerked his eyes back to meet hers. She squinted at his pupils. "What have you taken?"

"Nothing." Daniel pulled away. He mumbled out a story about drinking a few beers last night and falling asleep. He hadn't taken any drugs. He was acting strange because he hadn't realized how late it was. He wasn't sure how his clothes had gotten so dirty. He remembered to apologize a few more times. Angry at the sight of him, his parents let him go to his room at last.

CHAPTER 7

Beep.

"Where are you, Daniel?" Angie's recorded voice lashed out at him. "Why did you tell your parents you were out with me last night? What happened to that big essay you had to finish? Call me as soon as you get this."

Beep.

"I'm at the hotel, where are you? Look, people are talking shit, and we need to get some things straight. Call me, okay? I love you."

Beep.

"Hey. It's Misty. Look, I'm really sorry. I didn't want to scare you. I mean, I guess I probably figured you'd be scared. Just, I couldn't just tell you and make you think I wasn't crazy. Maybe now you think I'm something worse than crazy, I don't know, but . . . Jesus, now I'm babbling." She tried to laugh. "I had this whole thing ready to say, and I'm getting totally off track, but . . . I'm not working tonight, for once, so if you want

121

to talk or whatever. Or maybe you don't want anything to do with me ever again. I don't know. Just whatever, okay? Bye."

Beep.

"What's the matter, Daniel? Too busy skanking around with Misty Sandlin to be with me? Yeah, I heard all about that. The ceremony's starting in half an hour. You better get here, and you better have some damn good answers, or it's over. Got it?"

Beep.

Angie had left the last message a minute ago. Daniel thought about calling her, trying to explain something, but it didn't seem worth the trouble. He rolled onto his side, staring at the row of trophies and plaques on top of the bookshelf.

The ballroom was draped in the school colors. Matching, fresh-cut centerpieces sat on every table. Boosters and team members trickled in. Oliver Robinson talked to Coach Jacobs in the corner. Keith fiddled with the dimmer switch, fine-tuning the glow of the blown-glass chandelier.

Angie wore a satiny dress that made her seem to float. Keith watched her shove her cell phone in her purse. One of the boosters called her name. Angie's expression snapped into a smile as she looked up, reaching out to shake his hand.

The night had unfolded like fate. Daniel had gotten Keith into the awards banquet, then asked for a favor. Instead of blurting everything to Angie the first chance he got, Keith had played it cool. He'd whispered in a few ears and trusted the rumor to diffuse across the school on its own. *Daniel's slipping it to that little hoodrat Misty. He's probably already given Angie crabs by now.* By the time Angie heard what people were saying, Keith's name wasn't even attached to it anymore.

She didn't break up with Daniel, though, and as the banquet approached, Keith almost lost faith. Last night, he'd held the phone in his hand, wondering if he should call Jessica Orr.

He'd loved Angie since ninth grade, though. Gorgeous and funny, she was the kind of girl nobody but his cousin had a shot at. Finally, Keith calculated that one more embarrassment, going to the awards banquet alone and leaving the same way, wouldn't make enough difference to matter. But no matter how slim the chance, one hour with Angie on his arm, one kiss, would make the night shine out from every other. Keith had dabbed on some cologne and headed out with a unsteady prayer on his lips.

Then Daniel vanished. Nobody knew where he was, but everybody suspected who he was with. "The boy's headed to Cornell," Spence had snickered. "Gotta chase some wild hares while he's still got the chance."

Now, Keith walked toward Angie. "H-hey. You look really nice."

"Thanks." She smiled at him, then her eyes flickered to the door as someone walked in.

"Me and Caesar fixed the sound system. Only one speaker was fuzzy, so we just unplugged it. But you've still got three, so it should be okay."

"Okay. Thanks." She glanced up again as two more boosters came in. A shadow of hurt crossed her face when she saw it wasn't Daniel. For a moment, Keith felt bad, almost slimy. But it wasn't his fault Daniel was cheating on her.

"Hey, if Daniel doesn't show up. I'm not really here with anybody, and I was thinking—"

"Thanks, but I'll be okay."

"I know. I just didn't want you to have to sit next to an empty seat all night." He motioned to the dais. To present the speakers, Angie would sit up there with the coaches, Oliver Robinson, and a place reserved for her date. "I'm not much better than an empty seat, but I just wouldn't want people to think you'd been dumped on your big night. You know how people love talking about crap they don't know about."

Angie gave a tired laugh. She beamed at him the way she beamed at Daniel. "You're a pretty good guy, Keith."

Daniel couldn't remember if he fell asleep or not. He lay in bed, ignoring sharp hunger pangs. He was still dressed, and sand from the furnace made the sheets scratchy.

For hours, he worked to make himself believe it had been a hallucination. Misty had fed him 'shrooms. They'd screwed him up so bad, he'd thought he was a wolf.

But he'd seen the paw prints. His paw prints. Even worse, Daniel could still feel it. Lying in his letterman jacket and Core 205s, surrounded by books and trophies, with an acceptance letter from Cornell in the desk, Daniel felt the wolf beneath his skin, eager to break loose again.

After supper, his mom came up carrying chicken and broccoli. He thanked her and apologized again. The conversation was surreal in its normality. His mom talked about getting called off work, and church tomorrow. She had no inkling what lurked inside her son. After she left, Daniel ate his chicken and realized nobody else would either.

Like Misty had said, even if he told people, they'd never believe him. And Daniel couldn't think of any reason ever to tell.

He could pretend it had never happened. Just delete Misty's number from his cell phone and ignore her at school. In the fall, Daniel would fly up to Ithaca and lose himself in the privileges and duties of a shooting star. The bluestone towers were so far away from the furnace. Maybe, eventually, he'd convince himself it had been a hallucination after all.

He called Angie, but she wouldn't answer, getting back at him for ignoring her calls all day. Daniel couldn't let Angie break up with him. He checked the time. The awards ceremony was over. Angie might stick around for the afterparty, though. With a chicken slice in one hand, he scrambled around his room, changing into his Hugo Boss shirt.

His parents hadn't said anything about Daniel's punishment yet, but he was sure he was grounded. Buttoning up his letterman jacket and shutting off the lights, Daniel prayed for his mom not to check on him again, reminding God what he was trying to get away from.

He lowered himself out the window, thin-soled dress shoes scuffing the house's clapboards, Daniel dropped the last few feet into the sideyard. Getting back in was trickier, but he'd done it before. Cutting across the overgrown lawn of the empty house next door, he jogged up the street toward the bus stop.

After the banquet, Angie peeled out of her dress and pantyhose, changing into an outfit the white-haired boosters wouldn't have approved of, a little shimmery fabric and lots of honey-colored curves.

Keith had spent years trying to imagine the banquet afterparty, but it wasn't a single party at all. Instead of a fixed group gathering at a fixed spot, bodies, music, and beer flowed through the hotel. Doors kept opening and kept opening. Keith and Angie met up with friends, lost them along the way, then found new ones. When the manager kicked everybody out of one room, they just scattered like beads of mercury.

Through the swirl of players, student reps, and gate-crashers, Angie stayed close to Keith. If anyone asked about Daniel, she gave them a half-sneering shake of her head, as if the subject wasn't worth talking about, and touched Keith's arm. Then a text message would send her and Keith dashing up to one of the veranda suites.

After a drink, she started dancing with him. Her body

brushed his. A glimpse of Angie's tan line had left Keith dry-mouthed and dazed before. But the stars had guided him to this frantic, free-floating party. When he pulled her close and kissed her, it was with a calm confidence that Angie and the whole night were his for the taking.

The blue line MAX trundled through the city Daniel had grown up in. It passed his old pediatrician's office, the shop where he'd bought the tie he was wearing, and Mabel's Beauty Shop and Chainsaw Repair. Daniel had accepted the sign at face value for years before somebody clued him in that Mabel's was a gay biker bar.

Daniel polished his shoes with his handkerchief and refused to look out the bus's window. He couldn't let himself wonder how many places like the furnace the night hid, secret places where reality was worn thin.

The bus hissed to a stop across the street from the Tutwiler. Daniel ran around the hotel's fountain and into the lobby. Three girls from school sat talking on one of the leather couches. He spotted Spence and Scotty getting into the elevator. Daniel shouted, and Spence stuck his hand out to hold the door open, shouting back, "Where have you been, man? Everybody's—"

"Is Angie still here?"

"Yeah." Spence glanced at Scotty, then pushed the button for the sixth floor. "Yeah, I saw her in Morgan's room last. Listen, though, nobody knew where you were, so your cousin kind of stepped up. But it's nothing, okay? So just be cool."

Daniel nodded, betraying as little as possible. He'd assumed Keith had let the thing about Misty slip because he was an idiot. It had never occurred to Daniel that Keith might actually have been plotting against him. The idea was almost funny. Daniel never dreamed his cousin had that big a pair.

The elevator opened, and Daniel followed strains of club music down the hall. Spence's backpack, full of the beer they'd bought from Charlie Say What, clanked as he and Scotty jogged after him.

A piece of tape kept the door from locking. Daniel pushed through the waving field of bodies, past empty plastic cups and set-aside awards, looking for Angie. She saw him first, scowling over Keith's shoulder. As they moved in time to the music, Keith wrapped his arms around Angie and pulled her close. She kissed him, but kept her eyes fixed on Daniel.

Angie wanted to make him jealous, which meant she still wanted him. He was Daniel Morning. Everybody had known he was the shooting star since he was seven. It might mean sinking a spit-polished dress shoe into his cousin's gut, but Angie and his real life were still his for the taking.

Daniel took a step forward, then hesitated. The wolf inside him, the wolf that was part of him, hated these preening humans. He hated Daniel for being so ready to play Angie's stupid game.

He stood watching Angie watch him. Last night, Daniel had torn through mud and weeds. He'd eaten garbage. He'd howled. And it'd been even better than Misty had promised.

Daniel wanted more of that mad freedom. He wanted as much as he possibly could, because once he headed for Cornell, he'd never find his way back to the furnace again.

Spence had seen Angie kiss Keith. He took Daniel's arm. "Forget about her, man. You don't need her. Come up to Claire's room with us. Both Jessica and Emi came with some guy, then ditched him. They're both already lit. Probably dancing half-naked by now."

Daniel shrugged out of Spence's grip and decided to let Keith play the shooting star for a while. "Thanks, but I'm getting out of here."

"What? No. Come to Claire's room with us."

"No, I need to go see somebody." He slapped his friend in the chest. "Go enjoy the show. I want to hear everything Monday!" he yelled over his shoulder.

Misty had kept her phone with her all day, even setting it by the sink when she'd taken a shower, but nobody had called except Val.

"Give him some time. We were all pretty freaked out too, at first." Val was with Eric, who was still sore about Misty bringing Daniel to begin with. In the background, Misty heard him grumble, "Better hope he doesn't try to shoot you with a silver bullet or something now."

Val told him to relax, then said to Misty, "Even if he

doesn't call, that means you scared the hell out of a jock with fifty pounds on you. That's pretty cool, right?"

"Yeah, I guess."

Misty suspected that part would be funny eventually. After hanging up with Val, she curled back up on the couch, watching Marc play video games. She wished she could go prowl. Misty wanted to strip off her human skin, all her wondering and tension with it. But Marc and Eric had church early tomorrow.

Her phone rang again. When Misty saw the number, she jumped up, took a deep breath, and pressed the talk button.

"Hey."

"Hey," Daniel said in a quiet voice. "I'm in your parking lot. Are you busy?"

"What? No. Just a second, okay?" Misty rushed around looking for some shoes, then gave up and headed for the door.

Her mom sat on the couch cutting coupons. "Where are you going?"

"Nowhere. I'll be back in a minute."

"Misty, don't go outside in your pajamas."

"I'll be back in a minute." She stepped out and saw Daniel standing under the security light in a dress shirt and tie. She dashed across the cold asphalt in her socks, her arms across her chest. Daniel didn't move. Eric's silver bullet joke flickered through Misty's mind, but she pushed it aside.

"You're all dressed up," Misty said. It was the only thing she could think to say.

Daniel nodded. He still seemed wary of her. "Yeah. Sorry I didn't call earlier. Had a lot to think about, you know?"

"It's cool."

They stood quiet, Misty dancing from one foot to the other. Then Daniel blurted, "Have you ever hurt anybody?" all as one long word.

"No. I swear. I *swear*. Last night, before I showed you all of this, you promised you'd remember everything you knew about me before."

"I am. I'm trying to, at least. But you're a werewolf."

"Wolves aren't evil. They're just strong," she said. "I wouldn't do this if it was bad, Daniel. I swear."

He nodded, and they slipped back into silence. Misty's teeth started chattering. "So, all this thinking you did today. You decide anything?"

"I've decided . . . that you're the most amazing girl I've ever met. And that I can figure out the rest as I go along."

The tension in her shoulders vanished. The cold vanished. Misty felt warm blood rush to her cheeks. She wanted to climb the apartment building wall, race through traffic, maybe rob a bank, just because she could. Instead, she looked up at Daniel and nodded. "Cool."

CHAPTER 8

Monday, Daniel moved across the government classroom to sit behind Misty. Mrs. MacKaye didn't like people changing seats, but Daniel was the shooting star, so she let it go. In the cafeteria, Keith had taken Daniel's chair beside Angie. She leaned close to whisper something in his ear, her hand resting on top of his. Knowing they were both watching him, Daniel sat at the wolves' table beneath the windows.

Eric glanced up. "Where's your jacket?"

"Not on the team anymore."

Nodding, Eric went back to his hamburger, and Daniel was in the pack.

Saturday night, Misty had sketched out how they'd become wolves to Daniel. Now, the pack told him more stories, where they'd gone, how fast they could run, and how sharp their predator's senses were. The whole time, Misty teased Daniel's foot under the table, pressing her boot down on the toe of his sneaker. Daniel thought of something else.

"So do I have to get a pair of boots?"

"Stick with the Cores, man," Marc said. "Those fuckers are high-speed, low-drag, Teflon-coated."

"Thanks, but . . ." Glancing under the table, Daniel set his foot against Misty's. "I'll get some boots."

Despite grounding him until further notice, Daniel's parents still expected him to go to his college classes. Tuesday, Daniel went with Misty to Al Army Surplus. Industrial shelving piled with survival gear and MREs rose over their heads.

Daniel bought a pair of tanker boots. He spent the evening walking around in them, feeling like a badass. Getting home, Daniel stashed them in a battered blue suitcase under his bed alongside his small stash of porn.

Thursday, the pack took Daniel on a tour of their Southside. They showed him the chain of graffiti tags steadily constricting the neighborhood. Val was proudest of the pair gazing down from the concrete apron of I-65. She'd had to climb over the guardrail to paint them, dangling a story above the asphalt, exposed on all sides except for her pack watching over her. They'd come out perfect.

"So, there aren't any other werewolves besides you guys, right?"

"Not that we know of."

"So what's the point, then? I mean, who are you marking your territory off *from*?"

Misty shrugged. "They're just something to do. Running

around got boring after a while. I guess they're just for us. To know this is our territory."

"Yeah, but nobody else knows it, so what's the point? It's not like they change anything. It's not like the police are staying out of Southside because of them."

Misty squirmed. "You're right, but . . . I can't explain it to you, exactly."

Eric spoke up from the passenger seat, telling Daniel, "You don't get it because when you go to school, everybody's always happy to see you. When you get home, your mom's probably going to have a big tray of chocolate chip cookies waiting for you." His voice had a hard edge, like he hated Daniel for that. "You don't get it because you've always belonged somewhere."

Trying to lighten the sudden tension, Daniel forced a laugh. "Not always."

"Well, some people never have," Misty whispered.

Daniel watched the glimmer of the passing city play across her face. He let the questions drop and squeezed her hand. Daniel realized this was more than a game to them. Given all the freedom he craved, they'd built brute versions of the family and home he wanted to escape, a pack and territory.

Misty and the others still didn't know about Cornell. Daniel had spent the week trying to come up with the best way to tell them. Now, after Eric's talk about belonging, he suddenly realized there wasn't one.

• • •

Somewhere in Misty's subconscious, A Midsummer Night's Dream played forever, its rhythmic verse like an underground river flowing beneath the waking world. The footlights never went dark, the magic never ended, and sometimes when she slept, Misty found herself back onstage.

"Believe me, King of shadows, I mistook. Did not you tell me I should know the man by the Athenian garment he had . . ."

The painted forest backdrop had become real trees. Gnarled roots broke through the stage boards and wound around the lights. Misty glimpsed Daniel perched in the branches above. Grinning down at her, he waved.

Misty half waved back and tried to regain her train of thought. ". . . the garment he had on? And so far blameless . . . proves my enterprise . . ."

Realizing nobody else could see him, Misty kept cracking up and forgetting her lines. Finally giving up, she fluttered offstage on glittering wings and dropped into the tree beside Daniel.

"Methinks I have a great desire to a bottle of hay: good hay, sweet hay, hath no fellow."

The play went along fine without Misty. She and Daniel hid beneath a canopy of leaves and deep green shadow. Daniel leaned against the trunk, and Misty leaned against him. His arms holding her tight, they laughed at Tyree stumbling around in donkey ears.

Daniel played with her hair, then stroked the tender spot

behind her ear. He kissed her neck, let his hand travel down, and Misty's alarm blared to life. It tossed her out of warm dreaming and onto her rumpled bed.

Misty jerked upright. "God, I hate you," she hissed at her alarm clock, slapping the snooze button to make it shut up. Pulling the covers over her head, she slipped back to sleep for a few more precious minutes.

On the way to school, Marc asked Misty to drive him to their dad's later. Marc's relationship with their dad wasn't as prickly as Misty's. He stopped by once a week or so to eat dinner and play their dad's Xbox. Their dad usually slipped him some money, too, which was how Marc got by without a job. He was still pestering her as they walked through the school's front door.

"I can't drive you to Ensley, then get to the deli by four, okay?" Misty said. "Quit asking."

"I'm not riding the bus. That car's as much mine as yours."

"Grampa told you—"

"Grampa told you," Marc mimicked.

"—when I have work—"

"Not until four!"

"That's not enough time!"

"Yes, it is!"

They bickered around in circles all the way to Misty's locker. Dialing the combination, she stopped answering and tried to ignore Marc. She tried to ignore the damp February morning, ignore the school's florescent light and harsh smells, and remember her dream.

Somehow, her fairy wings had been both real and part of a costume. Misty was also pretty sure her id had shortened her skirt by several inches. But what Misty remembered vividly was how happy she'd felt watching *A Midsummer Night's Dream* with Daniel. A sweet, perfect dream about a dream.

"Hoodrat."

The word sliced through the hallway clamor. Misty looked up and met Angie Walton's hard glare. Angie never broke her stride. She turned to whisper a joke to Daniel's cousin Keith.

Misty slammed her locker closed. "You got anything to say?"

Angie glanced back around. "Not to you."

"Good. Shut your mouth then."

"Or what? You'll burn my clothes? That's okay; we give all our old clothes to Goodwill anyway. In fact, that shirt looks familiar."

"Keep talking, and I'll steal your next boyfriend too."

Angie's coy expression melted like wax. "Know what?" She came up a few inches from Misty face. "You can keep him. I'd never touch him again, anyway, after he touched a nasty little mutt like you," she hissed.

Misty was half-black in a city where nobody pretended race didn't matter. She'd been called a mutt before, and—sinking her fingernails into her palm—refused to let Angie make her flinch. But then Marc shouldered Misty aside. "Bitch, what did you call my—"

"Hey!" Keith jumped in, shoving Marc into a bank of lockers. A sharp *clang* and the crowd jumped back on all sides, snapping open around them like a startled eye. Misty screamed at Marc to calm down, but Marc was already hurling toward Keith. Then Daniel appeared from nowhere, stepping between the tussling puppies.

"Both of you chill out." Holding Marc off of Keith and a head taller than either of them, Daniel spoke in a calm, almost bored voice.

"Your boy needs to watch his mouth," Keith said.

Marc cocked his fist back. Grabbing Marc's wrist, Daniel glanced at Keith. "Don't I owe you a beat down?"

Keith's bluster went cold. Still holding Marc's wrist, Daniel yanked him around and shoved him down the hall, getting him away from the scene fast before a teacher showed up.

"Man, that—"

"Shut the hell up, Marc," Misty snapped. "That wasn't over anything worth a damn. Just drop it."

"Wasn't over anything? That little—"

"I don't care." She did. But if Daniel knew what Angie had said, he'd think he had to charge back and defend her, too. "Just. Drop. It. Okay?"

Marc looked at her, confused and a little hurt, then grumbled, "Whatever." He started slinking up the stairs, then stopped. "So, seriously, can I get that ride?"

"Be in the car by three, or I'm leaving without you."

Marc went to homeroom, leaving Misty and Daniel alone together.

"Thanks. They'll probably expel him if he gets into another fight."

"No problem. What was that about, anyway?"

"Keith bumped into him and wouldn't apologize. Dumb boy stuff." And before he could ask anything else, Misty said, "So you ready to prowl tonight?"

"Yeah. I'm still grounded, though. I won't be able to slip out until after my dad goes to bed."

"We'll wait. Scared?"

"Uh . . ."

Misty nudged him. "You can say it. I won't think any less of you if you say it."

"As long as you're there, I won't be scared." Daniel smiled the same gentle smile Misty remembered from her dream.

"We'll look out for each other, okay?" she said.

"Okay."

"So you'll pick me up later, right?"

"Yeah. I get off at eight, so, like, eight thirty." Misty pulled to the curb. Her dad's car sat in the driveway. "He's home already?"

"I told you he's off today." Marc grabbed his backpack and climbed out. "See you later."

"Wait." Beating her fist against the armrest, Misty stared at the house she'd grown up in. "Let me go say hi, at least."

In the living room, Rebecca was tying her youngest daughter's shoe while talking to somebody over the phone. She barely glanced up as Misty and Marc walked in. Their dad was cutting up vegetables in the kitchen. A pot of chili simmered on the stove. "That my boy?" He turned and gave Marc a hug, careful not to smear his shirt with tomato gore.

Misty stopped at the kitchen archway. "Hey, Dad."

"Hey. Haven't seen—what the hell is that?"

"What's what?" Misty asked. Then she clapped a hand over her mouth. Misty hadn't visited since Thanksgiving. She'd taken her lip ring out then to avoid a fight. "Oh, yeah."

"Your mom actually let you do that?"

"Well, she wasn't exactly thrilled. Just don't worry about it, all right?"

"I'm still your father, you know."

After an already bad day at school, Misty couldn't keep the wolf from lunging. "You want to play daddy now? How come you didn't want to play daddy a few months back when Mom had to go to the food bank?"

This time, instead of being ready to pound somebody for Misty, Marc grabbed a Hostess cupcake and retreated into the living room to play video games. Their dad turned around, chucked a dirty spoon into the sink, and didn't say anything.

Staring at his back, Misty twisted the knife. It felt good. "Write Mom a check; I'll take this stupid lip ring out, right now. No? Guess you don't want to play daddy so bad, after all."

Misty left the kitchen to find Rebecca and asked, "Is any of my stuff still here?"

"I think there's a couple boxes in Leigh Ann's closet," Rebecca said. "Honey, I wish you wouldn't hurt Aaron like—"

Ignoring her, Misty walked down the hall and into the room that had been hers before it had been Leigh Ann's. She rifled through boxes of old clothes and other junk, pulling out a pair of fairy wings.

They were relics from the one moment her life had seemed truly magical. The rest of her Puck costume had belonged to the school, but Misty had made the wings herself out of coat hangers, blue pantyhose, and lots of glitter. She put them on and checked herself out in Leigh Ann's vanity. The wings fluttered when she hopped up and down, making Misty laugh until she snorted.

"I mean, she's biracial," Keith said. He and Angie sat on his couch. They had books, notes, and sheets of scratch paper spread out on the coffee table.

"Aw, 'she's biracial.' We all have to handle her like glass because she's biracial. Everybody has to watch what they say because she's biracial. Make sure we don't oppress her. Damn, I didn't mean it like that."

"I know. I'm just saying that's how she took it."

"I don't care how she took it. You think I'm a racist?"

"No."

Flipping her notebook closed, Angie stood up. "If you do, tell me. I'll leave right now."

"No, wait. Of course I don't think you're a racist," Keith said, trying not to make it sound too forced.

"Good." Sitting back down, she jabbed an equation into her calculator. "Besides, how can anything anybody says to her be racist? Misty doesn't even have a damn race."

Keith plastered on a grin, and they moved on. It wasn't like Angie actually believed in white supremacy or anything. She'd just called Misty that to make her mad.

The story had changed by lunch, though. Rolling her eyes, Angie told their table how Misty had gotten into her face, warning her to stay away from Daniel. When Lexi asked what she'd done to set Misty off, Angie turned to Keith. "Did I say one word to her?"

Keith hadn't wanted any part of it, but he knew enough to mumble, "Uh-uh."

"Don't worry about it," Lexi said. "She's just scared because she knows Daniel will get bored with her soon and come crawling back."

Angie made sure to tell everybody how Keith had stood up for her.

"Shit, yeah," Scotty laughed. "A man needs to take care of business sometimes."

Keith still didn't say answer, but he liked the sound of that. Over the past week, the school had watched him walking through the halls, holding Angie's hand and making her laugh.

The same envy he used to feel himself shadowed faces all around him. Since the awards ceremony, Keith had become limitless.

Inside, there was a pinprick of shame. Angie had acted like trash. He'd watched and done nothing. But people had finally stopped thinking of Keith as Daniel Morning's cousin. They knew he was a man in his own right, now. It wasn't worth throwing that away for a little hoodrat.

Besides, it was Misty's own fault, really. People wouldn't be so quick to believe Angie's story if Misty wasn't always walking around with a chip on her shoulder.

CHAPTER 9

Daniel was still grounded, but he got permission to go to the library Saturday by telling his parents about a scholarship he wanted to look into and promising to be home by noon. Long ago, he'd learned to work their fear for his future to his advantage.

After supper, his mom left for the night shift at the hospital. Daniel studied and waited for his dad to herd Mack and Fischer to bed, then go to sleep himself.

Daniel had gone to the library after school and checked out a couple scholarship guides. When the house was quiet and still, he stuffed them into his book bag along with his dirty Core 205s. Strapping on the tanker boots, he crept through the familiar dark to the kitchen.

He dropped three Cheerios and a splash of milk in a bowl and left it on the table. Daniel hadn't lied about being back by noon; he was just leaving earlier than his parents thought. With luck, though, his mom would clean up after him in the morning and assume she'd just missed him.

Misty and the pack had told Daniel about the *Amanita* covering the furnace complex. They thought the mushrooms were a voiceless, thousand-bodied god, a rot-eater god. Daniel wished it sounded ridiculous. Instead, the name reverberated so deeply, it had made him sick.

His parents didn't know what it was, but they discussed the god all the time. They called it blight and economic depression. They told stories over supper about somebody else's brother or husband losing his job or getting into trouble with the police. They searched for its face in newspaper bar graphs.

Now, with the shooting star folded up in his bag, Daniel slipped out, returning to the foot of the thing his parents had prayed and sacrificed their own ethics to let him escape.

The pack waited for him in the casting shed. When Daniel pulled in, Misty jumped onto the hood of his car.

"Hooray, you made it! We were ready to give up on you." She wore a pair of sheer blue wings.

"Sorry. Dad didn't go to bed until late." Taking Misty around the waist, Daniel helped her down. "Um . . . what's up with the wings?"

"How come everybody keeps asking me that?"

"She's been wearing them all day." Val shook a can of spray paint. "I kept hoping she'd stand too close to the grill and set one on fire."

"You wore them at the deli? Wasn't Ilie pissed?"

"I had my vest. I had my hair tied back. There's nothing in the employee handbook about fairy wings."

"Can we get going," Eric cut in. He crouched by the low fire with Marc and didn't look up as he spoke. "It's past midnight already."

Misty squeezed Daniel's hand and whispered, "Ready?"

Daniel didn't know if he was or not, but he kissed her forehead. "We're going to look out for each other, right?"

She nodded, and Daniel almost felt as brave as he was pretending to be.

Val was supposedly spending the night with Misty. Her parents didn't know Misty and Marc's mom worked third shift. Since Andrew's death, Eric's parents had lived in a dense fog, and Eric could simply slip out of the house without bothering with an excuse. The pack could escape their daylight lives easily; hardly anybody even noticed they were missing.

The pack stole through the streets. At first, Daniel lagged behind, pumping his arms and panting, struggling to forget his humanity. But the harder he ran, the faster his heart pounded, speeding up *Amanita's* effect. He outraced his family and future. The memories slipped away, until Daniel, under wolf skin, didn't know they'd ever been there.

They followed the expressway up Red Mountain. As traffic and city smells thinned, the pack grew anxious. Daniel felt it too; they were edging onto the fringe of familiar ground.

The peak of Red Mountain had been sliced through. The

expressway snaked between a pair of artificial cliff faces as it traveled south out of Birmingham. Beyond lay Homewood, Vestavia Hills, and the other over-the-mountain suburbs.

Val and Eric crept under the barbed-wire fence. Shifting to human shape, Val climbed the eastern rock cut. Fingers and boot toes found chinks in the petrified reefs and beaches and the artery of rust-red ore that had been the city's lifeblood. Val started to paint, claiming it for the pack. Their sign looked at home among the dark millennia of Birmingham-before-man.

Eric stayed below in case Val fell. Marc vanished, loping to the top of the western rock cut. Misty lay down in the dead grass of the expressway median, resting and watching the cars coming up from the city. Daniel padded back and forth for a while, then settled beside her. Her warmth and scent calmed him some.

Val scuttled across the rock cut, creating a string of wolf heads. The moon slipped down the sky. Halfway between midnight and dawn, the sun's approaching light began swallowing the weakest stars.

Getting bored, Daniel nipped and pawed at Misty, wanting her to play. She ignored him, keeping her head lifted, ears erect, eyes never moving from the expressway. Daniel had his muzzle buried in the thick fur of her breast when Misty jerked to her feet. She began making low *whuf, whuf* calls, loud enough to warn the pack but too soft to draw attention from humans.

The cruiser moved hawk-silent. More panicked than Misty, Daniel sent up sharper, snarling barks, turning tight circles and snapping at the air. Unseen, Marc echoed their alert, and Val began climbing to the top of the rock cut with Eric close behind.

A siren screeched. Lights flashed across the pack's sign and turned Val and Eric into silhouettes. A policeman jumped out of the cruiser. He was young and well-muscled under a bulky black coat. He shouted, fixed a flashlight beam on Eric, but wouldn't climb after them.

Val and Eric vanished into the scraggly pines topping the rock cut. The policeman was talking into his radio when a spray-paint can arced through the darkness. The cop scrambled back as it hit the cruiser's hood and burst.

In the cold, crisp air, Daniel heard Eric's laugh sink into a long howl. Val joined him. Then Marc on the far side of the rock cut. Then Misty and Daniel as they bounded out of the meridian and stood on the empty street.

The policeman jumped back into his cruiser. Through the glass, he stared at Daniel and Misty with wide, white eyes.

Daniel realized the hand-licker knew. He would never say it out loud, but he saw their sign, heard their howls, and he knew this city belonged to the wolves.

Leaving the others in the casting shed, Misty and Daniel climbed to the second story of the blast furnace's control house. It was too cold to pull out of their clothes completely.

The frosty air made Daniel's skin smolder when Misty kissed him. He tasted dry and slightly sweet, a little like sawdust.

Time raced away before they were pulled apart again. Ignoring hunger and exhaustion, they had wordless sex. Daniel was more sure, more skillful, than Andre. His muscles gorged with blood, but he never let his strength overwhelm her. Misty stiffened, and he slowed. A soft moan made him push forward.

After, with flies still unzipped and belts flapping loose, Misty nestled against Daniel's shoulder. His fingers ran lazily down her arm. In drowsy silence, they watched sunrise pour through the windows.

Daniel's fingers stopped moving. Lifting her head, Misty nudged him until his eyelids fluttered back open. "Can't sleep," she croaked. Neither of them had spoken a word since the ritual. "Need to be home soon. You're grounded."

She hadn't meant it as a joke, but they both grinned.

Daniel yawned and stretched. "Forgot somehow."

"I love you," Misty said.

He looked at her, just long enough to make Misty afraid he would stay silent. Then Daniel whispered, "I love you too."

Misty's fairy wings lay on the floor, dripping bits of glitter to sparkle in the dust. She didn't remember bringing them up here, but unsure what to say next, she grabbed them and busied herself pulling them on.

Daniel watched her, then said, "I never read *A Midsummer Night's Dream*. But isn't Puck a guy?"

"The boys were allowed to try out. I beat them."

Daniel laughed again and pulled up the hood of his sweatshirt. Blowing into her hands, Misty saw how thin her human fingers were, like twigs. She wanted her heavy, ice-striding paws. Daniel took her hands in his. "You were never in another play?" he asked.

"Just the one. Just a dumb thing." Misty shook her head.

He rubbed warmth into her fingertips and traced his thumb along the lines of her palms. They had to speak slowly, working the words out in their minds, before giving them voice. "You liked it, right? If you're still wearing your fairy wings. You were good if you beat all the guys."

Misty shrugged. "Kept getting into trouble. I got into trouble too much and couldn't do any extracurricular things. Maybe I would have tried out for the next play, but . . ." She shrugged again. She didn't want to talk about it.

Misty's parents had divorced when she'd been five. They remarried a couple of years later, only to have that marriage break apart when she was thirteen. They yelled a lot, but what Misty remembered were the long stretches of empty, angry nothing, the trip-wire-tense silence that made her afraid to speak herself.

Misty remembered acting out at school, screaming at teachers for the smallest reasons or for no reason at all. She remembered hiding in her room one night, slashing the head off her old teddy bear, yanking her polyester stuffing out, and never uttering a sound because she was scared and helpless and mad and there wasn't anything else she could do.

She wouldn't have survived without Marc. He sang songs and made dumb jokes just to smash the horrible quiet. Marc was the best brother ever. Misty had thanked God for giving her Marc at least as many times as she'd punched him in the neck.

And then Misty's English teacher asked her to be in *A Midsummer Night's Dream*. She'd been young, not much older than Misty herself, and eager to challenge her students. Misty hadn't known anything about the play except that it would let her escape her house for a few hours every week.

She got a part and threw herself into it. She painted sets and memorized entrance cues. When the school closed, she rode the bus to the library or just rode around until dark. Script in her hands, Misty taught her tongue and lips the inflections of the Elizabethan English.

Opening night, Misty forgot all her lines. She stood backstage, just trying to not puke on herself. Her cue came. She stepped into the glare of the spotlight, squinting at the silhouetted audience. They sat shuffling-quiet and waiting. She choked out the first word. Then the second. The third. And then the whole rhythmic rise and fall flowed out on her breath.

The King doth keep his revels here to-night. Take heed the Queen come not within his sight; For Oberon is passing fell and wrath. Because that she, as her attendant, hath a lovely boy, stolen from an Indian king. . . .

It hadn't felt like reciting from a script. Misty vanished.

Puck schemed and flirted and didn't know she was just a character in a play.

The audience applauded when she came out to take her bow. Misty's mom had beamed. She remembered her dad wiping his eyes.

They split up not long after that. Misty's mom moved them to the Southside. She had to get a second job, and Misty and Marc had to grow up fast.

Misty would have stayed in Puck's enchanted forest forever if she could. The play ended, though, and she returned to the real world, where she was a stray, where she was a mutt, where she could never act soft or silly because the spoiled little hand-lickers would turn vicious the moment they thought she couldn't defend herself.

But Misty didn't want to talk about any of that.

Daniel's eyes had drifted closed again. "Wake up. C'mon." She shook him until they snapped open. "Italy or Greece first?"

"Huh?"

Misty sighed and settled back into the crook of his shoulder. "After graduation. Should we go to Italy or Greece first?"

"Am I coming with you now?"

"You don't have any other plans after graduation, right?"

Daniel was quiet for a moment, then nodded. "Right."

"Well then? I'm headed to Europe. I'm offering to let you tag along. If you want to waste your life hanging around here, fine."

Daniel nodded. "I think England would be the best place to start. Give us a chance to get used to a foreign country, but they speak English and have Coke, so it's not like foreign, foreign."

"That's a good idea. Start there, then go south. What's cool in England?"

While they talked, Misty pressed herself against Daniel's warmth. She decided they could make the overgrown furnace complex their new enchanted forest. The fact that it was abandoned and mostly forgotten by the outside world only made it more magical.

Their hunger finally grew too sharp to ignore. Going back to the casting shed, they found Val and Eric had already left. Marc was asleep in the back of the Lincoln, an arm draped across his eyes. Without waking him up, Daniel and Misty left the furnace's solitude, hushed except the for songs of birds, and ventured back into the rush of the city.

They headed to Milo's. A Milo's burger was a skimpy, greasy thing drowned in barbecue sauce. They made most people queasy, but a small segment of Birmingham's population craved them for breakfast, lunch, and dinner. Misty was part of that dedicated minority, and since last night, Daniel realized he was too. Walking into the restaurant, he smelled the deep-fat fryers and his mouth watered. He ordered five, sucked them down one after another, then ordered three more.

Afterward, Daniel drove Misty home. He was learning Misty's tics. When he noticed her tugging on her lip ring, Daniel knew she wanted to ask something but was nervous. His words stumbled over themselves to reassure her. "So when can we go prowling again?"

"Not sure." She quit playing with her lip ring. Relief softened her features. "Don't worry. We always find a few hours to get away."

As Daniel pulled into her parking lot, Misty grabbed her fairy wings from the backseat. She kissed him and whispered "I love you" again.

Daniel managed to get it out a little smoother the second time and relished Misty's guileless smile when he did.

Heading home, Daniel rubbed his eyes to keep himself awake and sorted through everything that had happened last night. It was hard giving up his voice. Humans had an urge to talk, even though most of what they said was meaningless.

But in exchange, the rot-eater god gave its wolves sharpened perception and the stamina to run for hours. Driving through the sleepy Saturday morning, Daniel felt sorry for the people around him. They would go from cradle to grave with the world dulled by their anemic senses, as if their heads were muffled in gauze.

There was a deeper change too. Not speaking, not able to process the meaning of speech, opened a chasm of silence between the pack and humans. Daniel remembered the cop. The wolves hadn't cared about the man; they had no respect for his authority and no concern for his safety. The cop had been only a threat to drive back.

Daniel had shifted back into human skin once they'd returned to the furnace. The disguise had been thin, though. He'd smelled Misty, felt how warm she was, and didn't care that he'd held back those same urges a week ago or why. *Amanita muscara* obliterated everything except the sensations of two bodies pressed together in the cold.

At first, Misty had been lost to those sensations too. As more of her humanity returned, though, the more she wanted besides animal rutting. She'd daydreamed about Italy and elsewhere. She'd told Daniel she loved him.

Daniel didn't know if he loved Misty or not. He'd said he did because her scent had been thick on his clothes and there wasn't anything else he could say without crushing her. Remembering how to speak, he'd remembered how to lie, too.

But while Misty had talked about far-away countries, Daniel found himself wondering if he could ever really give up the shooting star's clear trajectory for the right to roam. Not for a few dark hours, but day and night forever.

Pulling over a block from his house, Daniel unbuckled his tanker boots. Grime from the furnace covered his jeans and hoodie. He took clean clothes and his sneakers out of his book bag. A minute later, trying to ignore how tight the fresh clothes seemed, Daniel walked through his front door and back into his normal life.

CHAPTER 10

Lying on the living room floor, Daniel helped Mack with his Sunday school project, making a whale puppet from an envelope along with a little paper Jonah for it to swallow.

"I forget. What color are whales?" Daniel asked.

"Red!"

"A red whale." He reached for the Magic Markers.

"With blue dots."

Their mom came from the kitchen with the portable phone in her hand. "That was your aunt Leslie. Is Keith going out with Angie?"

"Yeah."

"Your Angie?"

"Not anymore."

Mack talked about whales in his usual happy jabber. Neither Daniel or his mom listened.

"Since when? What happened?"

"Since a few weeks ago, and nothing happened. It wasn't

156

working out." Daniel busied himself filling in blue circles across the whale. "Are these dots big enough?"

"No. They have to be big. Big like this." Mack spread his arms wide.

"So who have you been spending all your time on the phone with lately?"

Daniel sighed. "A girl named Misty."

"Misty what?"

"Sandlin. You don't know her."

"But you're dating now?"

"Yes."

"And?"

"And that's it. I'm seeing a girl named Misty. Keith's hooked up with Angie. You're all caught up." Daniel kept coloring. His mom stared at the back of his head for a few seconds, then walked out of the room without another word.

The snap in Daniel's voice had silenced Mack, too. Daniel handed him a red marker. "Here. Start coloring his head, I'll start at the tail, and we'll meet in the middle, okay?"

In the recommendation letter Mr. Fine had written to Cornell, the vice-principal had praised, among Daniel's other virtues, his organizational skills. For years, his life had run on multiple timetables, hours set aside for studying and homework, for practices and games, for church, student rep meetings, and summer college application workshops. Some nights, Daniel lay awake, slicing the next day or week or month into neat blocks of time. After all that, leading a double life—keeping two schedules from colliding instead of half a dozen—was no sweat.

He needed to fill out a transcript form so the school could send his final grades to Cornell. To make sure none of the pack saw him, Daniel waited until they'd all sat down to lunch, said he needed to piss, then rushed to the main office. At home, Daniel planned his escapes days in advance, thinking up stories, covering his tracks, and once, handing his dad a permission slip for an invented debate tournament. And while his parents slept, the pack's sign closed like teeth around Southside.

Their howls scraped rooftops and reached a pit-deep fear in human chests. It was a fear rooted in the time before cities, when people huddled around fires, the watching darkness on every side. Now, they gathered beneath electric lights, but either way, the wolves' call made skin prickle with gooseflesh. Eyes darted around. Steps quickened.

Shifting into wolf skin, though, had nothing on the mysterious change that overtook a soul between Saturday night and Sunday morning.

In crumbling Birmingham, the churches stood as forts against the rot-eater god. The decay spreading around them only inspired congregations to sing louder, to offer up more, to scrub and polish the Lord's houses until they shone. While sunlight peered through jewel-toned windows, staining his skin lavender and pink, Daniel lifted his voice alongside his brothers and sisters in Christ.

The first week of Lent, Pastor Crowell reached out to Daniel on the church steps after service. "Well, young man?" he asked, squeezing Daniel's shoulder with his thin hand. "Your dad mentioned you got some good news recently."

"Uh, yeah." The milling congregation started glancing over.

"Yeah? Something about college, am I right?"

"Yeah, I got into Cornell."

"Daniel, that's just wonderful. We all knew you were somebody amazing. We can't wait until you get out there and show the whole world."

Mrs. Applebee, Daniel's second-grade teacher, hugged him. Friends, the youth minister, and people Daniel barely knew jostled to clap him on the back and congratulate him.

"I'm not sure we can let him go or not," Pastor Crowell told his parents. "You know how many girls sign up for our youth missions because Daniel's going to be there?"

Everybody laughed at that, and the press of smiling faces made Daniel smile back. He shook everybody's hand, thanked them for their prayers, and told them he wanted to study law. He tried not to look at the gas station across from the church, where the pack's sign stared back from the painted cinder blocks.

On the car ride home, his mom turned to look at him in the backseat. "That was nice, wasn't it? You know how much Brother Crowell thinks of you."

Daniel nodded, then cracked the window. His mom's perfume was supposed to smell like honeysuckle. To the wolf, though, the harsh chemicals weren't anything like the real honeysuckle blooming across the furnace. They actually made Daniel dry-throated and a little sick. Or maybe that was from being reminded he wasn't who people thought he was anymore, that he wasn't sure himself.

After getting home, Daniel decided to meet Bwana and Spence at the park. He'd barely seen them since he'd started prowling with the pack.

They got into a game with some middle-schoolers, with Bwana playing center on one team and Daniel and Spence anchoring the other. The ball was a perfect street ball. The color and slickness of mud, it made a slightly dull *whap* against the concrete. After the eighth graders went home, Daniel and his friends played horse, laughed over Keith dating Angie, and talked about Spence going to UAB.

Spence still had an application at Florida State, but the University of Alabama at Birmingham had offered him a full ride, some scholarship meant to keep the city's best and brightest from leaving. Bwana thought it was absurd that Spence would struggle to keep up a 3.8 GPA, then matriculate to a college four blocks from his house.

"It's not going to be like going to college at all. You already take chemistry there." McCammon High had a good relationship with UAB, and their chemistry classes occasionally used the college's lab facilities.

"I know, I know." Spence shot left-handed from the free

throw line and missed. Tossing the ball to Daniel, he said, "I'm going to wait until I hear from Florida, but UAB has a good engineering program, I'll have money to do something on Saturday nights besides eat cold pizza and beat off like you two broke fucks, and—"

"And if you forget your lunch, your mom can just bring it up," Daniel added. "She'll be, like, 'Sorry to interrupt, Professor, but my baby gets grouchy without his pudding cup.'"

"And I'll still be able to go out with Dad on jobs sometimes," Spence went on. "Oh, yeah. He wants to know if you're going to work with us this summer."

Spence's dad owned Greensweep Landscaping. Daniel had worked for him over the last two summers, planting trees and hauling rolls of sod.

"Um, I'm not sure if I can or not." Daniel wiped his face with the front of his shirt. "I may be swamped getting ready for school."

"Yeah." Spence gave him a sly smile. "And we know who you'll be getting busy—I mean getting ready—with."

Bwana laughed. "Actually, we've got a question about Misty."

Spence stopped dribbling. "No, no. Don't ask him that."

"What is it?" Daniel asked.

"Well, we were wondering. Does Misty have brown nipples like a black girl or pink nipples like a white girl."

The wolf bristled. "Fuck off."

"C'mon. We're friends, right?" Bwana wrapped an arm around Daniel's shoulders. "I'm just curious. I'd hook up with her either way."

"You'd hook up with her if she had one of each," Spence said.

"Is that it? Damn, Danny Boy, it'd be like she was winking."

Daniel sank a fist into Bwana's stomach, doubling him over. Fingers digging into the nape of Bwana's neck, Daniel pushed him down.

Spence jumped back. "Shit. Relax, Daniel. Shit."

On his knees, Bwana sputtered, "Sorry. I'm sorry, okay?"

Daniel let him go.

"He was just joking around! Christ! Where the fuck's your head at?" Furious, Spence whipped the ball at Daniel's chest. Daniel batted it away and walked off the court. Daniel realized he'd been growling deep in his throat, and he'd been ready to hurt Bwana more if he hadn't submitted. Crescents of blood dried under his fingernails.

Bwana had just been joking around. Daniel had told him and Spence juicy particulars about almost every girl he'd hooked up with. He knew plenty about Geneva and Claire. Bwana had just wanted to swap the same dumb, dirty chatter they'd swapped since ninth grade.

But Misty was different; she was part of the pack. Or maybe Daniel was different now. Or maybe, after weeks of seething at Daniel's human self, the wolf had been ready to lash out at any hand-licker.

The wolf or the shooting star. It was getting harder to remember which one was his real shape and which was only a disguise.

Since becoming a wolf, Misty had stopped going to church with Marc, Grampa, and Nana. She felt guilty about that but liked being home when her mom got off work. Misty usually made breakfast while her mom showered and, if she was heading to her dispatching job, changed into her uniform.

"So tell me something about this Daniel boy," her mom said, sitting down at the table with a soft grunt. She was barely thirty-six, but her joints were stiff and worn out.

"Not much to tell." Misty shrugged. "His name's Daniel. He's a boy. He's really sweet."

Lily jumped into her mom's lap. She fed the cat some bacon. "He have a lip ring too?"

"No. I pierced my lip because I wanted to." Misty had already explained this to her mom several times. "I didn't do it because of Andre, Daniel, or any other boy."

"Probably has a ring in his pecker."

"Mom! He does not have a ring in his pecker."

"And you're so sure of that how?"

Busted. Misty sopped up her yolk with some toast and considered her response. "I know to be careful, Mom."

Her mom sighed. She trusted Misty, but mostly because

she had to. "Just graduate, okay? Please? That's the only thing I've ever asked of you or Marc."

"I'm going to graduate," Misty promised. "Don't worry."

"Just graduate and never date a guy with a ring in his pecker. Do those two things, and I'll be happy."

"You know what would make me happy? If we could stop talking about peckers at breakfast. If we could hold off the pecker-talk until at least noon. Or better yet, never."

Her mom chuckled. Waving her fork at Misty, she said, "Honey, I've made some mistakes in my life. But, God as my witness, I never dated any guy with a ring in his pecker."

Misty covered her face with both hands, her shoulders trembling with laughter.

CHAPTER 11

Ice and snow melted away, anxious to return next year, as winter only lingered now in the long morning shadows. During spring break, while classmates scattered to Gulf Shores and Panama City, the pack prowled their city almost every night. During the lazy days in between, they lolled among the sprouting green of the furnace complex.

"By the way," Misty told Daniel one afternoon. "Just so you know. Marc has a crush on you."

Daniel asked, "Huh?" but the twins had started into a flurry of shoves and punches. Marc got Misty in a headlock, but she was still giggling.

"He's started wearing the same body spray as you," she said.

"So?" Marc snapped back. "I liked it, so I went out and bought some. That's not gay."

"Yes it is! It's the gayest thing ever." Misty twisted free. "If you went and had sex with another guy, it still wouldn't be as gay as sniffing my boyfriend."

Marc's face darkened. Daniel slapped him in the shoulder. "Don't worry about it. I started wearing it after Keith did."

Instead of making him feel better, Marc's face seemed to darken even more at the mention of Daniel's cousin. Misty stopped laughing.

"Maybe I won't wear it, then," Marc mumbled.

"What's your problem with Keith? That time he bumped into you in the hall?"

"Bullshit, he bumped into me. That—"

Misty cocked her fist back, making Marc cringe. "Well?" he yelled.

Misty groaned and turned toward Daniel. "That fight you broke up? It started because Angie called me a mutt. Keith was hanging on her, then Marc—it was dumb. Forget it."

"She called you what?" Every muscle tensed. Daniel felt his shoulders hunch, his legs ready to spring.

"I said forget it. I told Marc to forget it. How come nobody listens to me?"

"So what? That doesn't bug you?"

"Yes, Daniel, it bugs me." Her tone made it clear that Daniel would never exactly understand. "But there's nothing you can do that won't bring ten times more trouble down on you."

"I don't care."

"Well, I do! So forget it."

Werewolves weren't the only monsters that had roamed the night in Birmingham. The Klan once operated as an unofficial arm of the government, maintaining order with dynamite, assassinations, and an assurance that the police would quiet any witnesses. Frustrated blacks began answering back with rocks, bottles, and a certainty that the problems were nothing a few dead cops couldn't fix. The days of Bombingham were over, but they'd left the city with wounds that would never heal entirely.

Daniel and Misty stared at each other. Then Daniel said, "I'm sorry."

"You didn't do anything."

"I know, just . . ." Just he felt filthy by association. Keith was family. Daniel had dated Angie for a year despite how trashy she could be. He wanted to hug Misty but wasn't clean enough.

"I'm going to talk to Keith," Daniel said.

"No."

"I'm just going to talk to him."

Misty took his hand. They left Marc in the casting shed and walked quietly through the perfume of wildflowers haunting the air. After a minute, Misty said, "It did bug me. I was so pissed, I could barely see straight, just thinking about Angie. But then I thought about what you think of me." She nudged him. "What do you think about me?"

"I think you're beautiful. And amazing and exciting."

Misty nodded. "That's what I thought you thought. You forgot breathtakingly graceful, though."

"Well, breathtakingly graceful, of course. How did I forget breathtakingly graceful?"

"So I thought about what you thought about me. Then I thought about what Angie Walton thinks about me. Then I thought, *Who cares what Angie thinks?* Forgot all about the bitch. Okay?"

Daniel had hurt Bwana for insulting Misty and would have hurt Keith, too. A wolf had to protect his pack. But instead, he kissed Misty and whispered, "Okay." His cousin would never know how lucky he was.

They lay in the grass, heads propped on their hands. Misty asked questions about his family. She'd started dropping little hints lately that she wouldn't mind meeting them.

Daniel couldn't let Misty come to his house. His parents told strangers in elevators about their son the Ivy Leaguer; there wasn't a chance they'd go through a whole dinner with Misty and not mention it. Before long, though, Misty would start wondering what the big secret was.

Finally, Daniel said, "Hey, I've got to watch Mack Sunday. You want to go out and get ice cream, or something?"

"Yeah, sure."

Daniel brushed Misty's chin with a dandelion while he talked. "I'll pick you up after church. Twelve or so."

She nodded. "So you still go to church, huh?"

Daniel shrugged.

"That's cool. Marc still goes. I think about going pretty much every week. But . . ." Dropping her voice to a guilty whisper, she asked, "Don't you think God knows? About what lives here? What we do?"

"What? Think God's going to strike you down?"

"No," she said, annoyed. "It's just, I don't know, I don't want to go and sing and stuff if I'm not being sincere."

Daniel stopped teasing her with the dandelion. Misty sneered at herself. "It's stupid, I know."

Daniel promised her it wasn't. He kissed her, then found himself laying his head against her breast. Settling onto her back, Misty ran her fingers through his hair.

She was a better person than him. She was beautiful and everything else he'd said. She was kind, too, with hurt animals and people who weren't worth her mercy. But that fairy-like creature inside Misty was as hidden to the hand-lickers as the wolf. The constant drone of gossip around Misty drowned out her own delicate lilt. A stupid little hoodrat. She burned all her boyfriend's clothes once.

Daniel wished he could rest there forever, between the cool grass and warm sunlight, listening to the soft beat of Misty's heart.

Before heading out Sunday, Daniel poured his brother a glass of Kool-Aid. Girls loved the Kool-Aid-stain mustache. As soon as Misty saw Mack, she went into a daze, unable to take her eyes off him. She spent the afternoon cooing over him, hugging him, and pretending to be brontosauruses with him. Any gathering suspicions she might have had evaporated. Nobody with a little brother that adorable could possibly have anything sinister to hide.

Unfortunately, even though Cornell wasn't noteworthy to Mack, ice cream and a girl who gave him piggyback rides were. At dinner, he told their parents about his and Daniel's day.

Their mom looked at Daniel. "So Mack's met her? Well, at least we know she's not imaginary."

Hunched over his plate, Daniel shoved food into his mouth.

"So why's he the lucky one? Why haven't the rest of us gotten to meet her?"

Daniel knew what to say to smooth this over. He just didn't want to bother. "Because Mack actually waited until he'd met Misty before making up his mind about her."

"Daniel, we haven't made—"

"The hell you haven't. You've called Aunt Leslie or Bwana's mom. You came up with something to talk about for five minutes, then said, 'Do you know anything about this Misty Sandlin? Daniel won't tell me anything.'" There was a subtle flush to his mother's face. Daniel knew he'd caught her. "And probably ninety percent of what they told you was bullshit."

"Watch your mouth!" his dad snapped.

"Fine," his mom said. "I wanted to know about this girl, and you wouldn't tell me anything. What was I supposed to do?"

Daniel went back to his food.

"So Misty's not as bad as people say. Good, I never thought you'd get mixed up with a girl like that. So bring her over sometime. We can't make up our own minds until we've met her, can we?"

"I've asked her, but she doesn't want to."

"Why not?"

Daniel shrugged. "Because she doesn't give a damn what you think about her."

"That's it. You're through." His dad pulled Daniel's plate away and pointed toward the stairs. "I don't know what's gotten into you lately."

"Nothing." Leaving his family and heading to his bedroom, Daniel mumbled, "Something's getting loose."

Even wearing human skin, Daniel stood a step outside humanity now. Their constant chatter grated on him. When school started again, students dragging their bellies in the dirt for the teachers made Daniel sick.

Everybody had heard how he'd punched Bwana, and Daniel's old friends didn't want anything to do with him now. Watching them joke around with Angie and Keith, that was fine by him. He started wearing his tanker boots every day. He liked how rough and ready they felt. He liked how they set him apart from the hand-lickers.

But Daniel could only afford his revulsion because he'd already licked all the hands he needed to. Hidden in his desk at home, he had a letter from Cornell, a one-way ticket out of Birmingham. He'd earned it by keeping everybody who mattered happy and keeping quiet otherwise.

It was a subtle art, looking into somebody's eyes and seeing, deep down, what they wanted to believe. Smart people and distrustful wolves would swallow almost any story if they wanted desperately enough for it to be true. Daniel could slip half a dozen lies past Misty and the pack before lunch, his sweet smile never wavering as they gobbled them down one after another. Now, Daniel realized that after four years of being the shooting star, of delicate manipulations and outright bullshit, he couldn't remember the last time he'd said one honest word.

The days were running out, though. Soon, Daniel would have to choose between being a shooting star or a wolf, drop all the lies, and find his real voice. Daniel wasn't even sure if he'd recognize the sound of it anymore.

But before dread of that coming moment grew too much to bear, the pack always gathered, once again, at the furnace. There, Daniel stomped his boots until his feet turned numb, chanting, "Want to be a wolf! A wolf! A wolf!"

Around him, the others screamed, then barked and raised howls. "A wolf! A wolf!"

Sweat and tears from the smoke dripped onto Daniel's lips

and fell *pap, pap* to the dirt. Exhaustion and *Amanita muscaria* wrapped him in warm delirium. They purified the animal inside him.

Someplace far away. Steepled halls above Ithaca. Two brothers, a mother and father. Something he needed to do soon. Something that was going to hurt somebody. Daniel stomped his boots. The human dross oozed from his psyche and fell *pap, pap* to the dirt.

Daniel's skin shifted around his altered consciousness. Sight and sound flooded creature senses. Misty's gentle whines would bring Daniel running. He'd bow low and whine back. Trotting beside her, Daniel licked her muzzle, making her tail wag.

He knew she was his companion, that she liked biting his ears. He knew her strength and quietness. He knew how moonlight burned across her fur. Nothing else remained.

"Don't be mad."

"I'm not mad," Misty huffed. She lugged a box of green peppers to the stainless-steel sink in the deli's prep area. Val trailed her.

"Look, I'm just telling you what I heard, okay? Angie was talking to Geneva in health class. She said something about him going to Cornell. This isn't the first time either."

"I don't care what Angie says." Misty jerked around. "You know she's a damn liar. You know she's still in love with Daniel."

"I know, but . . ."

"But you believe her, anyway?"

"No. I don't know. I mean, maybe Daniel isn't exactly lying, but maybe he's not telling the whole truth either. I mean, isn't it kind of weird that he's so smart, takes all those AP classes, but doesn't have any plans after graduation?"

"He has plans." She started washing the tomatoes. "We're going to Europe, remember?"

Val sighed. "Before he met you. And also, you've never been to his house or met his family."

"I met his brother."

"Who's five!"

"So? Just because your boyfriend's paranoid, doesn't mean you have to think everything's a conspiracy too."

Val had finally asked the questions that had been floating through Misty's head for weeks. She refused to listen. She refused to wonder what Angie had been talking about. It didn't matter; Angie was full of shit.

"Look, Misty. I—" Val touched her shoulder, but Misty gave an angry jerk.

"Don't." She forced herself to take a breath. Val was her best friend, even if she tried to mother her all the time. "I know Daniel better than you do, okay? He wouldn't lie like that, okay?"

"Fine." Val walked off without another word.

Under the lukewarm spray, Misty cut bruises out of the peppers' flesh. Maybe she didn't know everything yet, but she knew the way Daniel touched her. She knew the way he looked at her. Those couldn't be lies. The hand-lickers didn't see anything in Misty besides a ragged stray. Daniel saw someone else, though, someone enchanted, as if she really were Puck in butterfly wings.

Misty couldn't stop believing in him, no matter what. Otherwise, she didn't deserve to have him believe in her.

CHAPTER 12

The wolf's animal reserve was with Daniel all the time now. He grew distrustful of crowds. Too much noise. Too many bodies to watch, all moving at once. Even before winter had broken, the pack began refusing the shelter of the school lobby before class, meeting around one of the concrete picnic tables lining the front walk instead.

One morning after spring break had ended, they sat there despite the fat drops of rain plopping to the grass. They yawned and blinked bleary eyes but didn't say much. First bell rang. A few stragglers rushed into the school. The pack still didn't move. After a minute, Marc said, "Fuck it. Let's skip."

Eric nodded. "You've got some good ideas sometimes, Marc. They should give you one of those genius grants."

"I'm in if you guys are in," Val said.

"Me too," Misty added.

They all looked at Daniel.

"What do you want to do?"

Misty snorted. "Not be here. That's enough, isn't it?"

"Yeah, but—"

"Daniel Morning, have you ever skipped school before?" Val asked.

"Yes."

"I don't mean playing sick and getting Mommy to write you a note. I mean out on the town, free as a bird, skipped school."

"Well . . ."

"Oh, that's so cute." She pinched his cheek. "No wonder the teachers love you."

"Such a responsible young man," Eric said.

Daniel brushed Val's hand away. "Okay, okay. But if you're gonna skip, why not at least wait for a nice day? It'll probably drizzle like this all day."

"Baby, I promise." Misty wrapped her arms around him. Their noses touched. "The weather's always perfect on a skip day."

The patter of rain shut people inside, leaving Misty and her friends to wander their own private city. Crisp air sharpened the sound of their chatter. Flower buds, such a pale green they were almost white, covered gray branches.

After stopping at a grocery store to buy some bread, they drove to Kelly Ingram Park. When they'd started talking about the movement in history class, Mrs. Turner had shown a photograph that had been shot in Kelly Ingram. It showed protestors in their Sunday best, their faces frozen in shrieks as fire hoses slapped them to the concrete.

The park lay on the old border between the black and the white sections of town, between the Sixteenth Street Baptist Church to the north and Bull Connor's police and firemen to the south. During the Battle of Birmingham, protesters, mostly pissed-off high school kids, Misty's grampa among them, marched day after day.

They emptied the schools and filled the jails. The cops hauled so many people off, they had to start holding them at the YMCA. No matter how many kids Connor arrested, though, hundreds more would cut class and assemble at the park the next morning. The sheer weight of the protestors' bodies ground the city to a halt and forced it to surrender, beginning the slow process of desegregation.

These days, Birmingham's battleground heart hummed with bees. Wet clover swished against boots and soaked jean cuffs as they passed the Civil Rights Institute. Glancing over, Misty remembered a youth group field trip she'd taken there years back. She'd bragged to the tour guide that Grampa had been in the movement. She'd been proud of him then. He'd seemed like Superman. He'd stood up for truth and justice. He'd changed the American way.

Walking through the park with her pack, though, Misty realized Grampa had been the same age she was now. He'd been just as scrawny, just as frightened about making a fool of himself, and just as aware of how pitifully he stacked up against the world's meanness. Because of all that, Misty's feelings swelled past pride into awe.

As they approached the pond in the center of the park, the ducks started quacking, pulling Misty back into the present. She and her pack started tossing them bits of bread. Val got down on her haunches to feed them by hand. In seconds, the waddling mob had swarmed, fighting over the bread. Val went down, covering her head from flapping wings and nipping bills.

"Help!"

Eric, perched on a bench beside Marc, shook his head. "I'm not getting down there."

"Help!"

"Sorry. You're on your own."

Val managed to get to her feet. She declared the two large, squawking geese bullies but fed them, anyway. She made sure the ducklings, toddling little puff balls, got some too.

"That's it. See?" Misty showed the ducks the empty bread bag. "No more. Seriously."

Daniel and Marc flung their last pieces into the pond and watched the ducks dive after them. The pack crowded onto the bench and spent a while trying to shove one another off. Then Daniel and Misty left the others.

An installation dedicated to the movement, two black walls, rose on either side of the park's flagstone path. Police dogs lunged out of their inner surfaces, forcing visitors to squeeze past the welded-steel snarls. Finding shelter from the rain under the animals, Daniel and Misty daydreamed about Florence and Istanbul.

When their conversation lulled, Daniel lifted his face to the drizzle and said, "You were right. This is a perfect day."

"Told you."

"So, is something going on between you and Val?"

"No. Just crap from work." Even though she and Val had both apologized since their blow-up, things had still felt edgy between them all day. That would fade, though. But now Daniel had reminded her of all the questions Val had brought up. With a nervous lump in her throat, Misty ventured, "So what about when we get back from seeing the world? Any plans?"

Daniel shrugged. "Think Ilie would hire me?"

"C'mon. You're, like, the smartest guy in school. You take all those advanced placement classes. But whenever anyone even mentions college, you change the subject. You really don't have any clue what you want to do?"

Daniel shrugged. "I know what my parents want me to do. I know what everybody says is the smart thing to do. But, no, I really don't know what I want to do. I wish I did."

He ran his fingers through his hair while he spoke. Thin frustration lines formed between his eyebrows. Misty watched him and was sure Val had been wrong. There was no dark secret. Daniel was just as confused about the rest of his life as Misty was.

"Well, you should at least think about college," she said. "You'd be really good at it, and you wouldn't have any problem getting in."

Daniel nodded, still staring at the ground. "So what about you? What do you want to do?"

"I don't know." She shifted on the grass. The damp was soaking through her pants, making her itch. "I'd suck at college, but . . . during the summers, when there are lots of forest fires, they hire people to go out and help the firefighters. I want to do something like that."

"You want to fight forest fires?"

"I don't know. I don't care what job I have. But I want to be brave."

Daniel laughed out loud. "You're a werewolf. That's not brave enough for you?"

"Yeah, but . . ." Wolves were brave, but only as long as they stuck to their pack, as long as they stuck to their territory, a few square miles of badlands that nobody else wanted. Since Daniel had come, Misty had started having dreams bigger than Southside. She didn't know if she had the guts to follow them, though.

Misty turned to watch an elementary school class file into the Civil Rights Institute. She imagined her grampa marching across the park, over the border of the black section of town and into the world.

Finally, she asked, "I told you Grampa was part of the movement, right?"

"No. Was he?"

She nodded. "Got arrested, almost got expelled. He's still got this kind of dent in his forehead where some cop hit him with an ashtray."

"An ashtray?"

"One of those big glass ones. They were processing him at the jail, and Grampa said something smart, and the cop grabbed an ashtray and smashed him over the head with it until it broke."

"Fuck."

"Yeah. But my point is, Grampa wasn't a wolf. I mean, it's easy to be brave when you've got inch-long fangs. Without *Amanita*, though, how does somebody stand up like that?" Misty rested her chin on her knee. "I want to be brave even when I'm not in wolf shape. Even if I quit doing the ritual altogether."

His struggle to figure out if he could ever truly become a wolf had consumed so much of Daniel. Daniel had been so distracted, wondering if he could become a wolf, he hadn't noticed Misty beginning to wonder if she could become anything else. Daniel told her he thought she was that brave already. Misty smiled, kissed him, then turned away without answering.

They listened to the drowsy rhythm of the rain and the sharp laughter of the rest of the pack. They sat with their bodies pressed together, their thoughts still worlds away.

CHAPTER 13

Daniel walked with Misty to government class. They passed a pair of swallows chirping on the window ledge outside. Halting in the crowded hall, Misty's eyes followed the birds as they hopped across the concrete. "I hate this place," she said.

Daniel put an arm around her shoulder. Apart from the humans filling it, the school building itself had begun making him feel anxious and boxed in. The air that settled in the hallways smelled stale. He didn't trust the florescent light. The first few weeks he'd been a wolf, Daniel kept planning to go to debate practices and student rep meetings, then changing his mind at the last minute. He couldn't stand being in that building any longer than he had to.

They left the swallows and started walking again. "I hate this place and absolutely nothing could make it any better," Misty went on. "Except a piggyback ride."

Daniel snickered. "Nothing else at all?"

Pressing her lips white to keep from smiling, Misty shook her head ruefully.

Daniel took his backpack off, and Misty hopped on. "And watch your hands. I'm a lady, you sonofabitch."

Bouncing up and down as Daniel wove through the crowd, Misty laughed like a child. She goaded him up the stairs and to pick up the pace. "C'mon, baller! Let's see that McCammon Falcon hustle!"

He made it through Mrs. MacKaye's door before his legs buckled. Daniel and Misty tumbled over each other and hit the floor, but neither of them cared. Misty lay on her back, laughing too hard to notice her skirt had ridden up to her thighs. "Ow!" She rubbed her head. "I bonked my—"

"Get up! What's the matter with you two?"

Daniel and Misty saw Mrs. MacKaye standing over them, the class staring at them, and remembered where they were. Climbing to their feet, they crossed the classroom to take their seats, their teacher's shrill voice following them.

"Are you in kindergarten? You're seniors. You don't know how to behave in school yet?"

They sat with their shoulders hunched, their faces passive. Wolves weathering a storm.

"Nobody cares what you do at home? Fine. But you're not going to act like stray animals in my class."

"Don't talk about my home," Misty said quietly, plainly.

Without responding, Mrs. MacKaye turned and walked

toward the front of the class. She showed Daniel and Misty her back, signaling they were nothing worth worrying over. The insult only infuriated Misty more. Suddenly, she was on her feet.

"Don't call me a stray! Don't ever insult my family, bitch!" Misty flipped her desk over. It crashed to the floor, making the entire class jump and Mrs. MacKaye whip around.

Daniel saw the teacher cringe from Misty's snarl. Her eyes were as wide as a frightened rabbit's. The prey-fear only lasted a moment, though, and it was the only satisfaction Misty would get from the fight.

Mrs. MacKaye remembered this classroom was her territory, and her mouth tightened into a wire-thin line. "Let's go."

Misty glanced over her shoulder at Daniel, still frozen in his seat. When he didn't do anything, she walked out of the class, headed to the main office. Mrs. MacKaye followed her. Just before the teacher disappeared through the doorway, she snapped, "Daniel, fix her desk."

As soon as they were gone, the entire class turned toward Daniel, watching to see if he would go berserk too. Daniel sat with every muscle tensed. He wished it was night. He wished he was hidden under wolf skin; then he could have chased after Misty, defended her, comforted her.

It was daylight, though, and he was the shooting star. He stood up quietly and tipped Misty's desk back onto its feet.

• • •

Mr. Fine grilled Misty on what had happened, if she'd called Mrs. MacKaye "b-word." Misty answered with grunts and shrugs.

Months ago, Angie had insulted Misty, but Misty had kept Marc and Daniel from doing anything about it. It was getting harder to restrain the wolf inside her. Now Misty watched how soft and gray the aging vice-principal was, how sluggishly he moved.

"Glare at me all day. See if I care," Mr. Fine said. Then he sighed and squeezed the bridge of his nose. "Misty, you just—you can't throw a fit every time somebody makes you mad. Okay? I talked to Mrs. MacKaye. Is this because she mentioned your home?"

"No."

Mr. Fine waited for more of an answer. He didn't get one. "Is your mom still working two jobs?"

Misty studied the carpet and didn't say anything. She was a wolf. She was strong enough to bear the hate of every slow, stupid hand-licker in this school. But the pity in Mr. Fine's voice humiliated her. It struck a precise resonance, making Misty's chin tremble like a wineglass about to shatter.

"I know that's got to be hard on you and Marc. I know it—"

"You don't know anything! You think you know everything. Everybody around here thinks they know everything, but they don't." She slumped back down in the chair. "Just give me ISS already. Jesus."

"All right, we'll do it the hard way. Once again." He pulled a pad of blue discipline forms from his desk. "You've still got two months until graduation. We can spend it making each other miserable, or we can try to stay out of each other's way. It's up to you, Misty."

While he filled out the form, Misty quickly wiped a tear from her eye. Never let anyone see you cry except family.

At lunch, Daniel told the pack what had happened. When Misty sat down with her tray, she just said, "Five days ISS," and started picking the lettuce out of her taco.

The others seethed. But Misty, her fury already spent, only sulked. Daniel hugged her, told dumb jokes, and tried to make her smile. Misty worried her lip ring and mumbled, "Mom's going to kill me."

"Look," Daniel said. "Sorry I didn't stand up for you or anything. I should have."

Misty gave him a sour look, but turned away without saying anything.

When school let out, Misty felt a little better but still didn't want to face her mom yet. They decided to hang out at Val's house before the girls went to work. Walking toward the parking lot, Daniel's phone vibrated in his backpack. It was his mom.

"Where are you?"

"Out with some friends." Daniel stepped away from his pack, walking into the chattering crowd so they couldn't overhear. "We're going to go play some ball. I'll probably go to Samford from there. Grab something to eat on the way."

"I talked to Dr. Byrd today."

Daniel asked, "Who?" Then he remembered Dr. Byrd was his sociology professor. "Oh."

"You need to get home. Now." His mom was so mad, she wasn't even yelling.

"Yeah, okay." Daniel hung up and jogged back toward the pack. He made up one more lie on the spot, telling them he needed to go babysit his brothers because his dad was working late. Nobody doubted him. Even though he'd let her down a few hours before, Misty gave him two kisses, one for him and the other for Mack.

When he walked through the front door, his mom came out of the kitchen. She started to say something, but Daniel cut her off. "So you're checking up on me at school too?"

"I called your teachers to see how you were doing and if there was anything we could do to help. And don't you dare act like I'm Mommy Dearest; you haven't been going to class!" She smacked him on the side of the head, hard enough to sting. "Do you know how much tuition costs? Or books? Where the hell have you been?"

"Out."

She smacked him again. "This is a real dumb time to act smart. Out where?"

Daniel sighed. "Mostly down at the Florence Deli."

She spread her hands in bewilderment. "Why?"

"Because Misty works there."

She started pacing the living room. "Do you have any idea of the chances you've been given? Any idea of the kind of man you can become?"

"Yes."

"Roll your eyes again, I swear I'll slap them straight." His mom lectured him for a solid hour, until his dad got home and took over.

"Do you know how much we've spent on tuition? And books?"

"Yes," he growled.

"Daniel, you have gotten where you are by the grace of God and years of busting your ass. And now you've decided to chuck it all out the window for what? To hit on some hot little juvenile delinquent?"

That finally made Daniel snap back. "No. I decided to chuck it because I was fucking sick of jumping through hoops for you! I got into fucking Cornell. What the hell else is it going to take to make you happy?" Spit flew from his mouth. His dad saw trashing Misty had stirred something inside Daniel. He didn't know what that something was, but it still frightened him.

"This isn't about jumping through hoops, Daniel," his mom said from the sidelines. "The first day you're at Cornell, they'll expect you to carry yourself a certain way. You're going to have responsibilities you don't have in high school. So you can go to college and learn how to act like a college student. Or you can hang out at a fast-food joint and learn how to flip burgers. Those

are your two choices, and you don't get to pick the second one."
She glanced at her watch. "Now get your books and get to school.
And when you get home, I want to see notes from each class."

"I'll try to take notes, but it's hard to concentrate sometimes." Daniel shook his head sadly, then pinned his mom with
a glare. "You know, because of this ADHD thing I've got."

His parents' anger went cold, and their hurt expressions
made him happy.

Upstairs, Daniel dug through piles of clothes to find his
textbooks. When he came back down, his mom was in the
kitchen, making him a sandwich.

"Here, take it with you."

Daniel pushed the sandwich away and walked out.

Driving through town, he played angry music, stylized
threats barking over stripped-down beats. Samford's campus
was over the mountain in Homewood. Daniel got as far as
the rock cut Val had tagged two months ago. Black against
the brick-colored stone, the wolf heads were just visible high
above the expressway lights.

Daniel pulled to the shoulder of the road. His stereo
still snarling, he stared at the signs marking the border of the
pack's territory. He tried to imagine going to Misty, confessing
everything, and telling her he was ready become a true wolf.
But Daniel had been lying to himself all these months just as
much as he'd been lying to the pack.

Supposedly, time slows down during a wreck. The instant

it takes for a tire to blow out and one car to hurl into another becomes an eye-blink eternity. People emerge with vivid memories of glass shattering, metal crumpling, and watching helplessly as the well-ordered universe explodes all around them. Daniel remembered the year his dad got laid off from Pfizer in the same terrifying detail.

His parents were mad all the time. They had to borrow money from Uncle Josh to keep the lights on. Daniel remembered his dad thanking Uncle Josh for the loan, then asking him to not say anything to Daniel's grandparents. He remembered when the refrigerator broke. Before, it would be a problem cured with a little cussing and pulling out the checkbook. With the bills already piling up, though, it was what made his dad finally break. Daniel remembered taking Fischer outside to play so they could pretend not to hear him crying.

When his dad got a job with GSK, things started getting better. But his parents emerged from that car-crash year with a new determination. The world would never spin out of their sons' control like it had theirs.

At the hospital, Daniel's mom emptied bed pans and changed wound dressings for him. His dad spent days on the road and slept in his car for him. They still didn't know how they were going to pay for Cornell except that extra shifts and years off their own lives meant nothing if their children escaped the rot-eater god.

Daniel kicked the underpanel of his dash. He kept kicking

until his boot smashed a hole in it. He kept kicking as chunks of plastic fell to the floorboard and kept kicking until he was exhausted enough to actually think.

He thought about Misty's troubled home and Eric, whose brother was dead. They knew as well as Daniel how easily life could go freewheeling. The only difference was they couldn't depend on the shooting star's charm, talent, and miraculous luck to get them through.

They had nothing to grasp on to except their pride and their pack. They had to be strong enough to defend both, day after day after day.

Daniel loved playing wolf with them, prowling the city and seeing how much he could get away with. The shooting star could take a cheap shot at Bwana on the basketball courts and skip school once or twice. But bawling out a teacher? Causing mayhem in class? Those things would get back to Cornell, prod them to reconsider their acceptance.

In Mrs. MacKaye's class today, it had finally come time to refuse dreams of escape, to wipe the bluestone towers of Cornell from his mind and stand by his packmate. Daniel had been afraid, though. He'd sat cowed and quiet.

He watched traffic speed by in both directions. He looked up at the pack's sign again, then headed to class. It made him sick, but Daniel knew that—no matter how much he had to cheat to do it, how many hands he had to lick—he was one of the blessed few who'd ever get to cross this border out of Birmingham.

CHAPTER 14

Daniel spent all Friday and most of Saturday trying to figure out how to tell Misty and the pack he was leaving in the fall. It was too late. No matter what he said, Misty would hate him. And the pack, to whom loyalty meant everything, would kick him out. And even worse than facing those fates was knowing he'd deserve them.

For a few months Daniel had slipped off his destined path and run mad. He'd seen a world—a lush world, as beautiful as it was harsh—humans didn't know. As soon as Daniel confessed who he really was, all of that would snap closed to him once again, this time forever.

Daniel decided to put it off until the end of school, maybe through the summer. He couldn't do much more harm than he'd already done. So, adding a few more lies to the already leaning pile, he took Misty out Saturday. He stole kisses from her and did whatever he could to make her smile. Every moment was sweetened by the knowledge that he'd betray her soon.

When night fell, they went to the furnace. Barn swallows had built mud nests in the eaves of the casting shed. They squawked and wheeled overhead while the pack smoked a bowl and waited for the mushrooms to cook.

Misty wore cargo pants and a tank top in the warm-as-skin night. Months of prowling had hardened the muscles in her shoulders and arms. Daniel relished how they felt under his hands. They talked about ISS, joking that Misty would come out with prison tats or her ears chopped off like Charlie Say What.

Crouched by the fire, Marc chuckled. "Know what we should do? We should tag that fucking school."

Eric grinned. "That'd be funny as hell if they didn't have security cameras everywhere."

"So where are we going tonight?"

Before Eric could answer, Daniel spoke up. "Let's tag the school."

"Seriously?" Marc looked startled somebody had listened to him.

"Security cameras everywhere," Eric repeated. "We go to that school. They'll recognize us on the tapes. And if we get caught shifting—"

"We go to that school. We know where all the cameras are."

He nodded at Marc. "Think you and me can get up to the roof?"

"Shit, yeah. No problem." Marc beamed.

Every sugary note Daniel had slipped into Misty's textbook had been a lie. The plush wolf he'd gotten her for Valentine's Day, the T-shirt he'd bought because it made her laugh, had all been part of pretending to be someone he wasn't. Getting revenge for Mrs. MacKaye's tossed-off cruelty might be the one real gift Daniel could ever give Misty.

This was bigger than that, though. Finally accepting that he, too, was a domesticated pet had only sharpened Daniel's resentment of the hand-lickers. Hidden under wolf skin, he could vent his anger at them, at his own weakness, in ways the shooting star never could.

Between the school and the girls' gym lay a paved courtyard where delivery trucks backed up to the cafeteria. From the corner of the roof, the glass eyes of cameras watched both entrances to the courtyard. All they recorded that night was a pair of large dogs padding across the asphalt.

Once he and Marc were inside the courtyard, Daniel shifted into human form, catching the can of spray paint as it fell from his jaws and shoving it into his pocket. Marc carried a piece of rebar scavenged from the furnace. Flowing between skins had become easier over the months. Underneath, Daniel's mind wasn't exactly human or lupine. Cunning as the first, relentless as the second, it had become more dangerous than either.

A metal roof covered the path from the school to the gym. With Marc following him, Daniel climbed to the top, then to a second-story window ledge. Fingers grasping the metal grills protecting the windows, Daniel inched to the corner of the building. It was easy if you were brave enough, or brimming with enough hate.

The school had been built just as televisions began replacing radios in homes. A pipe ran up the brick wall, housing coaxial cables and more wires than the school's architects ever dreamed it would need. Using grills, ledges, and the pipe, Daniel pulled himself upward.

Reaching the top, Daniel took the can from his pocket, sprayed the camera lenses until paint dripped into his face, then heaved himself over the lip of the roof.

After blinding the rest of the cameras, he went to crouch over Thirteenth Avenue. A car passed below. Once the street was clear, Daniel let out a low *whuf*. Marc swung the rebar into one of the floodlights washing the campus hill in a pallid glow. Two strikes and a shower of sparks dripped to the ground below. Marc moved to the next light and the next.

The school campus went dark. Daniel howled, and Val emerged from across the street. She shifted into human skin and pulled out a second can of spray paint. She wore a heavy work coat also scavenged from the furnace. With the collar pulled up, it looked like the shadows clung to her. She approached the sign at the head of the curving front drive.

McCAMMON HIGH SCHOOL
HOME OF THE FALCONS

She slashed a dripping black wolf head across the faded plastic, then ran toward the sign on the other end of the drive.

Daniel stalked along the edge of the roof. Below, Misty and Eric lurked, unseen but watching. When Marc whined, Daniel turned to see what was the matter. Marc pawed and sniffed at something in the middle of the roof and started yipping for Daniel to come look.

A circle of wood was nailed to the roof and caked with old tar. There had been an air-conditioning unit there a decade ago, the wood covering the hole where the duct work snaked down into the school.

Marc scraped at it. His muzzle yawned open, trying to form sounds a wolf couldn't. The effort pushed him back into his human form. "Books," he said, anxious to please. "I smell paper. Ink."

Daniel sniffed at the covering. It looked solid, but he breathed in the acidic scent of mold. Below the rotting wood, he smelled a classroom, its books and ammonia-scrubbed floors.

Marc smashed the heel of his sneaker down. There was a wet crack, and a small wound opened in the roof. He kept kicking at it. Daniel ripped at the ragged edges with his fangs. As the hole widened, a nest of beetles plinked to the duct work and scattered for deeper dark. Soon, Marc kicked through insulation and plaster into ash-colored light.

They looked down at evenly spaced desks. A neat row of extra-credit projects lined the windowsill. Daniel stared down at the classroom, all right angles and order. He wanted to avenge Misty. He wanted the pack to remember, even after he betrayed them and ran off to Cornell, that he'd been a wolf once. And he wanted to remember himself. Tipping his head back, Daniel summoned the pack.

A human couldn't have fit. The wolves, though, with lanky legs and narrow chests designed for plowing through snow drifts, were able to slink down the hole to a support beam and into the classroom.

Daniel led the way. Moving through the corridors, dark against dark, they disabled the cameras inside and broke into the nurse's office. They pulled on thick blue latex gloves to make sure no fingerprints were left behind. Then, with the school splayed as helpless as prey, they lunged for the kill.

They danced between human and wolf skins, between hands and fangs, depending on how they could cause the most destruction. The school's black-booted misfits tipped over trophy cases, cracked necks of fire extinguishers to send them rocketing up the halls, and broke into the cafeteria's cooler. Wolves gorged on frozen meat, bit through chair legs, and pissed on carpets. Glass shattered. Metal crumpled. Every tiny hate, every splinter-sharp rumor, every moment of frustration and impotence the pack had absorbed through four years of high school came bursting out all at once.

Eric knocked over a filing cabinet, hundreds of permanent records spilling to the floor. Daniel remembered somebody and pawed through the files searching for him. He passed the file he wanted several times until recognizing the name on the tab.

Morning, Daniel J.

He knew what the papers inside said without having to read them. Grades and scores and extracurriculars. A form stating he suffered from attention deficit/hyperactivity disorder. Letters of recommendation. Daniel glimpsed the word "Cornell" over and over.

Reaching out with a human hand, he grabbed Marc by the scruff of his neck, lifting him onto his hind legs and growling until Marc shifted out of wolf shape. Daniel took Marc's lighter from his pocket, letting the flame lick the corner of the file.

Daniel yipped joyfully while the shooting star burned. He waved the file in his hand, watching it blacken and crumble, then shoved it back into the pile. Flames ate other names. Laughing, Eric and Marc broke into more filing cabinets. Soon, the fire swept up the wall with the shape and *whoosh* of a wave.

Smoke detectors began screaming. Water sprayed from the ceiling but wasn't enough to douse the flames. A computer monitor imploded from the heat. The blasting, blistering air — how the furnace must have felt when it had been alive — pushed them to the far side of the high counter, then out into the hall. They had stacks of records in their arms, flinging them back through the double doors, watching discipline forms and class rankings burn. The pack danced while the school sank into chaos, into wilderness.

Misty had disappeared. Dropping to his paws, Daniel padded across the lobby. Hundreds of scent-ghosts drifted through the school, but he found his companion's easily. He followed it to Mrs. MacKaye's room.

Misty had the spray paint. She was decorating the walls with wolf heads. When Daniel came in, she turned.

"No stray." Misty chucked the can at Mrs. MacKaye's blackboard. "I am a wolf. I have a pack. This is our territory. Ours."

The effort to speak twisted Misty's mouth into a wide, snarling grin. Giving up, she snatched up one of the desks, swinging it against a window. It bounced off the metal grill. Slivers of glass sprayed to the floor and a warm breeze swept in. Misty grabbed the desk again as it crashed to the floor, busted a second window, kicked out a third, then flung the desk across the room.

The fury ended in hard pants and the angry grin fading. Her face became as inscrutable as the moon. "Not a stray."

Daniel nodded. The sound of shattering glass, Misty's

heaving breaths, and the fun of breaking things excited him. Taking Misty around the waist, he lifted her onto Mrs. MacKaye's desk. She swept clear a stapler, a coffee mug full of pens, and other litter.

Daniel pushed Misty's tank top up. Boot soles squeaked against the laminated wood. A wailing siren approached. He kissed her breasts, licked salty sweat from her throat. Spinning red and blue lights stirred the room's shadows around them. The school hadn't been as defenseless as it appeared; the smoke alarm had summoned help. Misty's lip ring, her tongue in Daniel's mouth, felt electric.

A spot beam swept the front of the school, halting at the broken windows. The harsh white light steadied on them, and they finally glanced up at the fire engine outside.

Time to go. Rolling off the desk and shifting into wolves, they slipped out of the room beneath the beam. Heading for the curving staircase, they heard the pack's voices farther up ahead. Eric was angry. Val spoke in hard whispers.

Misty barked, then howled, trying to get their attention. They just kept talking.

"What did this have to do with them?" Eric screamed. "This didn't have anything to do with them."

Crouched low, Daniel slunk across the lobby with Misty close by his side. Inside the main office, fire crawled across furniture and computer components. Smoke boiled across the ceiling, so black, a wolf's night-stalking eyes couldn't see through it. Scraps of burning paper swirled lazily through the doorway and into the lobby.

Daniel and Misty followed the voices to the head of the east hall. The others crouched in human shape surrounded by student files. Eric clutched one. Coughing, Val said, "They're coming! Coming!"

Marc snatched the file from Eric's hands, throwing it down. "Need to run. Sirens. We need to shift."

"I can't anymore." Eric beat his palms against the tiled floor. For a second, his skin twitched, then settled back around human muscle and bone. "That didn't have anything to do with them."

In the fire's agitated light, Daniel picked up the crumpled pages Marc had thrown. Sometime, Eric had drawn two portraits of the same man in heavy lines and ballpoint pen shading. Now, they were in his file, paperclipped to a sheaf of notes from the school psychologist. The man wore dog tags in one picture. Unable to read the name, Daniel recognized Eric's long nose and thin lips and knew they were pictures of Andrew.

Eric had to become an animal in his mind before he could become an animal physically. Memories of his brother clutched him, holding him in human shape.

Misty's voice joined Val's and Marc's. "Cruisers are coming. Plea—"

A diesel motor roared to life outside the lobby. Marc

scrambled back from the shriek of bending metal. The others flattened themselves almost to the floor. Flashlight beams bobbed through the windows, silhouetting firefighters in helmets and heavy coats. They were forcing their way into the school, prying one of the front doors out of its steel frame.

Flinging Eric's file into the inferno of the main office, Daniel barreled forward and shifted skin. Under fur, fangs, and flaring eyes, he threw himself against the door. His muzzle shattered the window. Glass cut his skin. He barked and bit at the wire mesh. The bulky shadows stumbled back, dropping equipment.

He'd only startled them. As he started driving the pack upstairs, flashlights already peered through the windows behind them.

Kneeling beside Eric, Val raised her voice above Daniel's snarl. "He can't—"

Daniel tore Val's sleeve, pulling her to her feet. He got Eric up too. The pack raced up the staircase. Skidding around landings and down the third-floor hall, they found the math room where they'd entered the school.

Stepping onto Mr. Nguyen's desk, Marc climbed into the ceiling. Inching along the support beam, he changed shape and crawled through the hole to the roof. Watching, Daniel realized what Val had been trying to tell him. The hole was only wide enough for a wolf's lean frame. If Eric couldn't shift, he was trapped.

Voices buzzed over radios downstairs. The firefighters were

UNLEASHED

inside. Misty stood on the desk but couldn't leave her friends yet. "Forget. Please," she begged Eric. "We have to go."

Eric knelt, slapping his palms against the floor again. "I can't! I can't! I keep . . ." He didn't say his brother's name, but it didn't help. "What did that have to do with them?"

Daniel saw the despair starting to spread. Val worried for her boyfriend. Misty worried for both of them, and Marc and Daniel for her. He had to do something before emotion kept all of them from shifting.

Pressing his face to the windows, Daniel took in as much of the campus as he could. Lights flashed everywhere now, cruisers and fire trucks that hissed like dragons. He studied the window itself. It was designed to only tilt open a few inches. Misty had bounced a desk off the ones in Mrs. MacKaye's class without breaking the metal grill. Eric was caged.

Daniel wiped warm blood from his mouth and winced at a stab of pain. When he'd thrown himself against the front door, a piece of glass must have lodged under his skin. He'd deal with that later.

Val was trying to comfort Eric even though he pushed her away. Daniel took her arm. "Police in the student lot." His teeth and tongue worked carefully to form the words. "Keep them back. Back from the west side."

"I can't—"

"I will get him out. Downstairs. Keep police away from west side."

Val tried to say a few words to Eric, but Daniel wouldn't let her. "Go!" He snapped at Misty, too. "Run! Run!"

The girls scrambled through the ceiling. The smoke from the lobby was rising to the third floor. The thickening haze made Daniel dizzy and his chest burn.

Dropping to all fours, he ran into the hall, ears pricked forward. He heard firefighters in the lobby, shouting mixed with the roar of fire hoses. Others moved upward in groups, searching for victims.

Daniel listened to heavy footsteps, the creak and clank of equipment on straps. Their gear made them move even more clumsily than other humans. It was designed to protect from heat, not fangs. Daniel could take one down easily, but four in a group would be hard.

The humanity left inside him cringed from the course his thoughts were taking. He couldn't kill the firefighters, but he couldn't let them catch Eric, either.

He ran back to Mr. Nguyen's room. Fear and rushing adrenaline made it hard for Daniel to shift to human shape. He struggled to hold it, the mirror opposite of the struggle Daniel once had staying in wolf skin.

Eric watched him, still slumped on the floor. Tears, from the smoke or over his brother, cut tracks through the soot on his face. Daniel grabbed Eric and made a stooped run to the doorway. They crouched on the balls of their feet. Around them, the school was pitch-black but alive with sound.

"Down stairs. Down west hall. Down hall behind the gym. Out fire door. The humans are carrying light. I'll run ahead. Kill their lights. Turn them blind, scared of the dark."

"But I'm huma—"

Daniel squeezed the back of his neck. "You are a wolf. You don't need to see to know where they are. Listen."

"I'm a wolf," Eric wheezed, and Daniel let go. In the stairwell, the clatter of footfalls hardened, growing louder and losing its echoes, as the firefighters neared the third floor. Daniel leaned forward, balancing on his fingers. "Down stairs. Down west hall. Down hall behind the gym. Out door."

"I'm a wolf," Eric whispered. "Don't need to see. I'm a wolf, wolf."

Flashlight beams, diffused through swirls of smoke, bobbed up from the stairwell. Daniel gave them a few heartbeats to enter the hall, then raced out. Shifting didn't feel like hiding under a disguise; it felt like ripping free of one.

Four firefighters walked in a line. Moving quick, silent, and low, Daniel lunged at the leader. By the time the man saw Daniel, he didn't have time to throw his arms up. He wore a flashlight mounted on his helmet. As they arched to the ground together, Daniel bit through its plastic, then jumped clear as the man crashed to the floor. He brought the second one down by his jacket, then slid, twisted, and bit into the thick canvas and rubber of the third's pant leg, whipping him off his feet. Tearing his light from its bracket like meat from the bone, Daniel flung it skittering into a corner.

The fourth firefighter stumbled back down the stairs. Daniel caught him at the landing, and the last light went dark. The man curled into a ball yelling for help and never heard Eric stumbling past in the dark.

Eric's footsteps sank toward the ground floor. Daniel rushed by like a hard wind. Another group of men jostled toward the stairs from the opposite direction as the gym, following distress calls from the first group. Daniel struck without a sound. Fangs cast awful shadows as they shattered lights.

Scattering the firefighters' line and plunging them into primal darkness, Daniel vanished again. He followed the unsteady rhythm of Eric's footsteps down the swampy, sweat-gagged hall between the gym and locker rooms. The fire door swung open. Eric staggered into the moonlight, and Daniel burst past him again. He barked and snarled. Spit flew from his jaws. He searched for the next human standing in their way, but there wasn't any.

Daniel and Eric half-ran, half-tumbled down the hill toward Seventeenth Street. Daniel wouldn't let Eric stop until they reached the Ronald McDonald House two blocks north of the school. Collapsing into the red mud, Eric coughed and heaved for breath.

Daniel heard the rest of the pack growling, keeping the police away. He sent up a baying howl, telling them they were safe. Their clamor fell off as they slipped back into the shadows and followed Daniel's call.

"The roof! The roof! The roof is on fire. We don't need no water, let the motherfucker burn! Burn, motherfucker, burn!"

At the furnace, Val and Eric sang while Marc told Daniel everything that had happened on the north side of the school.

"So I fly down the pipe. Like, so fast, it's burning my hands, and I drop the last few feet. Twist my ankle bad and just shout, 'Ow! Fuck!' As soon as I do, somebody comes running around the corner, and I know its gonna be one of the cops."

"Did he see you? See your face?"

"Shhh . . . don't talk." Misty straddled Daniel's lap. With his chin in one hand and tweezers in the other, she dug for the glass lodged in his lip.

Marc shook his head. "He comes around the corner, and I jump out as a wolf at him. Fucker screams, right? He's out of there. So I chase him all the way to the parking lot. He fucking jumps back in his car, locks the fucking door."

Daniel snickered, as much at how Marc's words tripped over one another as the story.

"Don't laugh, either." Misty tilted his chin higher. "Got it. I got it." Her hand trembling with care, she removed a half-inch-long sliver of bloody glass and held it up to admire. "Jesus."

She leaned down to kiss him. Rising, her mouth was smeared scarlet. Misty licked Daniel's blood from her lips and smiled.

Eric crept toward them. Sliding out from under Misty,

Daniel stood up. Eric glanced at him. He managed to mumble, "Hey. Thanks, man," before his eyes darted back to the dirt.

Daniel hugged him. Eric resisted for a moment before wrapping his arms around him. He just nodded instead. It wasn't a normal hug. He clutched the back of Daniel's shirt, like Daniel was the only thing holding him up.

"I'm sorry about your brother," Daniel whispered.

Eric's face was buried against Daniel's shoulder. He sniffed and tried to say something, but his voice quivered too much.

"But you've got a pack now. You know that, right? We're a pack." Until sunrise. Until the amnesic magic of *Amanita muscaria* wore off. Until he flew up to the bluestone towers of Cornell. But for the moment, in the thrall of the rot-eater god, Daniel believed every word.

They turned the music so loud it hurt and danced on top of the rusted machines. They howled and sang into the clear night. *"We don't need no water, let the motherfucker burn!"* Daniel sang louder than any of them.

CHAPTER 15

Misty woke up still exhausted. Lying in the foggy land between Birmingham and dreams, she felt *Amanita muscaria* growing inside her. The mushroom budded through organs like cancer and clogged her throat. She jerked upright, coughing until her chest hurt. It was just crud from the night before.

In the shower, Misty washed her hair three times, but the sooty smell lingered. Her mom and Marc were still in bed. After breakfast, Misty curled onto the couch and watched the morning news. They showed footage of the pack's sign slashing out the McCammon falcon and covering Mrs. MacKaye's room. The fire had wrecked the main office. A fire captain said it could have been a lot worse if it had gotten into the ceiling and spread.

Last night, Misty had felt drunk on triumph. It was almost graduation, and she'd given that miserable school a big, wet kiss good-bye. Staring at the TV, she waited for that rush to return.

She tried to force a chuckle, a sneer, anything, but she

couldn't push herself to hatred or happiness. She just felt leached dry.

There was a soft rap at the door. Misty saw her grampa in his blue suit through the window, and her mood brightened. Opening the door, she hugged him. The sweat and machine oil smells of the stamping plant clung to Grampa even when he wore his church clothes.

"Hey, girl. Missed you at church today."

"Yeah. Sorry," Misty said sheepishly.

"Where's your mom?"

"In bed. I don't know when she has to get up, but you want to wait? I can make some coffee."

"That'll be fine."

Grampa and Nana had never liked the way their son had left Misty's mom to raise two kids on her own. They didn't have a lot of money themselves, but they helped out whenever they could. While Misty poured water into the coffeemaker, Grampa stood in the living room watching the news report.

"Misty? What happened at your school?"

She hesitated. "Some—somebody trashed it, I guess."

Grampa shook his head, and that was enough to make Misty ashamed. Handing him his coffee, she glanced at the crescent-shaped depression on the side of his forehead.

He'd dropped to his knees and prayed in front of police batons. He'd been arrested and almost expelled. Even then, he wouldn't shut up, so they smashed an ashtray over his head.

They bloodied him, might have killed him, but they couldn't make him believe he was a nigger.

And Misty hunched under a pelt, spray-painted walls, and trashed schools. The rot-eater god offered revenge on anybody who treated Misty like some nasty little animal. All she had to do was prove them right.

Somehow, the wolf was both rebellion and total surrender. Misty finally managed a small, sour laugh. Nobody had ever told Misty the devil had a sense of humor.

Daniel's mom banged on his door to wake him up. He mumbled that he was up already, and after she went away, dropped his head back onto the pillow. There were no bird-songs outside his window. From that, Daniel knew the sun had already reached its peak in the sky.

Two soup cans lay on the floor. Coming home last night, he'd been starving, drinking the clam chowder cold along with several MoonPies. Throwing the garbage away, Daniel took a shower. The water swirled gray with ash and paint.

Standing under the hot spray, Daniel thought about last night. He hadn't planned on entering the school. He certainly hadn't planned on the firefighters and police. Remembering the chaotic rush of it all, he allowed himself a small, sated grin.

But now, Daniel had to make sure the pack's trail was swept clean. As his mental gears started clicking again, he let the shooting star take over, the brilliant Cornell-admit with excellent organizational skills. First, they had to dump their clothes from last night. Walking to the kitchen, he ran into his dad coming in from mowing the lawn.

"Well, good morning." His dad beamed with mock enthusiasm, then said, "Christ. What happened?"

Daniel touched the scabbed-over slash above his mouth. "Cut myself shaving," he said, too distracted to come up with anything believable.

His dad shook his head. "Damnit, Daniel," he said, walking away. He'd given up trying to get anything out of his son, and that was good enough for Daniel.

Getting a trash bag, Daniel went back upstairs, stuffed his boots and ruined clothes into it, then headed out, grabbing a few more moonpies on the way.

Grampa was still waiting for Misty's mom to wake up. Marc had emerged from his room, but he'd barely spoken, just hunched over a bowl of cereal without a shirt or shoes. Misty wanted to talk to Daniel. She left a message on his phone. When he called her back from his car, though, he was all business.

"Hey, baby, how's everything?"

"Okay," Misty said, even though she wasn't so sure.

"Good. Listen, we need to get rid of any evidence from last night. First, we need to throw away everything we were wearing."

"I already did. The smoke ruined it all anyway. Even my underwear was—"

"Where? In the Dumpster at the apartment?"

"Yeah."

"Go get it. We need to dump everything at the furnace. Nobody will look there even if they suspect us. Boots especially. Police can match shoe prints the way they can fingerprints."

"Eric's not about to throw Andrew's boots away."

"I'll handle Eric. Just get those clothes and let Marc know, okay?"

"Yeah, okay." Misty knew they needed to prepare for any fallout, but it wasn't what she'd wanted to talk to Daniel about.

"I'm on my way over. Love you."

"Love you, too."

Daniel showed up fifteen minutes later to pick up Misty, Marc, and a bag fished from the Dumpster. He'd already called Val and Eric, and the pack met at A1 Army Surplus before it closed.

Everyone at school knew the pack for their tanker boots. Showing up in sneakers Monday might seem suspicious. Searching for boots with a different tread pattern than her other pair, Val turned to Daniel "So this stuff about cops matching shoe prints to specific shoes. Do you know if they can do that or is it just something you saw on *CSI*?"

"You know what? I'd rather not find out," he answered.

Leaving the store, they drove to the furnace and tossed the evidence down the black mouth of an underground coal silo. Before Eric dumped his brother's boots, he wrapped them inside two plastic grocery bags. Daniel said they could retrieve them in a few months. Humbled since Daniel had rescued him, Eric accepted the compromise.

As night fell, they kept meaning to get something to eat but lingered at the furnace instead, talking amid the rising cricket songs.

"You should have seen it, man," Marc told Daniel about scaring the cop again. "He screamed like a bitch. Just screamed and bolted."

Misty watched her friends, her boyfriend, and her brother. Her pack of misfits. She remembered Val assuring her that wolves weren't evil, just strong. Misty had convinced Daniel of the same thing. But hiding under wolf skin made it so easy to do evil things.

"I guess it's about time to go home," Val said.

"Hell. Let's go hit the town again," Marc suggested.

They dithered and drifted toward prowling a second night in a row. Misty kept quiet. Even seeing how dangerous the rot-eater god could be, she still felt reluctant to venture back into the hand-lickers' world. She looked at one of the rust-skinned blast stoves. In the dark, Misty could just see the wolf head painted on its side. The sign surrounded them, marking the borders of their territory. Misty realized it was better at keeping them penned in than keeping imaginary enemies out.

Eric pulled his cell phone out. "Let me call Mom and tell her we're going to a movie or something."

Finally, Misty stammered, "Actually, I'm still pretty worn out. I'm just going to go home."

"C'mon," Daniel said. "We'll just roam for a couple hours. You can sleep when you're dead."

Misty gave him a halted laugh. "Actually, I've been thinking about not prowling all the time anymore."

None of the others said anything.

"I mean, I'm probably going to ask Ilie for some more hours. Start saving some money for when we go to Europe." She looked up at Daniel, hoping for support.

"Well, you can come with us tonight, at least," Eric said.

"No. I'm worn out. You guys go, though. You don't need me."

But they were a pack. The others started mumbling, no, maybe they should just get some rest. Misty started feeling bad. She insisted they should prowl if they wanted to. After a minute, Daniel took her hand and led her around one of the massive ladle cars.

"What's the matter?" he asked once they were alone. "Last night scare you?"

"Well?" Misty shrugged. "I mean, we almost burned down the fucking school."

"Misty, we did that for you. We did it because of what Mrs. MacKaye—"

"I know. I know." She folded her arms across her chest.

"But first we just ran around. Then we ran around and spray-painted buildings. Now, we're running around, spray-painting buildings, then setting them on fire? What's next, you know? And there's lots of things I want to do besides be a wolf. I mean, things we want to do, right?"

Daniel kissed her forehead and pulled her close. He started rocking her side to side. Her thoughts had been a briar patch all day. It felt nice to be held. "So what do you think?" she asked.

He nodded toward the others, goofing around like pups. "I think the pack needs you a lot more than you need them."

That made Misty smile. Then Daniel whispered, "I need you more than anybody, though."

"Yeah, right," Misty said, despite the hot rush of blood the words brought.

"Last night got out of hand."

"It's not just—"

"I know. But it did. I don't want to do anything like that again. Just prowling, though, just roaming the city, why should we give that up until we have to? You're right, we've got to grow up sometime. But we can at least wait until graduation, can't we?"

The way Daniel explained it made Misty think she'd blown everything out of proportion. It made her wonder why she couldn't enjoy being a wolf for a little while longer before moving on. "Yeah." She nodded. "Just no more fires, okay?"

"God, no. I've been coughing all day. When I took a shower, I swear, the water turned gray."

The lights of Birmingham swirled in Daniel's eyes like pinprick galaxies. Laughing, Misty could just glimpse herself there, reflected against the depthless green.

They decided to prowl. Gathering *Amanita muscaria* behind the casting shed, Daniel thought about what Misty had said. Their attack on the school had frightened her, how vicious it had turned, and how quickly. It frightened Daniel, too. He'd wanted to get the kind of revenge he never could in human skin, but if Eric had been arrested, he might have dragged them all down with him. Daniel could never have gone to Cornell then.

He was glad Misty wanted to move on, ready to be more than a wolf on the fringes of civilization. After graduation, she would travel to distant places and fight fires instead of start them. Daniel would head off to the bluestone towers of Cornell. The others would find their own places in the world.

No more arson, but Daniel couldn't bear to give up racing through the city, drinking in the night, until he absolutely had to. He, none of them, would ever be this free again.

He felt bad for promising Misty, once again, that he was going to Europe with her. But then, Marc turned up the music. They started to dance and scream, and once again, the rot-eater god's ritual washed away all memory and guilt.

CHAPTER 16

"I want to make this clear. This is your school. When somebody trashes it, they're trashing you."

First thing Monday morning, homeroom teachers herded their students to an assembly. Mrs. Wainwright, the principal, spoke from the podium. Two glowering police officers stood to her left. Mr. Fine and some guy in a brown suit stood to her right.

"Hey, guess who's in ISS. Claire Rollins." Misty should have been sitting with the ISS students. As traffic bottlenecked at the auditorium doors, though, she'd let herself get lost in the muddle and sat next to Daniel.

"What did she do?" Enjoying this unsanctioned time together, Daniel cuddled with her the best he could with the metal armrest between them.

"I don't know. I'm going to try to find out."

"We know some of the people in this auditorium were involved. We don't suspect; we know," Mrs. Wainwright continued. "And I promise you, everybody involved will be arrested soon."

Val sat on Misty's other side. "I bet Claire missed a spot when she was polishing Mrs. Turner's shoes."

Misty laughed into her fist. "Or forgot to change the batteries in her vibrator."

"Ew. You're sick."

"You know what it was? I bet—"

Mr. Nguyen appeared behind them. "You need to listen to this. All of you." He pulled Daniel's arm off Misty's shoulders, then vanished again. The pack straightened up a little in their seats.

"This is a zero-tolerance situation. If you were involved, we're going to find out. If you helped, we're going to find out. If you think you might have something to tell us, there's a very narrow window of opportunity for you to come to me or Mr. Fine and clear the air."

"Wish they'd left me in ISS," Misty whispered, eyes fixed forward. "'Least they don't lecture you there."

Daniel laughed. His fingers searched for Misty's again.

The guardians of human order huddled on the cavernous stage, insisting again and again they were in control. Between dramatic pauses, the clamor of staff searching lockers trickled in from the halls.

Daniel had spent the weekend worrying. Had they disabled every camera? Had they left any evidence? Once he heard Mrs. Wainwright's threats, though, Daniel relaxed, knowing he and the pack were safe. Predators stalked silently. Only prey made loud noises to try to scare predators off. The rush of getting away with it was almost as good as the demolition itself.

Misty returned to ISS after the assembly. She wasn't particularly surprised when, fifteen minutes later, an aide came and took her to see Mr. Fine.

The main office was full of workers ripping out the drywall and carpeting. In the meantime, the administrators had taken over the AV lab at the end of the west hall. On the way, Misty passed more maintenance people carrying toolboxes and spools of wire. Cardboard covered more windows than she remembered breaking.

In the AV lab, students, teachers, and a couple of cops tried to not knock over the outdated recording equipment. Three printers hummed at once, replacing the files the pack had burned from computer backups.

The secretary sent Misty into a tiny studio where the school used to put on closed-circuit news broadcasts. There hadn't been money in the budget for that in years, but the anchors' desk still stood beneath a McCammon falcon mural. Mr. Fine sat on the corner of the desk with a short stack of fresh student files, Misty's lying on top. A stocky policewoman stood nearby.

"So last Thursday, you got angry because Mrs. MacKaye called you what again?" Mr. Fine asked.

Misty fidgeted in the plastic chair. "I don't remember."

"Come on, Misty. What was it?"

"A stray," she whispered.

"That's right. Then somebody spray-paints dogs all over the school, particularly all over Mrs. MacKaye's classroom. That's a pretty big coincidence, isn't it?"

"So you're blaming me?"

"Well, who should we blame? If you want to get out of hot water yourself, this is the time to do it."

"I don't know who did it." Misty sat with her arms crossed. Mr. Fine told her to stop staring at the floor and look at him. The cop let him badger Misty for a while before speaking up.

"So why do you think this happened?"

"I don't know who did it. I already said."

"Yeah, but whoever it was, why do you think they tore up the school like this?"

Misty shrugged. Seconds passed by. The cop and Mr. Fine watched her and waited. "Probably mad," she finally said.

"Yeah? What do you think they were mad about?"

Misty opened her mouth, then hesitated. She wanted to talk. Even if it was in the vaguest terms possible, she wanted them to understand. That's what they wanted too. They both suspected Misty had played a part in wrecking the school. Now, the policewoman was giving her a little space to tell them about it, hoping she'd slip up.

The urge to fill the air with words that didn't matter was miserably human. Forcing it down, Misty shrugged again.

"Come on, you can't imagine anybody being mad at this school for any reason? It's that wonderful a place to go to?"

Another shrug.

They tried to squeeze her beneath silence and hard glares. The room was so quiet, Misty could hear her heartbeat. She summoned the wolf's patience, her calm resolve, and kept her mouth shut.

The policewoman opened a metal briefcase. "Let me see your right boot."

"Don't you need a warrant or something?"

"Yes," Mr. Fine said. "I'll also need to call your mom and have her leave work and come down. Do you want me to do that, or do you want to cooperate?"

Misty took off her boot and handed it to the officer. She'd known they'd check their shoe prints; she wished she'd remembered to wear socks without holes. As the policewoman rolled ink across the sole of Misty's shoe and pressed it down to a piece of paper, she asked, "So what's a cute thing like you need such ugly boots for, anyway?"

"I'm not cute on the inside."

The woman laughed. She handed Misty her boot and an alcohol wipe to clean off the sole. After she'd left to compare Misty's shoe print to ones they'd found on the roof and kicked-in doors, Mr. Fine assured Misty this was her last chance. Misty hardly glanced at him.

Even after the officer returned shaking her head, the vice-principal wouldn't give up. "We're going to talk to your friends next. Maybe you don't want to save your neck, but I bet one of them does. If they tell me how, say, you started the fire and they didn't know it would go that far. Well, you're not telling me your side of the story, are you?"

But Misty didn't have any friends. She had a pack. "Talk to whoever you want."

Mr. Fine shuffled through the files on the table, pulling a few out. "Let's see. Eric Polidari. We'll talk to him. Daniel Morning. If Daniel gets arrested for this, he can kiss Cornell good-bye. You sure he'll throw away his entire future over this?"

Misty sneered. "Cornell? That's just some stupid rumor."

Mr. Fine stared at her. He gave a small, snorting laugh. "Is that what he says?"

Even if Misty had wanted to speak, her mouth had suddenly become too dry. Still, she managed a tiny nod and had a tiny bit of faith that the vice-principal was trying to trick her somehow.

Mr. Fine opened Daniel's file and thumbed through the papers. "Let's see. His file was one of the ones destroyed. But the recommendation letter I wrote to Cornell was still on my computer at home." He laid a long letter on the desk. "And the central office had copies of the transcript requests he filled out." He showed Misty two photocopied forms. "That's Daniel's handwriting, right?"

The same looping strokes listing the receiving school as Cornell University filled the sweet notes she'd saved in her jewelry box.

"No, he isn't leaving. It's all bullshit. It's all—" Misty tried explaining, but rising sobs choked her every time she opened her mouth. She shoved the papers away, but Mr. Fine pushed them back under her nose.

"Look at the date, Misty. He signed this last transfer request a month ago. Look at the date. He didn't even tell you he's leaving in the fall. You really think he's going to risk everything to protect you?"

Mr. Fine pelted her with threats until Misty screamed, "Shut up! I wish you'd all just die! I wish you'd—I—" She wished the wolf could emerge, could lunge across the fake-wood desk and silence him. Misty stayed trapped in her pathetic human shape, twig-thin arms hugging her belly.

Finally, the policewoman touched Misty's shoulder and told Mr. Fine that was enough.

When the aide slipped into Daniel's trig class and handed Mrs. Schiff a note, Daniel knew it was for him. The administrators had gathered a whole herd of black sheep in the AV room, desperate to find their hidden enemy. Daniel leaned against a rack of old VCR tapes beside Val. Three skaters shared a private joke in one corner until the secretary snapped at them to be quiet.

"Misty's with Mr. Fine now," Val said, nodding toward a door with a cracked ON AIR sign above it.

A minute later, the door opened, and Misty stepped out with a cop. She wiped her nose with the back of her hand

and was shaking. Shouldering one of the skaters aside, Daniel went to her. After all this, the hand-lickers had hurt her again. He swore they'd pay. They hadn't seen what the pack could do yet.

"Are you going to Cornell?"

Daniel stiffened, her hand in his. It felt like being jolted awake, that panicked second before remembering where he was, who he was.

Mr. Fine told Misty not to say another word. Squeezing Daniel's fingers, she said, "You aren't. Just say you aren't."

"I'm . . ." He was a wolf. He was the shooting star. He was a natural charmer hiding a snarling animal hiding a miserable coward. And he was the one, not the hand-lickers, who'd brought Misty to tears. "I'm so sorry."

Her mouth opened, but no words came out. Taking her arm, Mr. Fine whisked Misty out of the room. Troublemakers, student aides, and cops watched the scene.

"Son of a bitch," Val said. "She had me convinced."

Daniel pretended he hadn't heard her. Mr. Fine reappeared a few seconds later. He crooked his finger at Daniel, ignoring the students who'd been called in before him, and led him into the studio. Without commenting on what had just happened, Mr. Fine asked the policewoman to take Daniel's boot print. As soon she'd left, the vice-principal smiled.

"You switched boots, didn't you? Pretty clever. That must have been your idea."

Now that it was all over, Daniel felt nothing but a bone-deep exhaustion. He busied himself pulling his boot back on. "I don't know anything about who broke into the school."

"Well, I do. It was you. It was Misty and all your new pals. Now, want to know why they vandalized the school?"

"None of them—"

"Why not?" He spread his hands. "They don't have any futures to waste, so they might as well get stoned and knock things over and knock one another up. Hell, that's what makes running with them so fun, right?"

Daniel arched his eyebrows. "And yet somehow their lives aren't transformed by your inspirational teaching methods."

"Come on, Daniel." Mr. Fine rubbed his face. "Nobody hates it more than me. I—every teacher here—does what we can. But I've been at this longer than you've been alive, and I know a lost cause when I see one. You're not one of them, though. You can leave this mess behind and still go on to great things. I'm trying to help you, Daniel, but now you need to tell me the truth."

"The truth." He spoke the word, listening to it roll down his tongue and wondering how much of the truth Mr. Fine would ever believe. He wondered if he even knew the truth anymore. "The truth is that something found your lost causes. You, every teacher here, everybody wrote them off. But something big and ugly found them."

Mr. Fine sighed. "And what's that mean?"

"They found paw prints on the roof, didn't they? Inside the

ceiling?" Daniel shrugged. "What's that mean? What about those phantom animals the firefighters saw in the school? Appearing, attacking, then vanishing again? What the hell does that mean?"

Daniel hadn't known if the cops and firefighters had told the administration about any of that until he watched Mr. Fine's eyes widen. His Adam's apple bobbed with a hard swallow.

"So you were involved. You're admitting that?"

"I'm trying to help you, Mr. Fine. Don't push this too far. Talk to anybody you want, take shoe prints if you have to, but after that, drop this. Pray you never find out the truth."

"Daniel, son, don't threaten me."

"I'm not. Like you said, I'm not one of them. Problem is, I'm not what you think I am either. What I was before."

"Then what are you?"

Daniel thought carefully, but finally shook his head. "I wish to God I knew."

The policewoman walked back in, but Daniel decided he was done talking. Getting up, he walked past her and out of the studio. Neither Mr. Fine nor the cop moved to stop him.

Keith had hoped they'd cancel school for a couple days, but actually, that upside-down Monday was better than sleeping in.

Everything and everybody was off-kilter. Because of smoke damage and broken glass, most of the front hall had been blocked off behind hanging plastic sheets. Without enough rooms, teachers held class outside, in the library, anywhere they could find space. Every window was propped open to get rid of the lingering smell of smoke. Cool spring air blew through the corridors.

In Keith's first three classes, Mrs. Ellison continued scolding her students where the principal had left off; Mrs. Crow showed a movie; and Mr. Healy popped his head through the door ten minutes after the bell, apologized, said he'd be right back, then never returned.

By lunch, working through the lunatic day had turned the whole student body a little giddy. All order felt temporarily suspended. Keith and his friends bounced through the breezy halls, as if even the school's gravity had weakened. When Scotty suggested going to the Hardee's up the street for lunch, Keith didn't think about what would happen if they were caught. He just realized what a sunny day it was outside.

At the restaurant, they compared rumors. So far, Keith knew of six people who'd been overheard in the bathroom admitting to the arson. One teacher's grade book had burned and she was giving all her students A's. If the school couldn't send your transcripts, no colleges would let you matriculate. Somebody had died in the fire, but the administration was keeping it quiet. Another teacher's grade book had burned and her students' grades for the whole period would come from the final. If the school couldn't send your transcript, you got to make up anything you wanted. Everybody was worried about prom.

Keith finished his cheeseburger and bought ice-cream cones for Angie and himself. Heading back to school, they fell a couple steps behind the others. Keith let his hand slip down to rest on the curve of Angie's butt, savoring the muscle and motion beneath a thin layer of denim. Angie held his gaze from the corner of her eye, tasted her ice cream, then said, "I was thinking. We should throw a massive graduation party."

"Cool." He nodded. "We'd need to do it at your house, though."

"Screw my house. I hate my house. It's too small. We need to rent a space. Get a real DJ and everything."

"Please tell me you're a pimp and not a ho."

"I don't know where we'll get the money yet, but think about it." She started skipping backward in front of him. "You throw the most massive, huge, big-as-God party right at the end of senior year and it's like every other party gets wiped off the map. Like, ten years from now, whenever anyone thinks about high school, all they'll remember is your party."

Keith grinned at that thought.

"Now, here's the genius part," Angie went on. "We don't throw it on graduation night. Everybody's going to have a party that night, so nobody'd come to ours. We throw it right before finals week. Everybody will be stressed, ready to bug out, and—"

"Hey, Keith." Up ahead, Bwana had stopped and turned. "What's up with your cousin?"

They were across the street from the school. Keith saw Daniel in the paved courtyard beside the cafeteria that always reeked of congealed fat. He paced in tight circles and kept gesturing and pointing, trying to explain something to somebody who wasn't there.

"Aww . . . he's sad because his little skeezeball got ISS again." Angie giggled.

Even if Misty had ISS, Keith wondered why Daniel wasn't with the rest of the ghouls he hung out with. Suddenly, Daniel kicked the fence surrounding the school Dumpsters. He looked ready to collapse to the asphalt.

Scotty clapped a hand over his mouth to keep from laughing out loud. "Guy's finally snapped."

Keith shook his head. "I don't even want to guess what that's all about. C'mon."

Angie told him more about the party. Keith had spent all of high school in Daniel's shadow. Last January, he'd finally made a grab for the brass ring. A little courage was all it took. Angie had fallen in love with him. Bwana and the others started treating him as one of the group. And today, Keith let his imagination soar even higher. Like Angie said, if the party was big enough and wild enough, it would obliterate four years of being Daniel Morning's tag-along cousin. People would finally see who Keith was; they'd remember him for the rest of their lives.

This weird day, it seemed possible. Almost anything did.

• • •

For once, Misty was glad to be in ISS. Even though there were a dozen other people in the room listening to her sniffling, Misty couldn't see any of them behind the high dividers of her carrel, none of them spoke, and she could pretend she was alone.

Misty sneered. She had a talent for deluding herself like that.

Clenching her jaw to make it stop quivering, Misty hunched over the busywork her teachers had assigned her. Even when her vision blurred with new tears, she kept writing. When the final bell rang, Misty gathered her things and handed the sheaf of papers to the ISS monitor. She'd answered every question with the same response: *I am a wolf. I am a wolf. I am a wolf.*

Outside, wisps of gossip filled the campus. A small audience gathered around a trio of boys crooning an R & B song, snapping their hips to the beat. Head down, Misty walked through the babble until a call stopped her cold.

"Misty, wait! Misty!"

Daniel took the front steps two at a time. He came within whispering distance but didn't touch her. He wouldn't look her in the eyes. "I didn't rat you out," he said. "You don't have to worry. You—the pack's safe."

Misty tried to say something but couldn't. Squeezing her arms across her chest, she started toward her car.

Daniel followed her. "Misty, I'm sorry. Will you just listen? I'm sorry. I didn't want you to find out like this."

"I told you everything! I—Jesus, I brought you into the pack."

"I know, I know. I should have come clean long ago. I was afraid you wouldn't trust me."

Misty whipped around, eyes narrowed for the slaughter. Daniel sputtered, "No. That's not what I meant."

"That's exactly what you meant. You might not have gotten your little pecker sucked if I knew. That's exactly what you meant."

"No. It's not. Please—"

The rest of the pack rushed up, scattering the passing handlickers. Marc shoved Daniel against the wall of the school, pushing his face close. "Missed you at lunch today."

"What did you tell Mr. Fine?" Val demanded.

"Nothing."

"Bullshit," Marc spat. "Everything you've said has been bullshit."

"No, it hasn't. It's just—"

"He didn't give us up." Glancing at the crowd, Misty hissed between her teeth. "You're going to give us up acting psycho in front of school. Get out of here."

They backed off. Marc and Eric headed toward the parking lot. Val tugged on Misty's hand to follow. For months, Misty had refused to ask Daniel, or herself, certain questions. When Val tried asking them for her, Misty had blown up. Now, she hugged her best friend, whispering, "Wait for me. I'll explain everything, okay?"

As soon as Val left, Daniel looked at Misty and sucked in

a ragged breath. "I'm so sorry. I should have told you. I should have told you a hundred different times. But I was worried you'd just see that one thing about me, that I'm going to some stupid college, and decide that's all I was. I was scared, okay? I was scared because you were the most amazing person I'd ever met. Before this wolf shit, this pack shit, you were amazing."

"Quit! Just quit. I was a gutterfuck."

"No. Misty, you weren't."

"Yes, I was!" More humiliating than any of it was that part of her still loved him. Part of her was still desperate to believe the brightest, most beautiful boy in school could really love her. Misty wanted that part dead. "Tell me the truth just once, Daniel. Tell me I was a gutterfuck. I was a stupid, gullible slut you could hump and dump once you went on to better things."

Daniel stood shaking his head, saying, "No, no." Little gaggles of hand-lickers watched them.

Taking a step closer to Daniel, Misty dropped her voice again. "Go to Cornell. Go back to your jock friends. Go back to Angie, for all I care. But keep your mouth shut. Stay out of our business, and we'll stay out of yours."

"Misty, please—"

Turning before he could lie to her again, Misty rushed up the sidewalk toward the safety of the pack.

CHAPTER 17

Daniel hadn't shown up at lunch, either too scared to face them, or maybe, after his secret was out, he just didn't care enough to explain. The pack had panicked, though, certain he'd spilled everything to Mr. Fine. Even after Misty told them the police weren't about to swoop in, they still felt betrayed.

"I told you he wasn't like us." Eric's face was dusky red. Tendons bulged from his neck. "But the pouty basketball star winks, and you get all stupid. 'Oh, of course we can trust him, look how pretty his hair is.'"

"Screw you!" Misty snapped back. "I wasn't the only one who got stupid over him, was I? 'Gee, Daniel, thanks for saving my butt in the school. Let's have a big, manly hug now.'" Turning, she hit Marc. "And quit nodding along with him. You're wearing the same damn body spray as Daniel, dumbass."

Marc rubbed his arm without answering. Eric punched the roof of Val's car, but he didn't say anything else.

Misty could almost smell the boys' admiration curdle.

Daniel was quick-thinking and confident. Everything seemed effortless for him. They'd all let themselves pretend they could be a little like him.

Daniel had never been part of the pack, though, just slumming. Once the game lost its thrill, he'd intended to leave them and their grimy city behind.

Misty had never felt more trapped by her crappy job than she did that day. Her world might be collapsing, but people still needed their panini Italianos and smoked turkey breast on ryes. All afternoon Misty punched the wrong buttons on the cash register and gave the wrong change.

One woman became personally offended when Misty didn't take the cheese off her vegetarian pizza. She hovered around the counter after Misty ordered up a new one. She'd told Misty she didn't want any cheese. She was lactose intolerant and couldn't eat cheese. She'd told Misty that.

Misty cracked. "Okay! I'm sorry, but I'm not trying to poison you."

Ilie took her off the register, sticking her in the back doing prep work. But she started thinking again while slicing up tomatoes, dropping them in a dirty bucket with half an inch of jalapeno pepper juice still in the bottom. Ilie, who usually bore her goofing off with Eastern Bloc stoicism, noticed the eye-watering smell, and it was his turn to crack.

"Throw this out, start over, do one thing right!" He stormed off, shouting, "I hope your mother dies on your birthday!"

Misty threw the bucket against the wall. Pulp splattered everywhere. Val and another deli drone froze, staring at Misty with wide eyes. Watching tomato slices ooze down the cinder blocks, Misty considered kicking in Ilie's office door, cussing him out, and quitting. Instead, she leaned against the prep table, burying her face in her arms. Without a word, Val got a towel and started washing off the wall.

Somehow, Misty stumbled through two more hours of slicing, stocking, and cleaning without collapsing into a sobbing heap. By eight, there was only one couple in the deli. Older, they were new to each other. She listened to them laugh. When the man finished his potato chips, the woman shared hers. Misty wanted to hit them. Instead, she finished scraping the brown gunk off the soda fountains, then went to poke her head in Ilie's office.

"Need anything else?"

Ilie was making changes to the week's schedule. Iron Maiden played on the little stereo on his desk. Shaking his head, he said, "Remember to clock out."

"All right." She lingered in the doorway. "Hey. Sorry about everything tonight."

"You got problems outside? So does everybody, okay? But in here, I pay you to work, okay?"

"Okay. Good night."

She turned to leave, but Ilie called her back. "Misty?"

"Yeah?"

"You're very pretty today."

"Huh?"

"You never come in without the dead girl eyes anymore. You're very pretty today."

Misty washed her eyeliner before coming to work, afraid she'd start crying again. Ilie told her she was pretty in the same hurried tone he told her to mop the floor. Still, it made her smile for the first time that night.

"Thanks. You're looking good yourself."

He let out the soft grunt that meant he couldn't tell if she was making fun of him or not. "Don't worry about Softhead. You'll find a new boy, no problem. And that thing about hoping your mother dies, I didn't mean." He shrugged. "It sounds funnier in Russian."

"Forget it. Good night, Ilie."

"Good night."

Val was already outside waiting on the sidewalk. Misty raced up to her. "Ilie just gave me a compliment."

"What?"

"He goes, 'You're very pretty today.'" Misty mimicked Ilie's gruff accent. "Then he apologized for wishing Mom would die."

"The nicest thing he's ever said to me is, 'At least you don't steal.'"

"How pathetic am I that Ilie feels sorry for me?"

Val hugged her. Misty rested her chin on Val's shoulder. "Did I really throw a bucket of tomatoes?"

"Just a small one."

Misty laughed, then Val said, "Hey. Let's go prowl."

"No." Misty pulled away. "The guys are ready to maul Daniel."

"Well, maybe not maul him. But we could make sure he knows you're not just sitting around feeling sorry for yourself."

Misty grinned but shook her head. "Come on, Val. We have to be at school in twelve hours."

"You're going to be in ISS. You need a full night's rest for that?"

"Or a shower?"

"So you'll stink. After everything else, you really care?"

Misty had wanted to quit prowling altogether. But if she went home, she'd lay awake all night in the empty apartment. Through the dark hours, the way Daniel smiled, the way he touched her and spoke her name would crush Misty. The wolf, though, would shake those fragments of dreams off like droplets of water. Misty couldn't escape who she really was.

"Screw it," she said. "Call Eric and see if he's up for it."

I was a gutterfuck.

Daniel stared at a blank page in his notebook. He'd tried to explain at school, but Misty had been too furious to listen. As soon as he'd gotten home, Daniel locked himself in his room to write her a letter. He couldn't let Misty think she'd been nothing but a piece of tail.

UNLEASHED

He started a line, scratched through it, started over, tore the page out, and started over again. The sun sank through an orange-and-purple sky. Fischer called him to dinner from the foot of the stairs. Daniel ignored him. Darkness fell before he got past the second sentence. He stared at the debate medal hanging on the wall above his desk, remembered it was for persuasive speaking, and sneered at himself.

Daniel paced the room. He started talking to an imaginary Misty. He tried opening with apologies, then with compliments. He told her she was beautiful, so full of heat and life, he'd felt more alive being near her. He could never forget her, but this was his one chance to become someone great. He had to take it.

Misty never said anything except, *I was a gutterfuck*. That silent answer smashed every pretty, spun-glass phrase Daniel came up with. Yanking the debate medal off the wall, he whipped it across the room.

Finally, hours after his parents and brothers had gone to bed, Daniel had nothing left except the sickening realization that Misty had been right.

She was full of heat and life, and Daniel had fed off her like a tick. He'd loved watching her build castles in the air but had no plans to stick around once they came crashing down. He would be taking his place among the real towers of Cornell by then. Misty had opened herself to him, revealing wonders and gentle enchantments, but Daniel had been too cowardly and obsessed with his own hungers to appreciate them.

"You weren't anything but a gutterfuck to me," he whispered. It was the most vile sin Daniel had ever confessed.

He unbuckled his boots. Leather straps and black rubber stripped away, his feet seemed fragile. Daniel studied them for a long time, then finished getting ready for bed. He was reaching for the light switch when howls pierced the quiet.

Daniel had never invited Misty to his house, but she knew he lived below Vulcan Park. Standing in his underwear, Daniel pushed back the window blind. Nothing moved on the street outside.

The unseen wolves let their pitches rise, then drop sharply. It was an instinctual trick, making it sound like Daniel was surrounded by dozens of hunters instead of four.

He forced himself to stay calm. If the pack had come to hurt him, they would have kept as silent as shadows. They only wanted to rattle him, have a little fun. Still, Daniel crept barefoot through the dark house, into bedrooms, and past his sleeping parents and brothers. He made sure every window was latched and both doors were bolted.

For close to an hour, he sat listening to Misty's mournful baying in chorus with the others. They wanted him to know, *We are still here. Our pack is still strong. You've made your choice. You don't belong on our streets anymore.*

CHAPTER 18

The days grew hotter. At school, smooth skin—arms, calves, and bare toes—appeared along with the buttercups. Before first bell, the pack hunched around their picnic table, watching over one another's shoulders.

One morning, Marc grumbled, "Let's just go."

"No," Misty said.

"I'm not putting up with this bullshit anymore. Let's just go."

Marc didn't want to skip class. He wanted to leave school for good. Misty imagined how free it would feel to just stand up and walk away, but she shook her head. "Mom wants you to graduate."

"So?"

"So she's put up with your whiny ass for eighteen years. So you're gonna put up with this for a few more weeks. So be quiet already."

Their mom had never finished high school, and she

dreamed of seeing Misty and Marc in caps and gowns. Misty once overheard her praying for them to graduate. It was a stupid thing to pray for, a piece of paper saying Misty had jumped through the hoops like a good little hand-licker. But their mom had broken her body for her and Marc. Misty could bear school a while longer.

Marc turned to Eric. "Let's just go."

Eric didn't bother looking at him. "It's less hassle just to go than it would be to drop out."

Suddenly, Val lifted her head. Eric and Marc turned too. The three wolves followed Daniel as he trudged past them up the sidewalk. Only Misty pretended not to notice him, studying the chipped edge of the cement picnic table.

Misty knew he was watching her from the corner of his eye. With her pack bristling around her, she risked a glance. Even ragged and worn thin, Daniel was still gorgeous. He'd shed his boots for white sneakers again, but he hadn't gone back to his letterman friends like Misty assumed he would. Instead, Daniel Morning, the prince of McCammon High, had spent the last two weeks scuttling along its walls like a rat.

He'd tried talking to her since their breakup. He kept leaving messages on her phone, but Misty erased them before giving in to the temptation of listening. She wasn't strong enough to hear Daniel's voice, to remember everything she couldn't have.

Misty couldn't stand hurting anymore. She let the pack tighten around her and keep Daniel away. She let hate cover her too-tender heart the way the wolf's tough hide enveloped her weak human shape.

The pack relaxed as Daniel slipped out of sight again among the crowd. "Little bitch," Eric muttered. "Little over-the-mountain-wannabe."

Misty gave a sneering laugh and rested her chin on her arms.

Workers pieced the school back together. Glass reappeared in windows, and classrooms reopened with fresh coats of paint. The police left without making any arrests. But most of the teachers still seemed to at least suspect it had been Daniel and the pack who'd broken into the school.

The day Misty got out of ISS, Daniel had gone up to her in Mrs. MacKaye's class and tried telling her about the things he'd been thinking about.

"Misty—"

"Leave me alone." Misty scribbled across the cover of her notebook, creating a dense black spiral.

"I'm sorry, okay?"

"I don't care what you are. Leave me alone."

"Daniel," Mrs. MacKaye snapped, pointing to a seat across the room. "Go sit behind Devynn."

"Class hasn't even started yet."

Walking up to them, the teacher hissed, "Give me a reason to get you two out of my class."

Afraid of landing Misty back in ISS and making things even worse, Daniel moved behind Devynn. Since then, he spent his days staying as unnoticeable as possible.

Sometimes Misty would glance at him across the classroom or before school. Daniel knew how deeply he'd hurt her. Every time he tried to apologize, though, she hunkered behind the pack and that damn pride he'd once loved.

He avoided the cafeteria and usually went to the library during lunch. Sneaking bites of a granola bar one day, Daniel overheard a couple girls talking about Keith throwing a party. Stealing his cousin's girlfriend had been good for Keith's self-esteem. Whenever Daniel saw him now, his hand rested on the small of Angie's back. He stood taller, and his laugh even seemed louder. Daniel remembered when he used to feel like that.

At home, he spent most of his time studying. Besides ditching his extracurriculars, Daniel had let his grades fall so badly, he might fail if he crapped out on his finals. It seemed surreal that, at the beginning of the semester, he'd been within grasping distance of valedictorian.

One day he came down to forage for food just as his mom walked in from the front porch with two iced-tea glasses.

"Your aunt Leslie was just here," she said. "You going to this party of Keith's?"

"Huh? No."

"Leslie and Josh were going to buy him a new car for

graduation. Now, he wants the money for some huge party instead."

Daniel ripped open a package of string cheese. "I don't know anything about it."

"Well, listen. We need to get up to Boaz soon while winter clothes are still on sale."

"I already have a coat."

"No, you have a jacket. You're heading up to New York, Daniel. People die from the cold up there."

"They do not."

"Do you know what hypothermia is? Frostbite?"

"It's not the Arctic, Mom."

She sighed, sick of arguing with him all the time. "Fine. When your fingers fall off and you need somebody to unzip your fly for you, you tell them I warned you."

She turned, started walking away, and then Daniel mumbled, "Misty found out I'm going to Cornell."

"What?"

He said it again. He felt pitiful confiding in his mom, especially after the way he'd been acting, but he didn't have anybody else to talk to.

"You just got around to telling her you were leaving?"

"Yes." He rolled his eyes. "Actually, no. She kind of found out by accide—"

Tea splashed his face. Jumping backward, Daniel yelped, "Mom!"

"What is wrong with you? Having fun with girls you don't plan on marrying is one thing. Outright lying to them is another. I didn't raise you like that."

"I know." Fishing an ice cube out of his shirt, he tossed it in the sink. "I didn't exactly mean not to tell her, it just—"

"It just what? Slipped your mind for four months? Daniel, that's enough time for a girl to get so wrapped around a boy, she doesn't know which way's up anymore. Then she learns you're leaving? How do you think she feels, Daniel?"

"She pretty much wants to kick my head in."

"I'd hold you down while she did."

"Okay! I screwed up, I get it. But what do I do now?"

"Honey, there's not much you can do." She started to pat his hair, then pulled back and wiped her damp hand on her jeans. "Misty feels played and angry and . . . Why didn't you just tell her when you started dating?"

"It's complicated. I didn't mean to get as involved as I did. I didn't mean to end up liking her as much as I did. As I do."

"And this is what all the sneaking around lately has been about? And why me and your dad weren't allowed to meet her?"

"Pretty much."

"Well, high school's over in a couple weeks. You'll go up to Ithaca, and it'll be a whole new beginning. Just remember how crappy you feel right now, and treat the next girl better."

Daniel nodded. He'd hoped for some other answer but was starting to see there wasn't one. He grabbed some more cheese and went up to his room, then stopped at the foot of the stairs. "Let's go to Boaz sometime this weekend."

"Sounds good," his mom said.

She couldn't get his smell out of her bed. Misty had snuck Daniel into the apartment enough times that the faintest essence of him lingered on her pillows and sheets. She used to love that. She drifted to sleep, feeling close to Daniel even while he was miles away. Then Misty learned that once he got home, the boy she dreamed of was just a suit Daniel pulled off and hung in the closet.

She'd washed her sheets twice, scrubbed the mattress with Formula 401, but his scent lingered. At least she imagined it did. Misty had started sleeping on the floor. Only soft humans needed soft beds, but it pissed her off, anyway. This was her room. Even after lying to her for months, even after she'd torn his grinning photo off the wall and thrown away every little gift he'd given her, Daniel didn't have the courtesy to leave.

Lying in the hushed dark, Misty twisted and kicked to form a warm nest in the pile of dirty clothes. She stared at the fairy wings hanging above the bed. Months ago, she'd pinned them up there by their shoulder straps. It was very sixth grade, and Misty woke up most mornings speckled with glitter, but she'd liked watching them turn slowly, silently overhead.

Misty rolled over but couldn't forget the wings were there. A tear snuck through her squeezed-shut eyelid. She didn't understand how Daniel could have been that cruel, to make her believe she could fly.

"Quit," Misty hissed at herself. She would not cry over some hand-licker boy. Climbing onto her bed, Misty yanked her wings down. One of the wires bent as she shoved them into the closet. Misty told herself she didn't care. Grabbing her cell phone, she called Val.

"Hey, baby," Val mumbled. "Can't sleep again?"

"Let's go shift in front of somebody. See what happens."

"Tonight?"

"Yeah." The thought alone made impish giggles rise like bubbles, effervescing Misty's black mood.

There were several seconds of quiet, only the gentle static of the open line. Finally, Val answered, "I'll call Eric."

In the darkened room, Misty found some jeans and pulled on her boots. Their leather was as battered as she felt, but a hell of a lot tougher. Buckling them, she crossed the short hall to rouse Marc.

Performing the ritual, Misty was the last to shift. While the pack raced around her legs, she beat her feet against the earth and screamed, "Want to be a wolf! A wolf!"

The bass throb, low enough to make reality shudder, filled her head. She let go of his name, his scent, and the way he laughed. Misty dropped to all fours, and nothing was left of her tangled emotions except a smoldering, voiceless anger spreading to all humans.

The hospital's parking deck glowed, harsh light against white concrete. Warm food smells drew the pack. Three medical students, their voices shaky and too-fast from caffeine, sat in a car cramming down an after-midnight dinner of cheeseburgers.

Eric slipped into human skin and out of the shadows. The white-coated students didn't notice him until he kicked one of their side mirrors off, sending it skidding across the deck. The woman in the passenger seat yelped. Calmly, Eric walked around to knock the driver's side mirror off too. Before he could, the man behind the wheel jumped out. Big and quick, he grabbed Eric's arm.

"Little shitheel, what the—"

Eric shifted, and suddenly the man was holding a wolf's paw. When Eric snapped at the air, the man cringed against the car. Even though the door stood open, he couldn't think enough to dash back inside.

The rest of the pack emerged. Boots thudded on the hood, then claws scratched against its metal. They growled at the two women inside, spit dripping to the windshield. The woman in the passenger seat screamed again, covering her head with her arms. The one in the back just stared.

Pushing it a little further, Misty slunk into the car. She ate the half-finished burger off one student's lap. The human started sobbing. Ignoring her, Misty dropped to the floor and ate some fries that had spilled around her feet.

Done with her meal, Misty let out an echoing yip, bounded out of the car, and the pack vanished back into the witching hour.

They shifted in front of a man dragging trash from a bar's alley door and some kids on a street corner, people nobody would believe, who wouldn't believe it themselves when daylight came. None of the hand-lickers attacked, and only a couple thought to run. Watching the pack remove their human masks, the hand-lickers' minds jammed. If the pack had actually been hunting, they would have brought down dozens.

The mushrooms began wearing off, and Misty remembered Daniel's name. The way he laughed. She found herself trapped in human skin by human thoughts, but the memories didn't cut as sharp as they had a few hours earlier.

They headed back to the furnace. Eric led the way with Val at his side, Misty and Marc a few steps behind. Eric glanced over his shoulder at Misty. "Those things were hunters once," he said. "They've traded spears for cities, turned soft. I never knew how soft. How unfit to rule."

Safe inside the furnace grounds again, the pack stretched across the cool grass to snatch a few hours of sleep before school. Misty had almost drifted off when Marc whispered, "Hey. Misty?"

"Hm?"

"I thought you didn't even want to prowl anymore. Now you're dragging us out of bed just to scare people."

Eric and Val lay curled together a short distance away.

Misty listened to their steady, sleeping breaths mingling. "Nobody made you come," she said.

Marc shrugged. "But I don't have anything else to do. You had a bunch of other plans, going to Paris and stuff."

"Well, plans change." Misty didn't want to talk about this.

"You don't need Daniel to go to Paris. You want to go, get on a plane and go."

"Shut up." Jerking off the ground, she cocked her fist back. "You don't know a damn thing about it."

"Fine. Sorry."

"Only talked about that stuff because he liked talking about it. What am I going to do in Paris? Go to a bunch of museums?" Misty sat staring into the darkness around them. Then, getting to her feet, she walked away from her brother.

She walked the railroad tracks to the blast furnace. Misty always felt small and timid at the base of the brick and coiling steel tower. She could almost feel the rot-eater god gazing down at her from above.

She started to climb, rising above the canopy of pine trees to the highest catwalk. Ducking into the mouth of the exhaust vent, Misty sat down where Daniel had first kissed her.

I've thought about, like, backpacking through Europe or something.

It had been a sad fantasy, pretending she liked being a stray. That she didn't even want a home; she wanted to go see the world.

Misty let out a weak snicker. It suddenly struck her that Daniel was headed to law school, not Italy. Chasing adventure through exotic lands had been just as much make-believe for him as it had been for her.

High school was almost over. Misty and Daniel had spent the twilight of childhood together, the last days they had left to play dress up and become anything they wanted. A shooting star could put on wolf skin. A stray could insist she was actually a fairy. And when that got boring, they'd act like fearless explorers instead. The only difference between her and Daniel was that Daniel never forgot it was just a game.

Her legs were asleep when Misty crawled out of the vent. She walked around to the other side of the catwalk. Under the lightening sky, she could barely see the outlines of her pack.

She depended on them, and, just as important, knew they depended on her. In the natural world, lone wolves didn't survive very long. Her pack was a wolf's protection and purpose. Even if it left a small hole inside her, all the silly daydreams she had to give up, Misty knew she belonged here.

CHAPTER 19

P rom came and went. Daniel spent the evening playing *RPM: Quarter Mile* with Fischer.

After church that Sunday, his family drove an hour north to the outlet stores in Boaz. Daniel got gloves, wool socks, and a coat so thick, he could hardly put his arms down. He balked at the poofy knit caps, though, telling his mom he'd rather lose an ear to frostbite than walk around in anything that stupid.

The joke made him remember the first night he'd met Charlie Say What. He'd been scared for Misty; she barely came up to the monster's chest. She talked about her mom, though, drawing a story out of Charlie about his own parents.

Daniel shook the memory out of his head. He'd chosen. He'd left all that behind.

His parents also bought him sheets and matching pillow-cases, a brushed-steel touch lamp, and a desktop CD player. Daniel didn't need any of that stuff; his old lamp and CD player worked fine. But his parents wanted him to have some new things when he got to Cornell.

At school, teachers treated Daniel like a thug. His old friends treated him like an outcast, and the outcasts treated him like a traitor. He went through most days without speaking a word to anybody.

With isolation came a slow clarity. Daniel had plenty of time to think about the fire, the double-edged gifts of *Amanita muscaria*, and how much control the wolf had seized by the end. Daniel had gone searching for answers about who he was and almost lost himself completely.

But even with that gut-tightening, hand-trembling realization, Daniel would sit in class, obsessively running his tongue over short cuspids and dull premolars. He didn't like seeing himself in the mirror. His reflection seemed repulsive, like he was covered in burns.

Four months of shifting skin had left Daniel a stranger to his own humanity. The rest of the pack had been at it before him, and if Daniel had neared the point of no return, they were forging even further.

In the mornings, the pack leaned against one another around their picnic table. Daniel rarely heard any of them speak. They just watched the hand-lickers with wary eyes.

Misty usually slept through government class. It meant she wasn't causing trouble, so Mrs. MacKaye was happy to ignore her. Her appearance became more and more savage. The second week before finals, she wore the same clothes three days in a row, steadily accumulating grass stains and splatters of mud. Not only did Misty spend most nights prowling, she must have started sleeping among the tall weeds at the furnace.

Thursday, Daniel waited outside the classroom for Misty. He needed to try talking to her again. He couldn't let her destroy herself over him. When Misty saw him, there was no more expression in her eyes than if somebody had left a chair sitting in the hallway. The hair on one side of her head was getting matted.

"Look, I—"

Misty stepped around him and kept walking, heading to the cafeteria. Daniel kept on her heels.

"Misty, please." It felt good to say her name again. "You're really starting to worry me, okay? You look like hell. When was the last time you slept in an actual bed?"

"You better go before the pack sees you."

"I don't care about them. And since when did you? What about Europe? About everything else you wanted to do besides prowl?"

"Changed my mind."

Fear hardened into anger. Daniel grabbed her arm. He had an urge to shake her. "Look, I'm a douche bag. I am. But I still know you've got a lot more to offer than spray-painting walls and eating fucking garbage."

"You don't know anything about me." She yanked free.

"You don't know what I've got to offer. You don't even know Marc's behind you."

Daniel hadn't been paying attention to the whirl of noise around them. Suddenly, he noticed the dull crack of thick rubber soles. He turned and almost bumped into Marc.

"Leave her alone."

"Relax. I'm just—" When Daniel touched Marc's chest, it set Marc off. Slapping his hand away, Marc grabbed him around the neck and chest, pinning one arm.

"You don't tell me what to do. You don't touch me." Marc's lips pulled back into a snarl. Daniel would have laughed if he'd thought Marc was mimicking a wolf. But walking upright, speaking human language, was the facade now. The tic revealed how thin it had become.

"Quit it, Marc," Misty said.

Daniel tried to twist away, but Marc held tight. Eric and Val edged in from either side. They wanted to hurt him. Daniel raised a foot to keep Eric back when Misty snapped, "Marc!"

Her brother let go. Daniel coughed and staggered a couple steps. People had started chanting, "Fight! Fight! Fight!" around him. Eric led Marc and Val through the crush of bodies. None of them glanced back at Daniel. Only Misty lingered.

"I won't stop them next time," she whispered before turning to follow her pack.

The idiots were still chanting, "Fight! Fight!" even though Daniel was alone in the circle. He had to vanish before a teacher came rushing up. Shoving through the crowd in the opposite direction as the pack, he ducked his head and pretended he didn't know what was going on. People laughed. "Got beat down, bitch." Daniel ignored them.

The hushed corridors of books made the library feel like a drowsy wood in the center of always-humming school. Since his exile from the pack, it had become his sanctuary.

Daniel set his bag on one of the tables but didn't sit down. He wandered, thinking about the evening after the fire. Misty had seen how serious their game had become. Daniel had convinced her to keep playing. He could have told her, could have told all of them, that they could be anything besides wolves ranging through a rusted-out steel town. Misty had loved and trusted him. The whole pack had. They would have listened.

His moment of greatness had come, not a diploma or money but true greatness, and Daniel had squandered it. All he had left were the bluestone towers of Cornell.

The past few weeks, he'd let go of everything he'd never had in the first place, returning to his destined path. Daniel didn't know if he wanted to follow it anymore, but he was, because it felt safe and familiar. Now, Daniel realized the penance for cowardice would be watching Misty letting go too. She traveled in the opposite direction as him but for the same reasons.

Masks from a decades-ago school play decorated the wall above the drama section. The sun had faded their painted lips and cheeks. Splits in the papier-mâché revealed yellowed newspapers beneath. Daniel skimmed the shelves. *The Merchant of Venice, The Merry Wives of Windsor, A Midsummer Night's Dream*. Reaching up, almost afraid to touch it, he slipped the slender volume from its place and sat down on the carpet.

Through the forest have I gone, but Athenian found I none, on whose eyes I might approve this flower's force in stirring love. Night and silence—Who is here? Weeds of Athens he doth wear: This is he, my master said, despised the Athenian maid; and here the maiden, sleeping sound, on dank and dirty ground. Pretty soul, she durst not lie near this lack-love, this kill-courtesy.

All the other characters kept silent, just words on the page. But Daniel heard Puck's galloping rhymes in Misty's voice and birdsong laughter.

On top of every other regret, Daniel wished he could have seen her kicking the dust off four-hundred-year-old lines, before gossip, lies, and hard lessons turned her snarling and suspicious. In his imagination, she bounded through the play's enchanted forest, completely fearless of the real world looming just beyond the footlights. No wonder she'd beaten all the boys for the part.

Churl, upon thy eyes I throw all the power this charm doth owe. When thou wak'st, let love forbid sleep his seat on thy eyelid.

CHAPTER 20

A week ago, Andre Swoopes, who'd never said two words to Keith before, had asked if he could DJ his party. That's when Keith realized the thing, what Angie had dubbed their Freak Out Before Finals, was growing even bigger than he had imagined.

Bigger and a lot more expensive. Keith had already burned through the cash his parents had given him and begun dipping into his savings account, years' worth of summer jobs and birthday gifts, to spend it on food and the loudest sound system he could rent. Like Angie had said, though, the party needed to be wild enough to make people forget every other party in the past four years, to make them remember Keith for the rest of their lives. That was worth more than money.

Tomorrow was the night, and Keith only had one more task left. Before, he'd show up at a party, see a cooler overflowing with beer, but never wonder how it got there. Keith wasn't half-stupid enough to ask his parents to buy alcohol for him. Luckily, Spence knew a guy named Charlie Say What, who could help them out. After school, he and Scotty drove with Keith to Center Gardens Apartments on Fifteenth Avenue.

"All right, whatever you do, don't stare. He's real sensitive," Spence whispered, knocking on the door.

"Sensitive about . . . oh . . ."

A gigantic man opened the door. He had nubs of pink scar tissue where his ears should have been. But Keith had clawed his way to the mountaintop. One more ogre wasn't going to keep him from the peak. Meeting the man's eyes, he nodded when Spence introduced him. They walked inside and started talking price and product.

"You have anything better than Natural Light?" Scotty asked. "Rednecks drink that stuff. We aren't going to a cockfight."

"What I got is what I got," Charlie rumbled. Keith suspected that, if they did want to go to a cockfight, he could help them out there, too.

They bought eight cases of Natural Light and some cheap cognac, enough to get the Orr cousins and half the girls who came swinging naked from the rafters. Scotty bought a little weed, too.

While loading it all into his car, Keith noticed Eric Polidari and his little buddy Marc step out of an apartment across the parking lot. Turning, he took two more cases from Spence. While Spence and Scotty went in for more, Keith wedged the beer into his backseat and covered it with a blanket.

In the corner of his eye, Eric and Marc seemed to be

walking straight toward him, but neither of them meant a damn to him. They were probably going to try to get invited to his party. Keith laughed to himself. Not a chance.

"Hey there, Keith," Marc said in a mocking voice. "We've been meaning to talk to you."

Needles scraped Keith's spine. He remembered that Angie had called Marc's sister a mutt last winter. Straightening up, he looked at them. They were both scrawny, but ready to fight. If anything, Marc looked angrier than he had the day it happened.

Keith's mind started racing. He, Spence, and Scotty could take Marc and Eric, no problem. Keith would still lose, though, if his friends learned what Angie had said or how he'd lied for her afterward. They wouldn't want to come to his party. They'd spread the word around school. Nobody would want to come.

"Call Misty a mutt now, fucker." Marc faked an open-handed slap to Keith's head. "Call her a mutt now."

Keith flinched, but didn't swing back. "Look. I—I don't have anything against you."

"Fuck you, you don't have anything against me!"

He didn't. Angie didn't either. She'd just been mad; she wasn't really a racist. But that split hair didn't matter to Marc.

It wouldn't matter to Spence or Scotty, either. Keith glanced over his shoulder at Charlie Say What's door. This could not happen. Not today. Keith was so close, and now these two little nothings were about to ruin him.

"What's up, Keith?" Spence and Scotty stepped out

carrying the last two cases of beer, trying to figure out what was happening. Eyeing them eyeing him, Marc shrugged. "So? Think I'm scared? Think I'm going to let you or Angie or anybody call my sis—"

Keith did what he had to, slamming Marc into the car before he could say another word. The kid barely weighed anything. The back of his head bounced against the metal, silencing him.

Eric punched Keith in the shoulder hard enough to send numb shocks into his chest. He was stronger than he looked. Cases of beer crashed to the sidewalk. Spence tackled Eric, heaved the geek up, and flung him down. While he and Scotty kicked Eric's wailing, fetal body, Keith dragged Marc to the asphalt. Marc grabbed his arm, scratched and kicked, but Keith had twenty pounds on him and a reason to fight. Pinning Marc with a knee in his back, he ground the side of his face against the curb.

It didn't matter who'd called who what. Marc had almost stolen everything from him. For that, Keith hated him. For that, he enjoyed the way Marc flailed, trying to scream. Leaning down so only Marc could hear, Keith hissed, "Fucking, filthy little mutt."

"Hey!" Charlie Say What emerged wielding a baseball bat.

"Let's go! Go!" Keith gave Marc one last kick, then he and his friends scrambled to the car. Charlie hit the roof with his bat, the jarring *crack* making all three of them scream. Keith peeled out, leaving Marc and Eric crumpled on the ground. Blood shone on asphalt in the bright May afternoon.

"Oh, shit. Are they moving?"

Spence squinted through the rear windshield. "Yeah."

They fell stone silent, listening for a police siren to come tearing through the quiet. Instead, people pumped gas at the Texaco across from the apartments. Kids skipped home with cartoon character backpacks. It was an ordinary day.

Somehow, Scotty had retrieved one of the dropped cases of beer before escaping Charlie. Pulling a can out, he popped it open and took a sip. "Fucker doesn't have any ears. How'd he hear us fighting?"

Keith and Spence cracked up. Reaching around, Spence took the beer. "Damn. What was that about, anyway?"

Keith shook his head. "Freaks just came up, started calling Angie a slut and stuff."

"Somebody starts talking about your girlfriend, man's gotta right to shut them up. Here, you've earned this." Spence handed him the beer.

Scotty grabbed another can. "They're the ones Daniel's been running with lately, aren't they?"

"Yeah, plus they're the ones who tried to burn down the school, even though the police can't prove it."

"Fucking vermin, man. Somebody needs to beat them harder than we did."

They toasted one another. The beer was warm and thin,

but tasted great. As his pulse returned to normal, an animal calm settled over Keith.

He'd clawed to the mountaintop. It was his destiny, where he'd always belonged, even when no one could see that except him. Tomorrow, he'd finally reach the peak. Nobody could stand in his way.

Val's phone rang. "I'm on break, Ilie," she said, flipping it open.

"Can I go on break too?" Misty asked.

Ilie shook his head. "Restock the display cooler before the rush."

Misty sighed but went into the walk-in cooler, loading a shopping buggy with armloads of premade salads and slices of pie. She didn't hate the deli as much as school. At least Ilie was more honest than her teachers. Misty worked, and he handed her a check every other Friday. He never expected any more respect than he could pay for.

As she pushed the buggy up to the front, Val crashed into her. "Eric and Marc got beat up."

"What? By who?"

"Keith Morning and some of his friends. Eric and Marc are at your apartment now."

Abandoning the buggy, she followed Val, still on her phone, around the counter.

Ilie yelled, "Where are you going? Hey!"

Neither of them looked back. Pushing open the door, they crossed the parking lot in a dead run. The deli was okay, but the pack was all either of them had.

Misty drove. She heard Eric's tiny voice snarl and spit over the phone as Val coaxed more details from him. He and Marc had been watching TV and spotted Keith, Scotty, and Spence across the way at Charlie Say What's place. They went over, got into a fight, and Charlie ran Keith and his friends off.

Marc was hurt bad. Charlie had helped Eric get him back home and made it clear he didn't want the cops involved.

Opening her apartment door, Misty heard a crash from inside. Eric stalked the living room, clutching his side. He'd kicked over an end table, sending a lamp and remote controls to the floor. A nasty cut curved above his cheekbone, but he seemed more humiliated than anything. Val tried to hug him, but he pushed her away.

"They don't know who they messed with, but they're going to learn." Snatching the small fan that stood in the corner, he threw it across the room. "They're going to learn."

"Quit wrecking my apartment!" Misty heard water running in the bathroom. She went to look, saying over her shoulder. "Just calm down, okay? Just—oh, Jesus."

Marc's face looked chewed. One whole side was black with drying blood. Blood poured from his mouth. It quivered from his lips in gluey tendrils. It dripped between his fingers and splattered white porcelain red. He tried wetting a wash-cloth, but his hands were scraped and shaking.

Taking the washcloth from him, Misty held it under the warm water. "What did they do?"

"Fucking Keith." His voice was thick with blood and sobs. Two of his teeth were broken. "Kei—" Marc motioned to his face. "Keith—"

"He was sticking up for you," Eric said, watching from the doorway with Val.

"How were you . . . ? Damnit, Marc, I told you to leave that shit alone!"

Marc didn't yell back. He didn't answer at all. He just stood cradling his raw hands against his belly.

Misty sat him on the edge of the tub and pulled his shirt off. Berry-colored bruises splotched his back. One across his kidney had left the crescent imprint of a sneaker. Misty washed her twin's cuts. His blood, diluted with tap water, ran down her forearms.

"Going to look worse than fucking Charlie now." Marc braved a weak smile, and they tried to laugh for him.

"We're going to get them, Marc," Eric said. "Don't worry. We're going to get them."

Val still stood in the doorway. "You said they're going to a party?"

"Yeah. That's what Charlie said."

Val nodded. She weighed every word carefully. "Angie's

been talking about it for weeks in health class. It's tomorrow. At Café Five Nine."

That stoked Eric's rage. "No more games," he chuckled. "No more hiding, no more scaring them just for fun. It's time to hunt!"

"Quit! Just calm down! Just everybody calm down!" Misty's voice shook. She'd been scratched and pricked countless times but still found herself clutching hope by its thorns. "We aren't . . . We can't . . ."

"We can't what? Kill them? Because it's evil?" Eric leaned close. Beneath the drying blood, his face was a meld of pity and disgust. "Look at Marc and tell me this world cares what's good or evil."

"Quit!"

"They're going to joke about this, Misty. They're going to go to their fucking party and brag."

"I don't care!"

Eric ignored her. "Because there's no such thing as good or evil. There's only predators and prey."

Misty shrank away from him and lashed out at her brother. "This is your fault! I told you to leave that shit alone! I told you months ago. You stupid dumbass, why'd you have to pick a fight with three guys, every one of them bigger than you!"

"Because you're my sister!" Fine red drops sprayed from Marc's lips. "It doesn't matter how many there are, how big they are. I can't let anybody talk to you like that." Marc shook his head. He had to choke out the words. "You're my sister, Misty."

Through Misty's life, Marc had been the one certain thing. He'd made her laugh while their parents screamed. He'd been there every night when Mom had to work. Even when she insulted him and was too big a bitch just to drive him to their dad's house, he stood by her. Even when it meant stepping into an unfair fight—letting Keith pound him as ugly on the outside as Angie had made Misty feel on the inside—Marc had never let her suffer alone.

The rest of them had needed *Amanita muscaria* to teach them the loyalty of wolves; Marc had been born with it. He was the best brother ever.

The hand-lickers, though, would never see anything in him except a mutt, a dirty stray somebody should put to sleep.

"There's only predators and prey," Eric said again, quieter this time. "You're either one or the other."

Months ago Eric had told Misty she couldn't trust Daniel, that Daniel wasn't like them. He'd been right. Later he said that if somebody wearing boots got into a fight with somebody in a letterman jacket, the other hand-lickers wouldn't care what the fight was about. They'd defend their own, no questions asked. Eric had been right then, too. He'd been right over and over, and Misty couldn't make herself believe in fairy tales anymore.

Misty finally let go of the thorns, and there was no more pain. She felt calm, a little light-headed.

Marc was still sniffling. Reaching out, Misty held him as close as they'd been in the womb. "Don't cry. We're done crying." Marc's blood smeared her face like war paint. "They aren't, but we are."

Both of the boys could have used a few stitches, but didn't need them. They cleaned up a little more, and Misty found some antibiotic ointment in the drawer. They were smearing it on their cuts on when the front door opened.

"Oh, dear Jesus," Misty's mom said, seeing the living room trashed. "Marc? Misty?" When she saw them, Marc and Eric battered, Misty and Val still in their Florence Deli vests, she halted. "What happened? Marc? Are you all right?"

Marc nodded but didn't know what to say. Misty handed him his blood-streaked jersey, telling him to put it back on.

"Misty?" Her mom had done the best she could, but childhood was over.

"Don't worry," Misty sniffed. "We're going to be okay, okay? And I love you. And you're a great mom, and none of this is your fault. Just please don't think that, okay? And . . . just . . . I love you. I love you." It wasn't enough, but Misty didn't know how words ever could be.

"I know you love me, baby. I love you, too," her mom said. "Just tell me what's the matter."

Misty slid past her. She grabbed Misty's arm, but Misty yanked her mom's hand away and, unable to look at her, led the pack out into the dying red sunlight.

CHAPTER 21

The last week of regular class, excitement swelled through the school until groups of students seemed moments from busting into choreographed dance routines like a Broadway chorus line.

Daniel kept to himself, though. Ignored by teachers, no friends left, he'd become almost invisible. The only thing he looked forward to was slipping into the library every lunch period. He read a little of *A Midsummer Night's Dream* and remembered what he could have had.

If we shadows have offended, think but this and all is mended. . . .

Friday morning, Zach Lee jumped onto Jason Arrington's car as he pulled into the parking lot. Zach whooped in jubilation while bouncing on Jason's bumper. Everywhere, people laughed loudly and hugged a lot. The pack was gone. A clutch of posing freshman girls had taken over their picnic table. Maybe a third of the student body had decided to sleep in, though, so Daniel didn't think much about it.

In the lobby, Keith and the others gathered near the trophy cases. As Daniel passed by, Spence called out, "Hey, tell your boys they owe us a case of beer." They all laughed, but Daniel didn't get it. He kept walking, pretending he had somewhere important to be.

His phone vibrated in his pocket. Recognizing Misty's home number, Daniel's breath caught in his throat. He ducked into a restroom where a teacher wouldn't confiscate his phone and thumbed the receive button.

"Misty? Hey."

"No. This is her mom. Is this Daniel?"

After a few bright seconds of hope, Daniel's mood darkened again. "Oh, hey. Yeah, this is Daniel."

"Are Misty and Marc at school?"

"I don't think so, no."

"Could they be there somewhere and you just haven't seen them?"

"I guess. I'll keep an eye out, but I think they're skipping. Uh, do you know Misty and me broke up?"

She did, but she was desperate. She told Daniel what had happened the day before. Somebody had beaten up Marc and Eric. Misty had talked strangely, and then they'd left. "Neither of them will answer their phones. I've called their grandparents, their dad, the police."

"Well, if I see either of them, I'll tell them to call you,

okay?" The bell rang. Chatter in the lobby outside began falling to a few voices.

"Thank you. Are you sure you don't know what's going on?"

"No, ma'am. I really don't, I'm sorry."

"I don't know who'd want to hurt Marc like that." She kept talking, reluctant to hang up on her last remaining hope.

Misty's mom was scared, but she had no clue how bad this really was. While he mumbled vague assurances, Daniel imagined a faceless somebody joking about beating up two losers, laughing so hard he never noticed the werewolves stealing up behind him.

"Oh, God." Daniel remembered Spence's senseless joke. He ran out of the restroom. "Keep calling Misty and Marc, okay? I need to go."

The lobby was empty, but Daniel knew Spence had Mrs. Crow for homeroom. Taking the steps two at a time, he skidded to a stop in front of the English class. Mrs. Crow was giving some pointers about the final. Through the window in the door, Daniel spotted Spence. Thin scratches covered his arms, there were scabs on his knuckles, and Daniel's somebody wasn't faceless anymore.

"What did you do to Marc?" As he jerked open the door, the whole class turned and Mrs. Crow froze. Daniel ignored them. "Spence, what did you do to Marc and Eric?"

Spence jumped out of his seat. "They stepped out of line, so we helped them back in. Got a problem? Come on."

He thought Daniel wanted to fight. "Spence, Listen to me. They're dangerous, and they're pissed off. The pack is ready to kill you."

"The pack? Is that what those retards call themselves? Bunch of shit packers. That's what kind of pack they are."

Muffled laughter broke the silence around them. Daniel glanced at the students' expressions. A few were amused, most were just baffled. Mrs. Crow had quietly left the room.

"Damnit, this thing's not over." He grabbed for Spence's beefy arm, but Spence jerked away. Werewolves were stalking him, but Daniel couldn't warn him. Spence had been his friend once. All Daniel would have needed to say was that he was in trouble and Spence would have believed him. That was a long time past, though.

"Mr. Morning, back off. You too, Mr. Cross." Mr. Fine strode into the room, followed by Mrs. Crow. The vice-principal pulled Daniel away from Spence. Leading him out of the room, Mr. Fine rambled about how he wasn't going to put up with this anymore. Worse than an outcast, Daniel had become a mute. He could shout as loud as he wanted, but nobody would hear him.

Twisting out of Mr. Fine's grip, Daniel ran. Flying downstairs and out the front entrance, he made it to the sidewalk. Then fear seized him. Beneath one of the now-empty picnic tables sat a fairy ring of delicate *Amanita muscaria*.

"No, no," he groaned, trying not to believe what he saw.

The door swung open. Mr. Fine was chasing him, running too hard to yell. Daniel crushed a few mushrooms under his foot and bolted to the parking lot. With the vice-principal still coming, he jumped in his car and headed for the furnace.

Last winter, Misty had left school too. First, she told Daniel she'd done it because government class was boring. Later, he saw how little regard wolves had for any authority above the pack. That still wasn't the whole truth, through.

Maybe the wolf had made her reckless enough to stand up, but she'd been driven by compassion, love, and everything that lit humanity from within. At least, everything that could, since Daniel and the rest of the class had sat as dumb and dull-eyed as animals. Misty had the strength it took to be gentle. No fangs or claws, no rot-eater god, could give anyone that.

But from what her mom had said, Misty was making her peace with the human world and wasn't coming back. Her brother had been hurt bad. She couldn't bear getting punished for having pity on a dog or falling for the wrong boy anymore. Misty was tired and ready to become just another wolf in Birmingham.

Daniel drove to the furnace. Pulling to the gate, he stepped out into the gnat-dizzy heat. Cupping his hands around his mouth, he called, "Misty? Marc? Your mom called me. She's really worried about you guys. I heard about the fight, Marc. You're pissed. You have a right to be. But if you kill somebody, you can't come back from that. How can you ever come back from that?"

Birds sang through the brambles. The only wolves Daniel saw were the pair painted on the main office warning him away.

"Listen, I know we're not really friends anymore, but maybe we could just . . . whatever, just talk or something." Wiping sweat from his face, Daniel opened the padlock and unwound the chain holding the gate closed. "I'm coming in, okay? I just want to talk, okay?"

The dense scrub burst open. Gray-and-white fur, furious barks, and Daniel fell backward screaming. It took a moment for him to realize he hadn't been bitten.

Daniel had known his packmates apart by smell more than sight. Now, he couldn't tell who stood at the open gate, only that the wolf was both beautiful and terrible, head hunched low between shoulders, spit dripping from snarling lips.

The wolf turned and vanished back into the brush, leaving Daniel lying in the gravel, every thudding beat of his heart a gift. Beyond the gate, the dense plant life shuddered as the pack joined together. None of them had been more than ten yards away, but the weave of shadow and sunlight, browns and ochers, disguised their outlines, making them almost invisible.

The wolves formed a single-file line. Daniel watched them curve southwest toward a hole they'd cut in the distant side of the fence. Somehow, Daniel got to his feet and got into his car. He blew through a red light to reach the hole blocks away, but the pack had made it there first and were already gone.

His phone started vibrating again. It was his mom. The

school must have called her. Tossing it in the passenger seat, Daniel circled the block, then the next, then the next. The city had so many cracks—alleys, storm culverts, abandoned buildings—he didn't know how he'd find them or what he could do if he did. He kept looking, though.

Morning turned to afternoon. His parents called twice more, but Daniel could face them later. He tried telling himself maybe the wolves would just seethe for a while, lick their wounds, then show up for school next Monday like nothing had happened.

Driving around the city, though, Daniel spotted red-and-white mushrooms blossoming in empty lots and in the flower beds decorating UAB Medical Center. There were more every hour, erupting like plague sores. Daniel could tell himself whatever he liked; the rot-eater god was rising.

CHAPTER 22

Café Five Nine was in an old building a block south of the Storyteller Fountain. The restaurant shared the street level with a jewelry boutique and a Middle Eastern imports store. They had an open mike night every Sunday on the second floor. Other times, they rented the space out for wedding receptions, art shows, and parties. Empty at the moment, the second floor was a puzzle box of brick archways, with lots of hidden niches for end-of-the-year, last-chance hijinks.

"Miss?"

Misty walked through spears of sunlight that came through high, circular windows and sparked dust motes. Chairs stood on small tables. A stage dominated the largest room, ringed by dark theater lamps.

"Miss? I saw you come up here."

A stairwell led to the space's separate Highland Avenue entrance. Misty knocked. Val, standing on the sidewalk outside, knocked back.

"There you are. You can't get out that way. That door's locked."

Turning, Misty climbed the stairs again. The waitress stood at the top. "You're not supposed to be here, anyway. Would you like me to . . ."

Marc's blood had dried around Misty's eye and stiffened wild strands of hair. Misty refused to wash it away yet.

"Are you okay, honey?"

Shoving the waitress aside, Misty crossed the second floor again, then walked back out through the clinking silverware and easy lunch talk of the restaurant. She described the layout to Eric. He listened and mulled over angles of attack. The restaurant closed at ten. That door would be locked after that, and only the Highland Avenue entrance would be open.

They walked around the building. Somebody had tried to turn the alley into a courtyard with park benches and a concrete birdbath, but it didn't get enough sun for much to grow. Now, two motorcycles stood there and the birdbath was missing its bowl. *Amanita muscaria* surrounded a serene statue of Saint Francis.

Val motioned toward the power meter clicking on the rear wall. "We could take out the lights first, like in the school. Then they—"

"No more hiding, no more keeping to the dark." Eric shook his head. "No going back."

At dusk, the pack returned to the furnace; Daniel wouldn't

linger there after nightfall. Eric sent Misty and Marc for mushrooms while he and Val started the fire.

A copperhead, coiled up waiting for a rat, felt Misty approach. Deciding he didn't want anything to do with her, he wove off through the grass. Misty ignored him and gathered mushroom caps in the front of her shirt the way she'd gathered daisies when she'd been young. Red clay clung to her boots and stained her fingers orange. It streaked her skirt and bare calves.

Marc made a *whuf* sound with his human throat. When Misty turned, he tossed a mushroom into the air. Taking a lurching sidestep, Misty caught it in her shirt. She let out a triumphant laugh, and Marc grinned, flashing the gap-toothed smile Keith had given him. The side of his face was scabbed and still swollen. Misty felt another jab of hate every time she looked at him.

Gathering a few more caps, she walked toward her brother. "Once this starts, we won't have much time before the cruisers come. Eric will want to push it too far, stay too long, but we stick together. Find Keith first, then Spence and Scotty. Make sure the rest of them leave for college or wherever and never come back. Then we disappear."

Marc nodded. "What about Angie?"

"I'll take care of Angie."

"What do you think we're going to do after . . . after tonight. Are we just going to live here or—"

"We're going to stick together. And we're going to be okay."

Marc nodded again, and Misty dumped her mushrooms into his shirt. They'd gathered six or seven for each of them, double what they'd ever eaten in one night before. "Go back to the shed. I need to check on something." Marc started for the casting shed, then Misty added, "Hey. Thanks for not . . . when Daniel came by this morning. Thanks."

"Don't let him mess this up," Marc said.

"He won't."

They split up. Pulling her phone out, Misty walked into the building housing the row of tall, still engines.

The pack had spent months slipping farther and farther past the borders of civilization, but they'd always come back eventually. This time, their exile would be permanent. They weren't meant for the human world. They all accepted it. And maybe they'd even suspected it before the rot-eater god had given them the power to transform into their true selves.

Still, there had been a few humans who'd treated them humanely, a few who'd never shoved them aside or looked down on them. Misty had already said good-bye to her mom. When Marc had disappeared earlier, the rest of them pretended they didn't know he'd gone to call his and Misty's dad, probably their grandparents, too. Val had also slipped away for a few minutes while they'd roamed the city. Only Eric seemed prepared to leave and never look back.

Misty had turned her phone off the first time her mom tried to reach her last night. There were more than a dozen messages, but she didn't listen to them. Calling Daniel, she hoped his voice mail would pick up.

Halfway through the second ring, he shouted, "Misty!"

"Hey."

"Listen. I know about the fight—"

"Don't worry about any of that."

"I'm worried." He tried to laugh. "Where are you? What's going—?"

"You may have been right. When you said I wouldn't have trusted you if you'd told me you're going to Cornell. I might have decided I didn't like you very much, and it wouldn't have had anything to do with who you were, just who I'm not. Just jealousy, I guess."

"I'm so sorry about that, Misty. I'm so—"

"Be quiet, Daniel."

He stopped talking. Listening to him breathe, Misty watched night settle across Birmingham like ash.

Finally, Daniel whispered, "Misty?"

"I just wanted to tell you I don't hate you. I just wanted you to know that."

"Okay. So let's meet somewhere and talk, then. Or if you don't want that, that's fine. But just tell me—"

"Bye, Daniel."

"Wait! Misty, wait. I've been thinking, you know, and fuck Cornell. That's what my parents wanted. I want to be with you. I love you."

Misty wiped her eyes. "Don't do this to me again. Please."

"I'm telling the truth! I don't want any of that stuff. I want you. I just want you."

Misty could hear traffic noises in the background. He was still looking for them. But Daniel could have given up Cornell anytime. He hadn't, because—even if he hated it sometimes—he was a shooting star, just like Misty was a wolf.

"Go home," she said. "You need to stay inside tonight."

"No. I know you don't have any reason to believe me, Misty, but you have to. You have to. Please, Misty." He kept talking, saying her name over and over.

Closing her eyes, Misty looked inside herself. Daniel would hear any uncertainty in her voice. Finally, she cut off his rambling. "I'm glad I met you, despite everything. But get in our way tonight, and I'll kill you,"

"Misty . . ."

"It's time to grow up. Bye, Daniel." She turned her phone off before he could call her back. Slumping in the doorway, Misty breathed deep. She took a minute to get control of herself, then stood up and walked toward the firelight wavering through holes in the casting shed's roof.

Heat made the pack's faces drip sweat. Val fed the fire with pieces of art, color studies and crayon portraits she'd taken home as the school year wound down but never bothered pulling out of her backseat.

Misty shoved a tempera still-life into the embers, watching it turn black and curl up like a dying spider. The pigments made tongues of flame burn green. She wished she could go home just long enough to tear the posters and pictures cut from magazines off her walls. Misty imagined burning all her nice clothes, her books, a pair of wings made from bent coat hangers and pantyhose.

Streetlights flickered awake. Filling the city with the metallic reek of ozone, they signaled the end of childhood.

Val turned on her stereo, the slides already set to reduce music to a single, maddening beat. The wolves began their stomp-dance around the flames. Eric scooped two mushroom caps off the slag. As he chewed, he yelled so loud, his body shook. "Break! Everything!"

Misty, Val, and Marc joined him, screaming though the sweltering dark. "Break everything! Break everything! Break everything!"

"Shit!" Daniel threw his phone against the dashboard. "Shit! Shit! Shit!"

He'd meant it. Telling Misty he wanted her, that he'd give it all up for her, he'd meant every word. Listening to them spilling up from his chest, Daniel knew he'd finally reached bedrock truth. But after layer beneath layer of lies, it was too late.

Defying the relentless fall of night, defying the wolf who'd driven him off that morning and Misty's promise a few minutes ago, Daniel kept searching. Blood and slaughter were coming to Birmingham. Even if others were just as guilty, Daniel had played his part in calling it down. He didn't know if he could stop it anymore, but if he ran away now, Daniel would become the most refined breed of monster, one with perfectly clean hands.

He stopped by Florence Deli, but Ilie didn't know much. He went to Val's and Eric's homes, but their parents were just as useless. Desperate, Daniel went by Misty's apartment, hoping for any clue her mom hadn't told him earlier. She wasn't home, though, probably out looking for Misty and Marc herself.

Standing on the porch, Daniel glanced over at Charlie Say What's apartment. Spence had joked Marc and Eric owed them a case of beer. Suddenly, Daniel remembered introducing him and Bwana to Charlie months ago.

Running across the parking lot, Daniel pounded on Charlie's door. Nobody answered, but he could hear the TV. "I know you're home! Open up, or I'll kick the door down. I swear to God!"

The deadbolt snapped back, and Elsa appeared. "Charlie's pretty pissed with you guys," she said.

"So the fight was here?"

"Yeah, it was here." Behind Elsa, Charlie sat on the couch, flipping across channels. "That kind of shit brings the police. Tell your friends, they ever—"

"It's going to get worse." Daniel shouldered past Elsa into

the apartment. "The kind of shit that ends up on the front page. The kind where the cops hunt down everybody involved. If you go to prison again, what will they cut off this time?"

Charlie exploded off the couch. Before Daniel could step back, the ogre had a hold of his throat, heaving him to his tiptoes.

"I'm trying to stop it, okay?" Daniel croaked. "You need to help me."

Charlie studied him for a second, nodded, then dropped Daniel back to his feet. Daniel smelled weed on his breath and wondered how Charlie moved so fast stoned.

Yesterday, Spence had come over with some smart ass Daniel guessed was Scotty and another boy named Kevin.

"Kevin? You mean Keith?"

"Maybe. He was the one throwing the party."

Daniel's brain dug for a barely listened-to conversation with his mom. He almost laughed. Somehow, it was actually worse than he'd imagined. Half the school was going to Keith's stupid party.

"So what? They see Eric and Marc and just go beat them up?"

Charlie shook his head. "Marc and Eric saw them. First Marc got up in Kevin or whoever's face, then all of them were fighting."

"Why would— Oh, shit," Daniel said, remembering Marc's grudge with Keith.

"Sorry. Aren't you and Misty split up, anyway? Thought

you were a college man now. Getting out of this shithole."

"We did. I am. It's a long story. I need to go, okay?"

Charlie nodded. "Just keep the cops off my ass."

"And keep Marc and them out of trouble," Elsa shouted as Daniel rushed out. "I love those kids."

Streetlights had begun flickering awake. For the first time since he'd been six, Daniel was afraid of the dark. Back in his car, he found his phone on the floorboard and thanked God it hadn't broke when he'd thrown it.

When Keith answered, his greeting was drowned out by thumping music. The party had already started.

"Keith, you have to get out of there."

"Just a second—hey, it's Daniel! Everybody say hi!"

A chorus of shouts rose up. "Thanks for warning us about the pack!" Angie laughed. "We're all looking over our shoulders now. Covering our butts!"

Spence must have told them about Daniel's panicked blowup in school earlier. Ignoring Angie's mocking, Daniel asked, "Where the hell are you, Keith?"

"Daniel wants to come to the party! Should I invite him?"

A second chorus of boos.

"Sorry. I think that's a no."

"This isn't a joke! They're coming. They're coming now!"

"Yeah, well, we've seen how your friends fight. Not too worried."

"What's up, Daniel?" Suddenly, Scotty had the phone.

"Just wanted to tell you that, uh, when we were beating the shit out of those two little queers, it felt really, really good. Okay, bye!"

Keith chuckled. "It really did."

"Yeah? Why don't you tell everybody what the fight was about, then?"

Keith kept the phone to himself this time. "That doesn't matter anymore," he said, the exuberance gone from his voice.

"Yes, it does! It's going to matter a lot if you don't get everybody the hell out of there."

"Listen to me." The music faded behind Keith as he stepped away from his friends. "This is my moment. I wasn't about to let Marc steal it from me, and I'm not about to let you."

"Steal it? Keith, you beat a guy bloody for sticking up for his sister."

"Yeah, well, it won't be shit compared to what we do to you or your little pack if you show your faces tonight. And, just so you know, I make Angie lick my balls, and she fucking loves it." Keith hung up.

Daniel swore and punched the steering wheel. He had to get to that party. Uncle Josh and Aunt Leslie would know where it was, but Daniel only had Keith's cell number in his phone, not any for his parents. Keith lived on the far side of Twentieth Street. Daniel's own house was closer. Speeding home, Daniel tried to park and ran one tire onto the lawn. His dad stood at the window.

"Where have you been?" he demanded as Daniel barreled in.

Daniel ignored him. In the kitchen, Daniel's mom was reading to Mack at the table. "Damnit, I'm supposed to be at work right now!" she snapped.

"When you talked to Aunt Leslie about Keith's party, did she say where it was?"

"What? No. Mr. Fine called this morning. You've been suspended for the rest of the year. Do you realize that? Do you even care anymore? They're letting you take your finals in ISS, and thank God for that."

His mom's address book sat on the windowsill beneath some cooking magazines. Letting the pile topple to the floor, Daniel flipped through it and started dialing Uncle Josh's number.

"I'm talking to you, Daniel." His mom tried snatching his phone away. Daniel dodged her.

"Hello?"

"Uncle Josh? It's Daniel," he panted, out of breath. "I need to know where Keith's party is."

His uncle hesitated. "Listen, Daniel, I know there have been some hard feelings between you boys lately. Over Angie and everything. They'll probably heal with time, but maybe it's best if you don't—"

"Shut the fuck up and tell me where the fucking party is! Something bad is about to happen, and we're running out of time!" Before, Daniel could have teased it out of him, but all his charisma had chaffed away hours ago.

"Café Five Nine. On Twentieth and Highland," his uncle stammered. "What do you mean bad?"

"Very bad. Call Keith. Try to get him to shut it down. Please."

"All right, but—"

Daniel hung up, knowing his uncle didn't have a chance. He thought about calling anybody he could to warn them, but by now, everyone at school knew Daniel Morning, their shooting star once, had snapped.

He could abandon the problem to the police, tell them minors were drinking at the party, somebody had a gun, anything. While the pack closed in, though, the cops would waste time rounding the partygoers up, collecting names, and giving Breathalyzer tests. They'd keep their senses sharp for all sorts of human dangers, but nothing like what was coming. Daniel would only be inviting more lambs to the wolves' banquet.

His parents stood glaring at Daniel. His dad's face was dusky red. "We've been calling you all day," he said. "Where have you been? What do you mean something bad is about to happen?"

"I'll explain later. I—I have to go." Daniel sidestepped them.

"No! Stop! This has been going on for months, and it's

stopping now!" His yelling made Mack start to cry, but his dad was too angry to notice. "You sneak out of the house. You come home with cuts you won't explain. When you are here, you act like a little snot. They could have expelled you for the stunt you pulled this morning. You damn near threw away your entire future."

"I'm sorry."

"You'd better be sorry. Get to your room. I can't even believe I have to tell—"

"I love you," Daniel whispered. "But I have to go."

His parents forgot they were mad at him. "Daniel, what's the matter?"

The rot-eater god was rising. Uncle Josh couldn't stop it, the police couldn't stop it, and Daniel couldn't stop it either. Misty had revealed her beauty to him, but Daniel hadn't been brave enough to hold on to it. She was, though. Daniel had to believe Misty still was.

Turning, Daniel ran out. His parents shouted after him. Daniel didn't dare look back.

CHAPTER 23

They'd tried warning them. The pack's sign watched from walls and overpasses, from everywhere. Any other animal would have known what lived here. Even the crackheads—brains charred, more twitching animal left than human—stayed away from Southside.

But the rest of the hand-lickers never noticed. They kept hurting the pack. They kept pushing the pack until they had nowhere left to retreat. The hand-lickers were blind and arrogant in their blindness. They'd forgotten to be afraid of wolves.

Break everything.

The chunk of brick smashed into a windshield. Tires squealed, metal crunched into concrete, but the pack had already slipped back beneath the shadows. None of them turned to glimpse the wreck.

They ran everybody off the streets, chasing them until they collapsed. Fathers grabbed kids. Boyfriends left girlfriends behind. While the manager of a gas station cowered behind bullet-proof glass, wolves tore into candy bars and packages of beef jerky. They padded onto a bus. The driver and passengers scattered, leaving the bus to block traffic.

Glass shattered. Humans yelled. Sirens filled the night. The pack stalked through the pandemonium driven by something too cold to be hate anymore. The only thing left was an instinct to defend territory, to teach the hand-lickers to be afraid again.

The bluestone towers of Cornell were so far away now, Daniel couldn't even see them in his mind's eye anymore. He stood waiting behind Café Five Nine. Police sirens wailed to the north. Overhead, a DJ sampled an old Motown hit, chopping and screwing it into an oozy beat that seemed to drip down the wall into the alley.

Looking up, Daniel saw Zach dancing. Emi pulled Claire into a corner to whisper some secret. He stayed hidden in the shadows below. If Keith saw him, he'd come down, flanked by Scotty and Spence, and the night would go from bad to hopeless. But as old friends flitted past the windows, Daniel whispered their names to keep his courage. He remembered who they were and who they could be, if he succeeded.

The banshee sirens drew closer. Daniel stomped more mushrooms to pulp. Even though *Amanita muscaria* filled the alley, he didn't eat it. Daniel couldn't kill the wolves, and forced himself to remember who they were too. Their pelts hid fear, anger, and hurt, but nothing evil.

Amanita muscaria couldn't help Daniel now, and the shooting star's magic was just as useless. The faith Daniel could conjure with a bedeviling grin was gone.

But he could speak. As a wolf, Daniel had only barked and snarled. As the shooting star, he'd probably said even less. Letting go of all his other gifts, Daniel finally had a voice.

Blue lights flashed across the bell tower of the Methodist church. Despite the sirens, the scrape of claw against pavement seemed deafening. Rangy shapes and burning gold eyes emerged from around a building on the far side of the alley. They'd been moving upwind, and Daniel knew they'd caught his scent long before he'd heard them. Stepping into the light from the party above, their pelts turned jaundiced yellow.

Daniel stood in the middle of the alley, between them and the door leading up to their prey. He kept his hands open and in plain view, watching the wolves spread into a half-circle around him. They stopped, out of arm's reach but close enough that any one of them could lunge and bring Daniel down in an eye blink. Only suspicion made them hesitate; they couldn't figure out what he was up to.

Daniel had never been so aware of how fragile his muscles and bones were, his whole existence held together with spider silk.

"If—" The word came out raspy and small, the creak of

old leather. Daniel finally had a voice, which the rot-eater god ripped from its wolves, which hand-lickers were rewarded well for keeping muzzled. He had a voice and one chance to see what made powerful men and dark beings so afraid.

Swallowing, Daniel tried again. "If we shadows have offended, think but this and all is mended. That you have but slumber'd here. While these visions did—"

Growls turned into angry barking. Misty peeled back her lips, displaying bone-splintering fangs. Daniel raised the shaking words above the pack's tempest. "Appear! And this weak and idle theme, no more yielding but a dream. Gentles, do not reprehend: If you pardon, we will mend—"

"Kill you!" Misty screamed. "Told you I'd kill you! Nothing but a play."

"A *Midsummer Night's Dream*," Daniel whispered. "You were Puck."

"No! Nothing but scraps of breath." Misty was human but just barely. She slammed her palms against the ground, trying to shift back into an animal, trying to forget Puck, trying to forget what a miracle she was.

Daniel refused to let her. "If you pardon, we will mend: and, as I am an honest Puck, if we have unearned luck—"

Eric shed his wolf skin. He grabbed Misty's face, forcing her to look at him, not Daniel. "Traitor. Used you. Gutterfuck. He'll save his real friends. He'll throw you away again."

"I did use you, Misty," Daniel said. "And there's no reason

you should stop this for me. But the rot-eater god wants a sacrifice. You know I'm not good enough." He pointed to the stairs behind him. "Nobody up there is. It's hungry for Puck, for the piece of you that was onstage that night. The piece that stood up for a hurt dog when nobody else would. That's going to go see the world one day. It's hungry for the piece of you that nobody can turn into their pet or their monster."

"Good!" Misty screamed, then shook her head. "Puck can't survive here, Daniel. This isn't her enchanted forest. It's too hard."

"I know it's hard. It's a hard, mean place; I can't tell you how scared I am of it. And the only speck of enchantment I've ever found anywhere is inside you, Misty. I'm a lying, sack-of-shit coward, but even I know that's worth fighting for."

Eric kept shouting, "Predator or prey! Predator! Or! Prey!"

Daniel began reciting again. "If we have unearned luck now to 'scape the serpent's tongue, we will make amends ere long. . . ."

Like an incantation, the words touched cold ash inside Misty, making it blossom with the scent of tempera-painted backdrops, set-pieces dripping plastic ivy, and the beach-warm glow of footlights. In a tired voice, she began saying the words with Daniel: "Else the Puck a liar call: so good night unto you all. . . ."

Around the corner, Misty saw the door leading up to the party.

She still hated them. They'd hurt her brother. She was nothing but a mutt to them. But she couldn't sacrifice herself to get revenge.

"Give me your hands if we be friends, and Robin shall restore amends." As they finished, Misty let a smile emerge, as fragile and as relentless as the first spike of green shouldering up though damp soil.

"Marc?" Misty whispered. "Let's just go, okay?"

Marc glared at Daniel, his muzzle fixed into a snarl. When his sister spoke, he turned. Glancing at her, then back at Daniel, then back at her, he gave Misty a soft, uncertain whine.

"You can't do this, Marc. I need you."

"Whatever happened yesterday," Daniel added, "I know all you wanted was to stand up for Misty. Because that's the kind of man you are. But, Marc, if you do this. Go up there and hurt someone else's sis—"

Eric lunged. Daniel clutched his pelt, trying to push him back, but animal ferocity crushed him to the pavement. Long teeth sank down, tearing the words out of Daniel's throat.

Misty heard herself screaming as Eric's head whipped side to side, intent on snapping Daniel's neck. Suddenly, she was on her feet. The toe of her boot struck just below Eric's ear. Eric scrambled back with a surprised yelp.

"He wasn't going to hurt us!" Misty dropped to her knees beside Daniel. His too-quick breaths sounded like a sponge being wrung dry.

UNLEASHED

"Our chance!" Eric was human again. Blood blackened his mouth and ran down his chin. He grabbed Misty's arm, but she yanked free.

Daniel clutched his throat. Laying her hands on top of his, Misty felt the torn skin and cartilage of the wound underneath. Pink foam bubbled from the corner of his lips. His eyes bulged, but he didn't see her.

"This is our chance! He's a hand-licker! Why did you listen?" Desperate to finish the kill, Eric kicked Misty in the back of her head. The blow made her vision fog, but Misty took it and shielded Daniel's body.

Eric yelled, "Traitor!" Ignoring him, Misty didn't budge. Then his arm wrapped around her throat, and she realized she'd become the traitor now.

With a knee on her back, Eric bent Misty double until her flushed-hot face was pressed against Daniel's clammy one. She could hear music and the chatter of classmates from the party above. It started to sound miles away.

Misty struggled for air, struggled to call out for her brother, but she couldn't and didn't have to. Marc, wolf-loyal long before any ritual had turned him into one, was already bounding through the air.

Marc bit through the flesh of Eric's arm and snapped bone. They both fell, twisting, kicking, slashing to the ground. Eric shifted, and two wolves tumbled across the alley. With a limp foreleg, though, Eric wasn't much of a match.

Pulling her shirt off, Misty pressed it against Daniel's wounds. The gurgling noises made Misty want to sob. He scraped his heels across the pavement, trying to roll over. He was drowning in blood. She tried helping him get onto his side, but couldn't lift his slack weight.

"Val. I need help, Val."

Val had stayed out of it so far. Every muscle tensed, she crouched ready to spring somewhere. She look at Misty and Daniel, then at Eric and Marc.

"Val, please. He can't breathe. Please."

As Val's throat changed shape, the words clattered like gravel. "I didn't—didn't think it'd look like this."

"Don't think about that now. Just help me."

Misty pulled and Val pushed Daniel onto his side. It helped a little, but his breaths were still faint.

"Marc! Call 911. Go around to the restaurant and get some towels or something."

"Fucking never hit my sister! You fucking never!" Marc held Eric's thrashing wolf shape down, wrenching his broken leg every time he tried to get up.

"Marc! Get off him and go!"

Marc scrambled back from Eric. Eric limped after him, but Marc was gone from the alley before he'd managed five steps. If he tried to attack the party now, he'd hardly be able to get up the stairs, much less chase anybody down. Watching his pack abandon him made it impossible for Eric to hold wolf shape himself.

"You're nothing!" he screamed. "Nothing but strays sneaking around someone else's territory. Begging for scraps."

He kicked Daniel's splayed leg. Val yelled, "It's over! Stop, Eric! It's over!" She motioned to Misty that they should get Daniel away from him. Misty wrapped her arms under Daniel's, Val took his legs, and they heaved him up.

"They treated you like strays for years, and they were right. If you don't have the guts to fight back, they were right to treat you like strays."

Misty and Val carried Daniel halfway around the building. Suddenly, voices surrounded them and hands reached out to help them lift Daniel. The restaurant staff had been closing up, but Marc had pounded on the window until somebody came. While Keith's celebration went full-throttle above them, they carried Daniel to a bench in front of the restaurant.

The same waitress Misty had shoved earlier that day gently pulled her aside and draped a jacket across her bare shoulders. Misty didn't know if the woman recognized her or not.

An ambulance came. Then a fire truck. The sidewalk whirled with paramedics carrying canisters of oxygen and firemen rushing in with a stretcher, bellowing for the waiters to clear back. None of the humans noticed Eric standing in the mouth of the alley, cradling his arm.

Val begged him, "Please, you're hurt. It's over. Just let it go."

Eric looked at her. He looked at Misty with the waitress's arm around her and at Marc telling the paramedics something.

"The police will be here in a second. There's no point anymore." Val held out her hand. "C'mon, baby. Let's get your arm fixed."

"I loved you. I thought you were strong." Eric wiped his eyes, then returned, alone, into the night.

Val looked at Misty, but Misty didn't know what to say. Marc rushed up and whispered, "Taking him to UAB. I told them a dog attacked him but ran off."

Misty nodded. She watched Daniel being loaded into the ambulance. One of the paramedics was pumping air into his lungs. Misty could hear how scared they were by the way they shouted back and forth. On the stretcher, Daniel lay so still, she couldn't imagine him ever moving again.

Daniel had worked Keith's dad into a panic. Keith stopped him from calling the police, though, telling him Daniel was still mad about losing Angie. Deep down, he wasn't so sure. He kept glancing over whenever someone new came up the stairs. What if Daniel's friends did show up and try to start something? What if they ruined his party?

But before long, the air was dizzy-hot from dozens of bodies. Everybody was dancing. Scotty, his belly flopping, bounced onstage beside Andre. Couples slipped off to dim corners.

Suddenly, girls who'd made excuses when he'd asked them out before were whispering in Keith's ear. Guys who'd thought Keith was a suck-up and a clown, if they thought of him at all, now shouted his name from across the room. Keith shone like a star.

"Quit worrying about those losers," Angie finally hissed. "So what if they come? They just hate us because they know they can never be us."

She was right. Keith had fought hard for this, had gambled everything. This was his moment. He knew in his heart nothing could stop him. He smiled and kissed Angie. He noticed flashing lights outside the windows. Figuring it was a traffic stop on the street below, it slipped out of Keith's mind as he let himself be swept up in the swirl of music and shouts and skin.

CHAPTER 24

D aniel sank down, down. Below human reason, below animal instinct, until his heels touched the yawning, colorless void, as patient as forever.

He fought against it, breaking the surface in a bright white somewhere. The woman had blood on her hands. She pushed a humid plastic tube down Daniel's throat. Daniel tried shrinking away from her, but people held his wrists. The more he fought, the more blurred figures appeared. They clutched his wrists, ankles, and shoulders. Daniel was surrounded by machines and wires.

"Daniel! Relax, Daniel!"

"Let's give him some Pavulon, please. Ten milligrams."

Daniel's body grew lead-weight numb, his limbs too heavy to lift. The shouting faded. Staring at the drop-panel ceiling, Daniel surrendered to the nothingness rising around him. He stopped thinking, stopped knowing, and it finally slipped Daniel's mind that he existed at all.

He heard a murmur from the darkness. Unable to make out her words, Daniel recognized his mom's voice. Then his dad's. Listening, he wished he could see them again. Slowly Daniel realized the darkness was as thin as his eyelids.

Daniel opened them, tried to sit up, but the lack of air made him weak. The tube was still in his throat. When he reached for it, his parents yelled and grabbed his hand.

"Stop, Daniel! You can't take that out. The vent's helping you breathe. Just breathe, honey. Just breathe."

Daniel inhaled. There was a soft click, and cold air flooded his lungs. The clear tube fogged as he exhaled.

"There you go. Just breathe like normal. You're fine, honey. You're fine."

His parents squeezed his hands and rubbed his chest. Daniel gulped down oxygen until his head started to swim. It was so delicious, he almost cried.

He stared around a hospital room. His parents' eyes were purple-bagged, but shining. He didn't know where his brothers were. Outside the window, the sun either rose or set. Daniel had no idea if he'd been gone for a few hours or a few days.

He tried asking a question, but the tube blocked the flow of air across his vocal cords, and he couldn't make a sound.

"It's a ventilator," his mom answered, anyway. "It's protecting your airway. Your larynx was damaged and you aspirated a lot of blood, so they need to keep you on the vent for a while. But you're fine. Okay, honey?" She kissed his forehead. Daniel felt her tears dab his skin. He believed her, but she kept saying, "You're fine. You're fine," assuring herself as much as him.

His dad went to find Daniel's nurse. His mom didn't bother waiting. Checking his pupils with her penlight, she asked, "Think you can write?"

Daniel nodded. She handed him a notepad and pen from her purse, then quizzed him on who the president was, what his address was, and how much was four times four. Still full of painkillers, focusing enough to scrawl the answers made him sweat, but Daniel convinced his mom he didn't have brain damage.

"Do you remember what happened?"

Daniel touched his neck and felt the stitches holding the skin closed. He remembered the alley being yanked out from under him. He remembered dense muscle, hot breath, and Eric's fangs biting off his scream. He shook his head, though, not knowing what his parents thought had happened.

"You were attacked by a dog. You were going to Keith's party, you were in the alley behind the café, and a dog attacked you."

Daniel turned to a clean page in the notepad. *Anyone else hurt?*

"No, just you. Isn't that enough?"

Don't lie.

"You were the only one it attacked. I promise."

The wolves hadn't killed anyone. Misty hadn't fed herself

to the rot-eater god. Daniel nodded, then laid his head back on the pillow. The pain didn't go away, but its jagged edges softened a little.

UAB Medical Center rose above Southside like a sea monster, its glass-and-steel tentacles winding for blocks. The corridors teemed with doctors who knew all the body's secrets. Pharmacies stored drugs that kept hearts beating decades after they should have stopped. Behind sliding-glass doors sat sage machines, able to peer into every organ. Almost lost among acres of medicines and monitors there was a small, plain room that contained subtler wonders.

Designed to welcome all who needed it, the chapel wasn't decorated with icons of any particular faith, no crosses, statues, or gold-scrolled books. Six benches faced a wooden table that could serve as a lectern or altar. But the room was draped in quiet, and somehow that was enough to make the space sacred.

Wearing green scrubs borrowed from the hospital laundry, Misty slipped in during a Catholic Mass being celebrated by four people, including the priest. Sitting in the back, she listened to them recite the "Our Father" together before taking Communion.

A couple hours later, the family of somebody named Tony met with their pastor. They begged the Lord to comfort Anthony and give them strength. Lost in their own problems, none of them seemed to noticed Misty was there.

Misty didn't pray. She'd come one staircase away from murder. She'd gone to the party ready to be destroyed, ready to watch her brother and friends be destroyed. The idea of asking forgiveness made her stomach cramp. For now, Misty just sat and thought.

Puck was a character. She'd vanished as soon as the stage lights went dark. But she'd left something behind, one last open-mouthed laugh in the face of any hurt or heartbreak that may come.

It was just a tiny spec of Puck's magic, but this hard city couldn't grind it down. The flames of the rot-eater god's ritual couldn't burn it. Nobody, not even Misty herself, could destroy it.

Misty played with her lip ring. Grampa must have carried a speck like that marching toward the waiting police line, knowing they could arrest him, beat him, but never teach him his place. And while her joints stiffened and her body wore out from too much work, Misty's mom found the will to get up day after exhausting day. She held something unbreakable inside her.

When the pager went off, Misty jerked. A nurse had given it to her so she'd know when Daniel woke up. Misty's stomach cramps returned, but she left the chapel and rode an elevator to the ICU family room.

"Hey, guys. Dan—"

Marc and Val sat side by side, eyes closed, their heads

resting against the wall. Marc's cheek was one snore away from settling against Val's shoulder. Letting them sleep, Misty headed into the ICU.

When the nurse on duty came in, she didn't have much to do except repeat everything Daniel's mom had already said.

It was just past seven, the evening after the attack. Daniel had almost drowned in his own blood, the surgery team vacuuming three hundred milliliters of it out of his lungs. He was still at risk for chemical pneumonitis. That meant that, for a couple days, he'd be breathing through one tube, while a second fed him gray, high-calorie sludge, and a third pumped steroids and antibiotics into his arm. But everyone reminded Daniel he was young and strong. Flesh would knit itself together, infections could be treated, and he'd be on his feet soon.

"You'll be good as new by the time you head off to Cornell," the nurse said.

Daniel nodded, trying to smile around the tube.

She gave his foot a playful slap. "Gosh, your mom's been telling us stories about you for years. It's nice you finally came up to visit."

His parents laughed, but Daniel didn't hear her. Through the room's glass wall, he saw Misty walking lightly up the hall. Stopping at his door, she peered in at Daniel with his family.

"Misty! Come in, come in." His mom coaxed her in and

gave her a hug. They must have finally met while Daniel had been unconscious. "Where's your brother and . . . ?"

"Val? They kind of nodded off." Misty motioned toward the family room.

"Misty's the one who saved you," Daniel's dad said. "You remember that at all?"

Misty dropped her eyes to the floor, but Daniel nodded. He could never forget; they'd saved each other.

After another minute, his parents decided to grab dinner from the pizza place downstairs before it closed. His dad leaned down to squeeze Daniel's shoulder. He whispered, "I love you so much." His mom couldn't speak. After they filed out behind the nurse, Misty was still staring at her boots.

"You're parents are pretty cool."

Daniel nodded. They could be. He started writing. *Eric?*

"He disappeared once the ambulance and police came. We decided to stick around. Me, Marc, and Val. In case he decided to come after you, but—"

Daniel shook his head. *Eric won't attack alone.* Wolves, natural or magical, drew their strength from the pack.

"Yeah, I hope you're right. So how do you feel?"

Like I got gored by a unicorn.

"Or maybe mauled by a werewolf?"

Don't be dramatic.

That finally got a grin out of her, which made Daniel laugh, sending choppy puffs of air through the ventilator in

weird little hoots, which made Misty laugh, which made
Daniel laugh harder, which made the hoots even louder,
which made Misty laugh even harder. The absurd cycle had
them trapped until Daniel's chest started to burn. He forced
his breathing to slow down.

Thank you.

"Same here." Misty squirmed a little more. "Sorry."

Same here. It was getting harder to write legibly. *I wasn't
lying when I said I wanted to be with you.*

Misty smiled at that but said, "Still, I mean, Cornell. We'll
have all summer, though, and then you'd be home for . . ."

Daniel shook his head and started scribbling again. *I really
don't know what I'm going to do after graduation now.*

"Yeah. Me neither." Misty sat down in one of the chairs by
Daniel's bed. "I've been doing a lot of thinking today, though,
and I've realized how long I've spent looking for somewhere to
belong. But I've hardly been anywhere besides Birmingham,
you know? I've been thinking about going backpacking through
Europe or something."

Daniel's ventilator hooted. *Wow. Where would you go?*

"Gosh, I don't know," Misty said, trying valiantly not to
smile. "On one hand, you want to go to London and Paris and
see all the famous stuff like the Eiffel Tower. But then, it'd also
be cool to just wander around and not even worry about where
you're going to wind up, you know?"

That's what I'd want to do—Just get lost somewhere.

"Yeah." Misty nodded. "That would be cool."

They had their first conversation all over again. Except this time, neither of them was playing make-believe.

The legions of mushrooms that had threatened to overwhelm Birmingham began shriveling away. Ilie grumbled when Misty and Val showed back up at the deli, but it was less of a pain to rehire them than train two new idiots. At least they didn't steal.

Misty visited Daniel after her Monday finals. Keith's party was already legend. Everyone talked about it, whether they'd actually gone or not. They were all so busy trading gossip, hardly anybody noticed both Daniel and Eric were missing.

As promised, flesh healed and infections were fought. On Thursday, Daniel was taken off the ventilator and moved out of the ICU. It still hurt too much to speak and he had to stay in the hospital for a while longer, but he managed to eat a few bites of real food.

Daniel missed the graduation ceremony. Later that evening, though, Misty, Marc, and Val came up with the video Val's dad had shot. Angie delivered her valedictorian speech to loud applause. Watching her, Daniel felt the wolf gnaw at his insides, wanting to get loose just one more time.

Then, in the parking lot after the ceremony, the camera turned to Misty and Marc. Marc laughed through a mask of puckered wounds. Misty shouted, stuck her tongue out, and hugged her parents while her mom cried. Daniel knew he could be watching both scenes or neither. He'd chosen well.

Daniel's mom took pictures of him in his hospital gown and mortar board, Misty perched on the bed beside him. Then Val added Daniel to the end of the video.

Sunday, his mom asked if he felt up to seeing his grand-parents and Keith's family. Daniel said sure, and once she'd left, he climbed out of bed for the first time in days. Pins and needles stabbed his legs. It took two minutes to get across the room and dig his cell phone out of the bag of his bloody clothes.

Still dressed for church, his family kept the visit short, full of lame jokes and assurances that Daniel looked good. Despite the questions bubbling underneath their strained smiles, neither Uncle Josh nor Aunt Leslie asked about the strange night. As they started to leave, Daniel called his cousin back. Keith knew what he wanted to talk about and softly slid the glass door closed.

"Was it worth it?"

Daniel's voice was a rasp, and Keith had to lean close to hear him. "What?"

"Was it worth it? Your damn—" A wet cough felt like claws scraping his chest. He had to breathe deep through the nasal cannula before he could speak again. "Your damn party. You stab me in the back. Fine, maybe I had it coming. Then, Angie calls Misty a mutt, and you don't do anything. Then, you're so scared people will find out you didn't do anything, you beat down Marc before he can tell them. Honestly, was it worth it?"

"Yeah." Chuckling, Keith shrugged. "What do you want me to say? That I'm so sorry I whipped poor little Marc's ass? I threw the wildest party in school! People will remember me for years. C'mon, Daniel, you were the shooting star once. Would you have let a kid like him get in your way?"

Daniel thought about it. "No. I wouldn't have let anybody."

"Well? I'm the shooting star now. I can't let anybody either. I'm too big to worry about a couple of mutts."

Daniel nodded. He knew how easy he'd slept when all his silences and small cruelties served a greater destiny.

Keith shrugged again, then turned to leave. "Take care."

Once he was gone, Daniel pulled his phone out of the tissue box sitting beside his bed. Peeling tape off the earpiece, he heard Spence's tiny voice swearing.

"You catch all that?" Daniel asked. He'd made sure to sound extra miserable when he'd told Spence the whole story. Spence thought he was paranoid, but there was just enough friendship left between them for him to humor Daniel.

"That fucking bitch. I don't do anybody's goddamn dirty work. I can't wait to see that—"

"Don't beat up Keith." Another coughing fit made Daniel's shoulders convulse. "If I wanted to see Keith get his ass handed to him, I could have gone to a lot less trouble. Trust me. You need to make it up to Marc."

"How?"

"He needs a job. He's lousy at reading and math, but he likes being outside."

"You want me to get him a landscaping job with Dad? Come on, man. You've done it; you know that's hard work."

"He'll love it. You owe him the chance, Spence."

"Yeah. I can talk to Dad at least."

"Good. You got something to write down Marc's number?"

There was a pause as it sank in that the only way Spence could absolve himself was to apologize to Marc Sandlin. "Yeah, give it to me," he finally said. After copying the number, Spence added, "Listen, Daniel. I know there's been some dumb shit going on lately, but most of that stuff, I was just joking around, you know?"

"I know. Take care."

"Okay. Feel better, man. Seriously."

Daniel hung up, doubled over with another cough, then lay back down. He and Spence weren't exactly friends anymore, but they were cool.

When Daniel got home at last, he just wanted to sleep. There was one thing he had to take care of first, though. He'd known it since he'd watched the graduation video. Misty, Marc, and Val had risked—they were risking every day—telling the world who they were instead of letting the world tell them. Daniel hoped he had that sort of strength too. Calling Cornell's admissions office, he told them he'd cheated on the SATs.

Then he told them again, speaking slower. Daniel was put on hold, transferred to somebody else, went through everything step-by-step a third time, and was put back on hold. This didn't happen very often, apparently, and nobody knew exactly what to do with him.

His fourth confession was to the dean of undergraduate admissions. After convincing her that, no, this wasn't a crank call, and yes, he was certain he didn't have a learning disability, the full thunder and wrath of that centuries-old institution came hurtling down. But after facing a pack of werewolves, that sounded a lot like one middle-aged woman muttering about how disappointed she was.

"This is a very serious situation, Mr. Morning. I'm—"

"But you understand, at least, right?"

"Yes, and I'm going to have to take it up with the admissions board. I'm afraid you've put your future here in serious jeopardy."

"Okay. Let me know what they say." Daniel turned off his phone and sank into his own, familiar bed. He dreamed peaceful dreams for seventeen hours.

A few days later, Daniel got a terse letter from Cornell saying that, due to the recent discovery of academic dishonesty on his part, they were revoking their offer of acceptance. They included the number for their attorneys if he had any questions.

When Daniel told his parents, his mom jerked to her feet.

"No, no. They what? You what?" Her body tensed with the instinct to protect her child, but there was nowhere to lunge.

"They yanked my acceptance. Because I cheated." Scars across the cartilage of Daniel's windpipe had hardened his voice, probably forever.

"But you didn't cheat," his dad said. "I mean, call and tell them it was our idea. Put it all on us. Then—"

"I'm not a kid anymore, Dad. Whoever's idea it was, I went along with it."

"Damnit, Daniel!" His dad swallowed his anger and tried again. "I know you weren't comfortable with this, but doors like this don't open for many people. I don't want you to give up a great future just because of what we did."

"I know. But maybe sometimes being great means being ready to give a lot up."

"What?"

Daniel remembered waiting in the dark alley, listening to the pack coming. He'd never stood farther from the bluestone towers of Cornell, and if his parents knew, they never would have been prouder of him. Daniel shook his head. "Cornell can't make me great. It can make me more money, make life easier, but you already taught me how to be great, to work hard, push myself, trust myself. To take responsibility for my actions. But now I have to learn how to be good, and nobody can teach me that. I have to figure it out by myself."

His dad didn't say anything. His mom hugged him. "Daniel,

honey, you are good," she whispered. "You're wonderful."

He kissed her forehead. "I'm getting there."

Daniel wasn't afraid of losing Cornell anymore, but that didn't mean he wouldn't have liked to have gone. They might have admitted him with his real scores. He'd never know. He could apply to other colleges in the fall, though, and in the meantime, he'd decided to wander a little, the one thing shooting stars could never do.

Birmingham inchwormed into summer. No matter how scary it had become, Misty still missed prowling the city with her pack. Then her passport arrived in the mail. Sitting on her porch, Misty held the slender blue book and felt its mystery. She flipped through crisp pages waiting to be filled with entry and exit stamps, with Paris, Florence, and anywhere else she decided to go.

She stopped yearning for the ritual's magic after that. She'd never wanted to hurt anybody, she'd just wanted some excitement and a few blank pages to fill in herself.

Marc went to work for Spence's dad, planting shrubs and hauling bags of peat, coming home every evening covered in sweat and dirt. The pay was good, the guys at work were teaching him to play pool, and he took every chance he could to walk around with his shirt off.

Daniel started physical therapy for the torn muscles in his neck and got a job at the deli. Just as he was starting to accept that nobody could wear a harvest gold vest and a name tag without feeling like a tool, it was time for Misty and him to quit.

When Ilie handed Misty her last paycheck, she blinked a few times, then said, "This is, like, twice what it should be," she said.

Ilie started writing on a Post-it note. "In Russia, there's city called Tolyatti. Horrible city, nothing but old churches and Russia's largest ammonia plant. The oldest church is the Transfiguration Cathedral, right in city center. My parents went there. I did too, before I left." He jotted down the name of the city and church in English, then had to pause, remembering how to spell them in Cyrillic letters. "You and Softhead go, light a candle for me, and we'll be even. Please?"

"Yeah. Sure." It threw Misty to hear Ilie say please. "Wait. Don't we need visas to go to Russia?"

"You'll have to bribe some people. Don't worry. Bribes are very reasonable in Russia."

Misty nodded and stared at the Post-it. "So, I've always wondered. When you left Russia, you could have gone anywhere. Why the hell did you come to Birmingham?"

Ilie spread his hands. "What? This is Magic City!"

They both laughed. Fiddling with his stereo, Ilie fell quiet for a while, then said, "There are easier places to live. So easy, nobody has to really believe in anything. Birmingham? You better believe in something, and you better never forget." He shrugged. "I'm fat and old, Misty. I run a deli. I deal with teenagers all day. What do I have except what I believe in?"

Misty smiled. "Ilie, that's very poetic."

He grunted. "Also, I grew up in fucking Russia. I just wanted to live somewhere warm."

"Take care, Ilie. Thanks for putting up with me."

He grunted. "You too."

Val and Daniel were waiting for her in the parking lot. "What was that about?" Daniel asked.

It had taken Misty a while to get used to the delicate rasp of Daniel's once honey-sweet words, but eventually she'd decided it added character. Kissing him, she handed him the Post-it. "We've got a mission."

As she told them about her paycheck and what Ilie wanted, Val made a face. "God, you suck. It's bad enough you're leaving me, but now you get a bonus?"

Misty laughed. Over the summer, Val had grown even more bored than usual with the deli. Misty suspected she'd move on too, before long.

Val's mood brightened a little when they met up with Marc. "C'mon, man. When are you going to let me give you cornrows?"

"I don't know. You really think they'd look cool?"

"Yes, I'm telling you. Just grow it out a little more."

They walked through the humid summer night, smoked a bowl, and didn't mention this was the last time they'd get to hang out together for months. The statue of Vulcan stood at his anvil high above the city. A church was having a late choir practice. The doors propped open to let some air in, quavering blue notes of "Hand in Hand" escaped, fluttering into the dark like moths.

"So you'll keep an ear to the ground for Eric while we're away, right?" Daniel asked.

Both Marc and Val nodded. Val had gone to the furnace twice looking for him. Not only was Eric not there, the *Amanita muscaria* had disappeared too. But Birmingham was full of dank ruins where the rot-eater god could bide its time. They'd all had bad dreams about Eric gathering a new pack around him.

"I don't know what we'll do if we find him," Marc said. "It's not like the police would listen to us."

Val crossed her arms. "I hope if we find Eric, we won't need the police. If I could just talk to him . . . I don't know."

"You could convince him. I'm sure," Misty said, glancing up at Vulcan again. "Just keep looking, okay?"

Birmingham, built on fire and ore, didn't raise its children so much as forge them. The city had seen firebombs and riots. Werewolves had raced through its streets, howling for blood. A few lines of poetry had held them back, though, because Birmingham tempered love and faith every bit as unyielding as its steel. The rot-eater god might fester at its edges. Eric might recruit more wolves. But as long as there was a voice left, singing, swearing, laughing, and refusing to fall silent, hardheaded Birmingham would stand.

Misty only got a few hours sleep that night, but when her alarm clock went off, her eyes snapped open and she sat up in bed without any grogginess fogging her mind. She took a shower and got dressed. Her hands shook buttoning her shirt.

Her mom was already cooking breakfast. Misty was too nervous to eat, though. Milling around the kitchen, they talked about small things, the apartment Marc was thinking about renting. The couple who'd moved in upstairs. That Misty should be drinking orange juice instead of Pepsi.

"You scared yet?" Her mom asked. "I wouldn't do it. Go off someplace where I don't even know what people are saying."

"Yes I am, and you're making it worse."

"No." She rubbed Misty's back. "You're a lot tougher than me."

After Marc had finished Misty's breakfast, Misty kissed her mom and promised to be careful, then lugged her huge backpack out into the morning gloom. Marc drove to Daniel's house. Misty watched the still-dreaming city pass by.

While Daniel double-checked to make sure they had everything, his dad said, "While you're over there, why don't you check out some of the universities they—"

"Dad . . ."

"I'm just saying, a semester abroad could—"

"Dad," Daniel said more firmly.

"All right, all right."

Daniel said his good-byes and climbed into the old

Lincoln. At the airport, Marc helped them pull their backpacks out of the trunk. Misty squeezed him tight. They'd never spent more than one night apart before. "Just stay out of trouble, okay? Please?"

"Yeah, you know I will. So you think Val will go out with me?"

"What? You think Val's weird."

"She *is* weird. But she's kinda cool, too, you know?"

Misty rolled her eyes. "When you stood up for me to Keith and them, and then to Eric—after all that, Val said that she'd always thought you were funny and liked hanging out with you, but she'd never realized how noble you were underneath."

"Noble?"

"Yes. Go talk to her before she remembers what a thick layer of dumb-ass there is on top."

"Right, but that's the word she used? 'Noble'?"

"I love you. Bye." Misty kissed his cheek and shoved him aside. She walked with Daniel through the sliding-glass doors, then rushed back out. "When you talk to her, don't wear so much body spray!" Misty yelled across the drop-off lanes. "You smell the way a porn set looks!"

Marc cupped his hands around his mouth. "That's what I'm going for!"

Misty walked back in without an answer.

The airport was full of sleepy-eyed businessmen and the aroma of coffee drifting from a little café. Sitting together,

Misty and Daniel held hands, rubbing and gently pinching each other's fingers. Neither of them said much.

Then their gate opened, and they got in line to board. Misty couldn't take her eyes off the jet. She could hear it rumble and hiss through the concourse window.

"We really don't know what we're doing, you know?" Daniel whispered. "Honestly, we could be in way over our heads."

Misty snorted. "Story of my life."

"So if this adventure goes bad, think maybe I could carry you to safety this time?"

She laughed and remembered that awful, bloody night, lugging one hundred sixty pounds of slack basketball player out of harm's way. "We'll see."

They showed their tickets to the flight attendant and walked down a ramp into the belly of the plane, curious and nervous and thrilled to see what happened next.

Here's a taste
of **Kristopher Reisz**'s first extraordinary tale:

It was after ten on a nothing-better-to-do Thursday night.
Hanging out at the gas station, Gilly sipped a Diet Coke and
listened to Sam recount the three-way battle she'd gotten into
with her mom and stepdad.

Sam crashed on her brother Josh's couch a lot, escaping the
ground-glass angers at her own house. She had a key, but Josh's
roommate was a thug-wannabe full of crude words and wormy
stares. Sam didn't trust him alone, so she went to the Texaco
where Josh worked and waited for him to get off at midnight. If
she called, Gilly always came up to keep her company.

"Okay, so you pin it up there, and your mom sees it first,
right?" Gilly asked, trying to get the details straight.

"Pinned nothing. I glued it up there." Josh had stepped out

back to smoke a cigarette, leaving Sam in charge. As she talked, she straightened the rack of charm necklaces sitting on the counter, separating the pot leaves from the Grateful Dead bears.

"You did not."

"Hell, yeah, I did. That mother—"

Both girls looked up when the electronic door chime sounded. The homeless man walked into the store trailing the smell of something gone sour. His skin was burnished brown like antique wood, stretched thin across knuckles and the knots of his collarbone. A tamed crow, sleek blue-black, nestled in the crook of his arm.

His name was Meek. Gilly had seen him panhandling around Birmingham before but only once up close.

After church one Sunday, her family had stopped at McDonald's for breakfast. Meek had been there, the crow perched on top of his battered rucksack. He wanted to get some food but only had a handful of change. The manager kept telling him to go, saying he couldn't be there with the bird, anyway.

As Gilly's family walked in, the homeless man turned and smiled at her dad.

"'Morning, Officer Stahl."

"Hey, Meek."

Her dad stepped into the argument and calmed the manager down. He wound up buying Meek an Egg McMuffin and a cup of coffee while the old man waited on the sidewalk.

"You know that guy?" Gilly's little sister Caitlin asked after their dad came back inside.

"Oh, yeah. Meek's been a legend since before I joined the force."

"What's he a legend for?"

"Says strange stuff sometimes," he said through a mouth full of biscuit. When Caitlin pressed him on what that meant, he shook his head and shrugged. "Just strange stuff. Stuff that gets in people's heads."

Now, as Meek entered the Texaco and approached the counter, Gilly noticed the milky blue cataract eclipsing his left eyeball. He said hello in a soft mumble and asked Sam for a pack of Marlboros. She rang him up, stabbing at the cash register keys with one careful finger. Gilly kept quiet, watching the crow watch her.

"That'll be four eighty-six, please," Sam said.

The old man made a show of patting his pockets. He shook his head. "I'm sorry. I don't have any money."

"Well . . . I can't really let you have the cigarettes, then," Sam said. "Sorry."

"Suppose I gave you something better than money?"

Sam scowled at him. "Like what?"

"Well?" Meek looked down at his pet bird. "What does she want?"

Gilly glanced at Sam, then at the silent alarm button underneath the counter. Sam just tried not to laugh. "Look, man—"

The crow fluttered off Meek's arm and landed on the counter. Both girls jerked back. Talons scratching across glass, the bird regarded them for a few seconds.

"You want to go home," Meek answered.

Sam smirked. "Not quite. Actually, I'm—"

"I know what you want too, honey." He turned toward Gilly.

"What's that?" She wanted him to leave. His eye, like a dead fish's, grossed her out. It made her squirm when he called her "honey."

"You'd burn the world down to become beautiful, wouldn't you?"

"What the hell?" Sam stared at him. "You're walking around telling people who's beautiful and not? You don't have any fucking teeth, crackhead."

Meek shrugged. "There's a difference between pretty and beautiful."

The comment made Gilly smile despite herself. She glimpsed someone new beneath the desperation and the tobacco-stained whiskers, someone who'd been charming once, someone poetic.

"Whatever," Sam said. "Look, if it was my store, I'd let you have the cigarettes, but it's not. So—"

"I'll pay," Gilly said.

"What?"

Pulling a five-dollar bill out of her pocket, Gilly offered it to Sam. "I'll pay for the cigarettes."

Sam glared at her and took the money, handing Gilly fourteen cents change.

"Thank you." The cigarettes vanished into the pocket of Meek's ratty coat.

"So, now what?" Sam asked. "You read her palm or something?"

He scooped the crow off the counter, cooing to it. "Aruspicy's better," he whispered.

"Huh?"

"Reading the entrails of an animal sacrifice."

"Huh?" Sam looked at the bird in his hands, then jumped back, smashing into a rack of cigars and rolling papers. "Whoa! No!"

Hollow bones cracked and popped. The crow screeched. One free wing flapped madly. With steady, calloused hands, Meek tore the bird in two.

"You motherfucking psycho! Get the hell out. What the fuck's wrong with you?"

Kool-Aid-bright blood pattered to the floor. It ran down his wrists and stained his fingers slippery black. Intestines and tea-colored organs dangled from the crow's body. Meek dropped the halves of the bird onto the counter and began poking through its guts.

Sam's shouting brought Josh charging out of the back. "Hey, motherfucker. Hey!" Grabbing Sam, he jerked her away from Meek, putting himself between his little sister and the old man.

Meek stirred the crow's guts with his fingers, ignoring the brother-and-sister torrent raging on the other side of the counter. Gilly stood silent against the wall. She stared at the dead bird. Its polished obsidian eyes still watched her.

Meek looked up. "The Witches' Carnival is stopping in Atlanta tonight."

"Get out. Get the fuck out now!" Rounding the counter, Josh snatched Meek by the shoulder of his tattered coat as Meek snatched the torn-apart crow off the counter.

"Yeah! Take your fucking bird with you," Sam yelled after him.

Josh almost had him out the door when Meek raised the mass of feathers, bones, and guts to his lips. He kissed them. The bird cawed sharp and angry. It beat its wings. Gilly and Sam both screamed as the crow fluttered up to perch on his shoulder.

Meek turned toward Gilly. His blind eye seemed to pierce her chest. "Run fast. Leave everything behind. And you can catch them." Stepping around Josh, he shuffled off into the night.

The episode left Gilly so rattled, her hands shook for an hour. She'd been certain Josh would murder Meek. They helped Josh clean crow's blood off the counter and killed another hour until the third-shift girl showed up.

After Melissa finally arrived, Josh started his final check of the store. Gilly and Sam told Melissa about Meek, his crow, and the Witches' Carnival.

Melissa snorted. "My cousin has sworn for twenty years that he met the Witches' Carnival down in New Orleans once."

"You think he really did?" Sam asked.

"'Course not. He just drinks too much."

Gilly started for home around twelve thirty, the only person on the highway. The image of Meek's eye, the color of a gathering storm, floated through her brain and made her skin crawl. She tried to figure out how he'd made tearing up the crow look so realistic. All three of them had been fooled. She turned up the stereo to keep from falling asleep. Her thoughts drifted toward the Witches' Carnival.

Rock is dead. Punk is dead. Everything's dead.

Hollow-eyed girls and empty-headed boys drifting through neon constellations. Hipster ghosts haunting black-light dance clubs.

They were in New York before that. There's always something ready to explode in New York. And the San Francisco thing before that, dirty feet and grotty acid rock. They skipped out before it went sour.

And before that, howling nights in Mexico City. Smoke-filled jazz clubs in Paris before that, getting drunk and stoned with black GIs who never bothered going home.

Before that, the Great War plunged Europe into darkness, lamp by lamp. But titles and peers held galas beneath twinkling chandelier light, certain the trouble would be over by Christmas.

Before that, Vienna. Before that, London and Berlin. Before that, Renaissance Italy maybe, or Beijing's Forbidden City or the music halls of the Ottoman Turks.

Nobody knew where they'd come from, but like dragons and angels, the Witches' Carnival tapped deep into myth and appeared in every culture. They were the Council of Spirits in China and the Wandering Lords of the Hindu Vedas. Homer wrote about the Lotus-Eaters, Shakespeare about Oberon and his court, and Jung explained the trickster archetype. According to what legends you believed, they might have invented tarot cards or could turn themselves into foxes.

Nobody knew where they'd come from, but they'd been everywhere, climbing the Jacob's ladder of man's history. They'd borne witness to autumn decrees and October days during the French Revolution and had a lovely picnic on a grassy knoll in Dallas.

A band of gypsies tramped across the earth, sweeping the bonds and boundaries of the modern world away with a brush of a hand. Nobody knew where they came from. Nobody knew where they'd turn up, but the Witches' Carnival was always headed somewhere. They moved on the edge of your vision and melted away like fog the moment you turned to look.

Gilly pulled into her driveway two hours past curfew. She knew she was in trouble and hardened herself to face it. Pushing open the door, she saw her dad sitting on the couch. Gilly didn't look at him. Keeping her eyes forward, she walked through the living room and down the hall.

Her dad followed her into her bedroom without a word. As Gilly flipped on the light, he held out his hand.

"Give me your keys."

Gilly handed him her key chain. It vanished into his pocket.

"When you learn to mind the rules, you can drive again," he said. "Until then, I'm keeping these."

"Fine." Gilly stared at her bed, the blanket twisted and kicked to the floor. Her dad stood behind her for several seconds. Gilly tried not to say anything else. She wanted him to think she didn't care. But as he started to leave, it snuck out. Gilly couldn't stop it.

"We weren't doing anything."

Andy Stahl turned on his heel. "I don't want to know what you were doing, Gilly. It doesn't matter. You're supposed to be home by eleven o'clock. Why can't you manage that?"

Because Sam was upset and needed someone to talk to. Because there were things she could tell Sam that her dad never heard. Because she was hanging out at a gas station, not in the projects buying crack.

"Okay, Dad."

"No, it's not okay," he said. Gilly hated when he did that. "I can't figure out how come you're the only person on Earth who doesn't have to follow the rules. I can't figure out how you got so lucky."

"I'm not." If she had kept her mouth shut, he'd be gone by now.

"That's right, you're not." He jingled the keys in his pocket. "And when you think you can be home when you're supposed to be, you can ask for these back."

Gilly still refused to look at him. "Fine. Whatever."

Her dad left, shutting the door behind him.

Afterward, Gilly couldn't lie down. She paced her room for an hour, yelling at her dad in a voice barely above a whisper. She jabbed a finger at her reflection in the mirror and said all the things she wished she'd said while he was there.

She told her dad that she'd been helping a friend. She didn't care if he punished her; she'd do it again tomorrow if she had to. She told him she was gay, and if he was going to freak out about it, fine, but at least he could admit he was freaked out. Gilly told him that she loved him, and how much she wished that could still be as simple as it had been when she'd been little. Gilly found herself standing by her window, looking at the road running in front of her house. It connected to the parkway. Take Interstate 20, and Atlanta was three hours away. If Gilly left now, she could get there by sunrise.

The Witches' Carnival was the name and shape given to every fantasy of running away and leaving it all behind. It was the fantasy of the open road, the fantasy of motion and speed until all your problems became a blur. But most importantly, it was a fantasy.

Gilly let the venetian blinds drop over the window. Undressing, she flipped off the lights and went to bed. The Witches' Carnival wasn't real. That couldn't stop dreams, glittering like sunlight across water, from closing around her as she drifted down to sleep.

The red-faced bluster of morning talk shows spilled out of the car's stereo. Gilly sat in the front seat beside her dad. As they neared the school, Gilly turned toward the student parking lot, searching for Sam.

Sam sat on the hood of her Civic. Colby was beside her, his arm around Sam's waist and one foot on the car's bumper. Alex and Dawn stood hugging belly-to-back. Everyone watched Sam. Forming her hands into a circle, she yanked them apart. Alex laughed. Dawn clapped a hand over her mouth and started walking away.

Sam wore her long-sleeved black shirt. She had on the jeans with the frayed cuffs. Through the car window, Gilly watched Sam brush strands of dark hair out of her eyes, tucking them behind her ear. She turned toward something Colby said and smiled.

Gilly felt her dad glaring at her. She dropped her gaze to her sneakers. "She's just a friend, Dad."

Andy Stahl pulled to the curb and didn't answer. "Me or your mom'll pick you up at three."

"I'll get a ride."

"Yeah. With me or your mom."

Curling her lip into a practiced sneer, Gilly climbed out and slammed the door. Pulling the hood of her sweatshirt up, adjusting the straps of her backpack, Gilly dragged her feet along the sidewalk until her dad was out of sight. Once his car had rounded the corner, she loped across the parking lot toward her friends.

". . . and Josh is just—hey, G."

"What's up?"

"Where's your car?" Dawn asked.

"Dad took it away for staying out too late."

"That sucks. How long?"

"I don't know. Until he stops being an asshole."

Sam grabbed Gilly's arm hard enough to hurt. "What the hell was that last night?"

Gilly shook her head and laughed. "Some fucked-up shit. That's all I know."

Hugging herself against the steel-gray weather, Gilly listened to Sam tell the story. Sam told stories with a dry intensity. She never edited her own embarrassing moments. If anything, she exaggerated them for comic effect. She even did decent impersonations of Josh and Meek.

Once she'd finished, Dawn said she'd seen a magician do a trick like that on TV. She figured Meek had killed one crow and had another hidden somewhere. Colby asked where a homeless guy bought crows in bulk. His guess was that Meek had trained the crow to lie limp, then splattered chicken guts around to make it look like he'd killed it.

"He didn't just kill it," Sam said. "He ripped the thing in fucking half."

"That's just what you think you saw. It's power-of-suggestion stuff."

The seven forty-five bell rang. Alex and Dawn said good-bye and hustled off for class. Sam looked at Colby, her fingers twining with his. "Hey, I need to talk to Gilly for a second, okay?"

"What about?"

"Nothing big." She kissed him. "I'll see you in Mrs. Badford's class, okay?"

"You won't even tell me what it's about?"

"Shit." Sam jumped off the hood of the car. Taking Gilly's wrist, she pulled her into the bright, chattering stream of people pouring through the school's main entrance.

Inside, students and gossip flowed down every hall. Lockers clanged. Sneakers squeaked across the green-specked tile. A cluster of boys near the Coke machines burst into thick laughter.

Sam leaned close, her warm breath brushing Gilly's cheek. "I'm going to go look for them."

"Who? The Witches' Carnival?"

"Wanna come?"

"Sam, he's just some sick fuck homeless guy. He pulled

the whole thing out of his ass." They stopped at Gilly's locker. She started dialing the combination.

"Did that look like chicken guts to you?" Sam asked.

"No, but . . ." Gilly pulled her algebra book out and shut her locker. They started down the hall again. "The Witches' Carnival is a fairy tale."

"Maybe."

"C'mon. If they're real and Meek knows where they are, why's he hanging around Birmingham doing magic tricks for cigarettes?"

"I don't know. He's a sick fuck homeless guy. They march to a different drummer."

Gilly looked at Sam. "You're thinking about going. Seriously?"

"I'm not thinking, I'm going."

"When?"

"Today. Now. I only came to school to see if you wanted to come with me."

The second bell rang. The hallway clamor rose, footsteps scattering off to class. Gilly and Sam stood motionless.

"What about school?"

"Fuck school."

"What about Colby?"

"Fuck him. There's no way he'd go. Probably whine. I'm not even telling him."

"Sam, it's not real."

"I don't give a fuck." She plucked at the strand of Mardi

Gras beads wrapped around her wrist. "One way or another, I'm leaving. I'm sick of living in the same house as Greg. I'm sick of spending every night at Josh's place."

Gilly chewed her lip. "Yeah." It was a sound to fill the quiet, meaning nothing.

"So come with me."

"I can't."

"Why?"

"Because . . ." Gilly didn't have an answer.

"Miss Grace, Miss Stahl, the bell's already rung."

They glanced up. The hall was nearly empty. Mrs. Schiff, Gilly's homeroom teacher, stood beside her door smiling a tight, unfriendly smile.

Sam and Gilly looked back at each other.

"You got until the end of first period," Sam said. "Then I'm outta here whether you're with me or not." With that, she started down the hall.

"Sam, c'mon."

Sam turned, walking backward and grinning a wicked, sharp-cornered smile. "Remember, G, if you ain't pretty, start trouble." Turning back around, she hurried to class.

"Miss Stahl, do you plan on coming to class today?" Mrs. Schiff asked.

Simplify the following exponential expression. Remember to write it so each base is written one time with one positive exponent.

$$(24 \times 3)(x - 5)$$
$$(6x - 20)$$

Gilly stared at her textbook, the page covered with numbers and symbols. She only had hazy ideas what any of them meant. Mrs. Schiff stood by the overhead projector and went on about integer exponents. The classroom's stuffy heat made Gilly's scalp itch. She ran her fingers through her hair, dyed a violent shade of red, and wiped a damp palm on her pant leg. She glanced at the clock, then her watch, then outside at the rows of cars filling the parking lot.

Gilly knew Sam didn't believe in the Witches' Carnival. Nobody did anymore, not really. But it was too wonderful a story to let go of completely. Sam wanted to believe in somewhere she could escape to, some real home far away from the peeling-paint split-level she shared with her mom and stepdad. She wanted to believe in it so bad, she'd fooled herself into trusting a rambling, half-mad crackhead.

The bell rang. There was a clatter of voices and chairs scraping across the floor. Gilly joined the rest of the class streaming into the corridor's din. Lockers were jerked open and banged shut. Kevin Carney bolted past her with two of his friends after him.

Gilly walked with her head down, trying to figure out what to do. She had photography next period in Mr. Byrne's room on the second floor. Instead of heading up the stairs, though, she found herself walking past them. The hallway ended in a steel door with wire mesh over the window. She stood and watched the student parking lot. Sam appeared a few seconds later, cutting between the cars toward her Civic.

She was really going.

Gilly thought about her dad taking her keys away for nothing. She thought about how miserable school was going to be without Sam around. She couldn't make herself believe in the Witches' Carnival, but Gilly imagined climbing out of days like a labyrinth and breathing fresh air for a while. The door swung open. Gilly heard the soles of her sneakers beat against the asphalt. A mean October wind scoured her face.

Sam had already ducked into her car. She saw Gilly and unlocked the passenger side door.

"All right. I'm going," Gilly panted, collapsing into the seat. "What the hell, I'm going with you."

"Fucking bitch." Sam punched her in the shoulder, then cranked the engine. "Why'd you act like that in the hall? I almost thought you really weren't coming."

"Sorry. You sprung it on me so all of a sudden, I was kind of stunned."

Steering around the wooden barrier guarding the parking lot's entrance, Sam slung out onto the street. Two wheels popped the curb, and the car's chassis jolted against the pavement.

Winter-bare trees lined the curving road leading away from school. Gilly watched them pass for a few seconds before speaking up. "Hey. Let's stop by my house on the way."

"What for?"

"Money."

"Cool. How much you got?"

"I'm broke, but you know my dad's a cop, right?"

"Yeah."

Gilly took a deep breath. She was already in trouble, she might as well enjoy it. "Did you know he's crooked?"

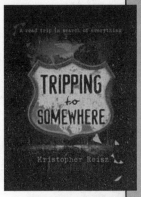